PENGUIN BOOKS

SCREAM TO THE SHADOWS

Tunku Halim was born in 1964. He is dubbed as Asia's Stephen King and by delving into Malay myth, legends and folklore, his writing is often regarded as 'World Gothic'.

His novel, *Dark Demon Rising* (1997), was nominated for the International IMPAC Dublin Literary Award whilst his second novel, *Vermillion Eye* (2000), is used as a study text in The National University of Singapore's Language and Literature course. He has also won first prize in a Fellowship of Australian Writers' short story competition and has had three consecutive wins in Malaysia's Popular-Star Readers' Choice Awards between 2015 and 2017.

His short-story collections include—*The Rape of Martha Teoh & Other Chilling Stories* (1997), *BloodHaze: 15 Chilling Tales* (1999), *The Woman Who Grew Horns and Other Works* (2001), *7 Days to Midnight* (2013) and *The Rape of Nancy Ng – 13 Nightmares* (2018). His other novels include *Juriah's Song* (2008), *Last Breath* (2014) and *A Malaysian Restaurant in London* (2015). His non-fiction books include *A Children's History of Malaysia* (2003), *History of Malaysia—A Children's Encyclopedia* (2009) and a biography of his late father, *A Prince Called "Charlie"* (2018).

Scream to the Shadows

Shadows
20 Darkest Tales

TUNKU HALIM

PENGUIN BOOKS

An imprint of Penguin Random House

PENGUIN BOOKS

USA | Canada | UK | Ireland | Australia
New Zealand | India | South Africa | China | Southeast Asia

Penguin Books is part of the Penguin Random House group of companies
whose addresses can be found at global.penguinrandomhouse.com

Published by Penguin Random House SEA Pte Ltd
9, Changi South Street 3, Level 08-01,
Singapore 486361

First published in Penguin Books by Penguin Random House SEA 2019

ISBN 9789814867153

Typeset in Adobe Garamond Pro by Manipal Digital Systems, Manipal

www.penguin.sg

CONTENTS

PART 3: DARK TECHNOLOGY

PART 4: GRAVEYARD VOICES

PART 5: MALAY SHADOWS

INTRODUCTION

Welcome to our theme park!

Be warned. This is no Disneyland with its ever-so-delightful Fantasyland, Adventureland, Mickey's Toontown and Mainstreet USA.

No, we have our own curated themes here. Ones for you to experience, enjoy and indulge in, all on your own, because this, dear friend, is no family outing.

And we're only open at the dead of night . . .

Now let me proudly share them with you.

First, allow me open the gates to the The Occult World.

As they creak open and you amble alone through the deepening shadows, you'll hear the hums, groans and scraping sounds of metal gears and levers, driving our enchanting rides from the other side. Tales from beyond the humdrum. The supernatural, the paranormal, can occur at any time, in any place. They may jolt us out of our routine or may reveal another existence, a dreadful one beyond our dullish day-to-day. These narratives come from that unsafe place, that dark other side where shadows and fangs so enticingly lurk. And perhaps, once there, the only thing you can sanely do is scream.

The first ride that awaits is *The Rape of Martha Teoh*, a tale about a dead man haunting his long-suffering wife, a narrative that I'm told is filled with *evil*. This is followed by *Malay Magick*, a story set in London and one that's gone through a recent maintenance upgrade. Then there's the beguiling *Black Death* and after the *Man on the 22nd Floor* experience, you won't be able to look at a strand of hair the same way again. So come join me and, as my VIP guest, we can skip the queues and have fun together hand in hand.

Next, we'll venture through the rusty gates to our second theme: Fragmented Minds.

Here you'll find tales where minds fall part. The human mind, as you so well know, my friend, can be a terrifying place. Its cold whispers, its ungodly machinations cause us to do terrible, awful, shameful things. Often, like a roller coaster, it runs off in a direction that we don't want to go, yet it hurls us screaming as it goes off the rails. If thoughts go bad, go haywire, then all things, especially the best ones, turn so dreadful and sometimes ever-so-bloody.

These rides are driven by madness. There's no need for anything supernatural, for nature itself can be twisted into its own loathsome forms. *Kyoto Kitchen*, for instance, was inspired by real events when a security guard kills two children. *The Black Bridge*, being one of my latest tales, was inspired by several days alone wandering the empty streets in an *onsen* town. In *Emil and the Lurking Shadow* we discover that we don't really know who to trust and after encountering

Ladiah, you'll never look at your maid the same way again. Or perhaps you may never employ one!

Then, hand-in-hand, we can happily skip into the Dark Technology section of our park.

Here you'll discover that terrors do indeed emanate from the tech world. Yes, out they drift like miasma from circuit boards, memory chips and embedded algorithms. Technology is no doubt disruptive, as anyone in the newspaper business will tell you, but it can also be destructive and so awfully deadly. I once wrote a story called *Hawker Man* and have since revised it into one called *Hawker Man and I*. It's right over there beside one of my favourite rides, *The App*, which is about what happens when technology rules our lives, a scary truth we're beginning to now realise. You must, of course, go for a spin in *Black Honda Jazz*. It may take you somewhere you don't ever wish to go. But before we leave this part of our park, do visit the gift shop and pick up *Mr Skull*. He's a soft toy that may well turn you into an internet sensation.

Feeling a bit chilly now?

That's because we've just ambled into our next theme, Graveyard Voices, and a mist is rolling across the pale headstones.

These places of the dead are such beautiful places, aren't they, my dear friend? They're serene and filled with bones and memories. But they're not places I wish to venture to at night, for even as I'm taking that selfie in the moonlight, I'll be wondering what creature watches, tongue licking its lips. And is that a soft singing I hear from beneath the freshly-turned soil? And what on earth is that sweet, floral scent?

These tales use the settings of the graveyard as inspiration. *44 Cemetery Road* was inspired by the Chinese superstition of the number 4 and if you combine that with the words 'cemetery' then you know that you're in big trouble. *Gravedigger's Kiss* is about a gravedigger with a mysterious secret while *Shrine* is a story about the eerie disappearance of some hapless village folk. It's a fast-paced ride and since there's no queue there right now, you should hurry on to it before the crowds arrive. And if you're strolling beneath the *Midnight Rain*, you'll discover that things are not always as they seem, no matter how alluring.

Finally, there's Malay Shadows.

Here you'll unearth stories that are influenced by the richness of Malay myths and legends, dark beliefs that may go back hundreds if not thousands of years into our primeval past. I recommend the *Biggest Baddest Bomoh* experience which is an old favourite but we've maintained it well, regularly checking its ageing gears and levers, while *Mr Petronas* may need to be thoroughly oiled. But they're still safe, my friend. I guarantee it. But things are somewhat riskier *In the Village of Setang* where were-tigers roam burning bright! We're so proud of this section of our park but once again don't forget to visit our souvenir shop for some Malay handicrafts to take home although I'd avoid the krises as I'm told that some of them are haunted!

So there you have it. Our glorious theme park.

There are twenty rides to enjoy. Some have been around for more than two decades but we've kept the rust off and given them a fresh coat of paint. Others are brand new and still sparkling like jewels in a crypt. Some are fast-paced, roller-coaster like, even. Others more leisurely. Some may be scary like a haunted house ride or a serial killers dungeon while others less so, but I'm sure none of them will take you into 'It's a Small World' territory. For you may then be quite entitled to demand your money back!

Please be careful in the park though. You can easily get lost if you take the wrong turn or go through one of the 'Staff Only' doors. I'm not too sure what happens in those shadowed places but those that enter never seem to come out. We've recently lost a few customers. But don't worry, you look like one of the more sensible types.

Anyway, you've got your ticket so don't be shy and come on in. I'll be here waiting, all dressed up in a suit and red bow tie, and ready to welcome you with my biggest brightest smile!

PART 1

THE OCCULT WORLD

1

THE RAPE OF MARTHA TEOH

He raped her but once. In darkened chambers, watched by a dark wooden clock.

Martha's almond eyes hopelessly transfixed upon a black wooden screen of dancing maids with gentle smiles, sweetly waving silk before clumps of bamboo; tears breaking the mother-of-pearl image apart. And the rhythmic pendulum—ticking—just beyond his grunting, panting; salty sweat trickling down her face, inhaling stale whisky breath; her mind reeling, screaming from his wicked intrusion. After an hour, crammed into mere minutes, Heng Wan slumped and fell away, singlet soaking, his white Robinson's underwear twisted around a long, hairless leg; snoring.

Martha whimpered in the Sunday afternoon heat haze which filtered through the louvred smoked windows, her breath still, her body daring not to tremble, instead tensing against itself, locked solid in a rigid paralysis. The red scroll that read *Happiness*, doubled, circled, grew to gigantic proportions, then sank to minute size and blossomed with

3

the word *Hate*. It was a lie. If she could say she hated him
with all her being, then she would be free.

Since that one singular rape she was trapped to him. What
should have been a time to despise and hate, only reaffirmed
her undying, blighted love for him. Heng Wan woke up,
stretched himself and laughed as if nothing happened.
Singing as he bathed himself, Martha could only look at the
ceiling knowingly resigned to her fate; her small, round face,
like putty, twisted in agony.

That was thirty-five years ago. Heng Wan was long
gone, dead of cancer ten years now. He came home one day,
coughed out blood and fell on the speckled terrazzo floor.
'He was only sixty-two,' everyone had said. Martha nodded,
grief-stricken, mourning for herself and a scarred life with
him. She closed her eyes and his face emerged. His wry smile,
sitting awkward on his hollow face, bright-lit eyes. The one
the ladies found so attractive.

And there were plenty more of those. It was not the
calls, quickly put down, with the dialling tone buzzing in the
eardrum, that annoyed her. Of course, it was maddening,
with at least two or three a day. It was the lift in his voice,
the gait in his steps, snippets of *Mack the Knife* whistled
enthusiastically (how that tune would cut her) every time
he was to travel outstation or would be out past midnight.
He would not be travelling alone, he would not be at
business dinners and drink without an escort. There would
always be a soft, slender hand on his bony knee and cool
whispers in his ear, in the dark corner of a bar as a waitress
approached, balancing a round of twelve-year-old whiskies,
ice cubes tinkling. Laughter, business cards exchanged for the

umpteenth time, another round of drinks. He was happiest away from her and didn't mind letting it show.

Martha would find lipstick on his collar, whiff remnants of perfume she never wore, and know. That was no problem for Heng Wan, he didn't care whether she knew or not. Sometimes, he would go out wearing a white shirt and return wearing a blue one. Sometimes, he returned home wearing clothes she never bought him and obviously not to her taste; modern, floral ties, colours clashing. Martha knew he had a wardrobe somewhere else; another home, another bed.

She had heard whispers, a mistress, a second wife, divorce. Martha knew better. Heng Wan would never divorce her. She was after all the perfect wife who somehow loved him, although she sometimes shuddered at his touch, and never mouthed the agony of his infidelity. If they had children, she would have been the perfect mother, but even without them Martha knew he was not going to leave her. And she was right.

The one who liked the floral ties was thrown out, after only two years of bliss. A new one, a Eurasian girl with hair to her hips, came along, and then another and yet another. Martha stopped counting. He was not going to leave her. She was an anchor in his sea of mistresses and one-night stands. She kept his home, ironed his clothes, made him delicious dinners on those occasions when he was tired or ill, and kept up the tradition of a family amongst the collection of antique rosewood furniture, marble tables and mother-of-pearl screens.

And then he died, leaving her alone with these memories. Not happy ones, for she loved him in a way that hurt her very being. Not a love that poured out of her heart but rather wrenched out of her wretched soul. An unhappy, tortured love that knew no way out of the hopelessness and despair. It was a prison of barbed emotion, that hurt every time she tried to pull away, to free herself from this person that was everywhere and in everything.

There was that one time when she could have left, after the singular rape, when she could have torn down the thick webs that suffocated and blocked her path and vision. But it only pulled her back, binding her to do his bidding. She knew then that her life was woven into the fabric of his ill being and nothing could make her tear herself away, whether in distaste, horror or hate. The coils of this seething love enslaved her to him, to the darkest corners of the house of which he was the master.

For ten years now, Martha had stayed on. Her sister Audrey had asked her to move in with her but Martha refused, this was where she belonged. His memory shifted here, within its very walls, echoing within the hazel-wood wardrobes, creeping by the iron accordion gates leading to the front door. Her thoughts of him swam in the humid air circling the now antique ceiling fan, his shadow elongating like bars stretching across the dining room floor.

His thin, knobbly fingers had touched it all. His presence permeated everything, submerged her in his being—bubbling in the corpuscles of her blood, spinning, entangling webs in the fabric of her soul. Everything but her heart. It spoke of truth—he was a liar, a cheat, an adulterer; but she did nothing about it then and did nothing about it now.

Martha, now grey-haired and frail, chubby cheeks long deflated, lines criss-crossing her sunken face, sat by the window as always, looking out across the garden, past the large *angsana* tree, to the rusty front gate with the initials THW. She'd been sitting here for hours listening to the clock tick, watching, with empty eyes, the minutes pass as evening strolled in and mosquitoes rose above the shrill of insects, beyond the mournful call to prayers.

The white clouds above the neighbouring houses took on a hue of dirty grey and small fruit bats swooped triumphantly through the air. Teoh Heng Wan was dusk, engulfing the day, seeping into every corner of dying light. Even with him ten years gone, she was trapped in his dark shadow. And shadows grew darker.

And then night came. The shadows in one particular corner by the red leather armchair, where he used to lounge before the television or read aloud from the paper, took on a heavy, watery blackness. The walls seemed to pull away in distaste, as the blackness grew, layer by sable layer. Every memory, every shred of his existence, every utterance or curse he hollered, drew together in a rancid, seething bonding. The air charged with a brooding malevolence and the inky darkness formed into a shape, tall and thin, quivering in the fading light. The blurred edges shrank away and there stood the unmistakable shadow of a lanky, slightly hunched man.

Teoh Heng Wan—still here—after all these years. It was perhaps the most natural, or unnatural of things. When his hunched figure first appeared three months after the funeral, Martha screamed and ran into the bathroom, locking herself in. She huddled in a corner, shaking and trembling, holding her head, certain insanity and its horde of diseases had found her. She didn't move from the cold, hard floor until the crack of dawn cast its first glimmer on the bathroom mirror. She had been planning to leave the house to live with Audrey, but after the appearance of his apparition those plans were laid to waste.

Every evening for ten years, just after nightfall, Martha sat like a bird with broken wings by the window in horrid fascination and dread, watching the despicable Heng Wan emerge from the inky blackness. Sometimes he did not manifest himself, those were the better days, but mostly he came. Sitting in the red vinyl armchair to gaze at her across the lounge through twin wells of penetrating blackness; goading in his mastery. No words passed but his voice in her said, you are mine, you cannot leave here, ever.

She would shudder, hands clutching tightly to the armrests, knowing she was trapped to him, to his memory, to this apparition. The dark figure would remain seated for about an hour or so, an hour in which Martha could touch every ghastly second that passed, and then without ceremony, the sable creature would dissipate into darkness. Martha, hands trembling, body shaking, would turn on every single light and feverishly pray he would not return. But he always did. And as the months passed, she became used to his nightly presence and soon it was like he never left.

Indeed he had not. He had always been there, just like tonight. Martha's eyes twitched, her eyebrows raised, her wrinkled, leathery fingers groped hopelessly for each other. Something was different, something was wrong.

Heng Wan should have in a singular long motion brought himself into his favourite chair. The red vinyl would creak as the apparition sat, as if adjusting itself into a comfortable position, to enjoy his dominion.

It did not. The figure hesitated. The murky head cocked itself into a position of thought, as if feeling out the house. *Something's here, Martha dear*, his voice whispered coldly in her head.

'What do you mean, Heng Wan?' she answered in a trembling whisper, her knees shaking.

The apparition took two steps forward, closer than it had ever been in those ten years. The figure was a watery darkness beyond the shadows, eyes like holes into a malignant black. It leered menacingly.

Martha's breath caught in the folds of her throat.

Someone's here, Martha dear.

And it laughed, an evil chortling of triumph and glee.

Young, nubile and innocent. Just how I like my women!

It turned and strode away, that gait in his steps, towards the kitchen, towards the utility room. Except it wasn't a utility room anymore. She cursed herself then, in a way she had never cursed before. How could she have forgotten! It was the maid's room!

Emma, the Filipino maid that Audrey had insisted she take over. You're seventy-two, Martha, far too old to look after this big house alone. And being the docile one, Martha didn't refuse, didn't even think about Heng Wan in the brightness or sanity of day.

How . . . how could she have been so stupid! With a face as white as ash, eyes wide in terror, she struggled out of her chair. Legs shaking, her head spinning uncontrollably, she was going to faint—but she pressed on . . . she had to help the poor girl!

Mack the Knife whistled enthusiastically came rushing down the corridor like a whiff of rotten fish. Heng Wan going out to a 'meeting' . . . going to meet his mistress. Heng Wan bringing out his fleshy knife.

Martha dragged herself down the corridor. As she passed her bedroom, the maids dancing upon the black wooden screen eyed her sympathetically, waving silk before clumps of bamboo offering to wipe her flood of tears that would inevitably follow. And the ticking, the infernal ticking of the wooden clock, the pendulum swinging madly, pounding nails into her head. She screamed and rushed to Emma's door, jerked and twisted at the handle but found it locked. She knocked with her fists frantically, calling for Emma to open it, to let her in, to run. But to no avail. All she heard was low gleeful laughter and Emma's young voice screaming out. Fear and pain in her hollering.

Martha fell to her knees, her fists warm and bleeding. Emma sobbing, begging for mercy that would never come.

And then silence. A dreadful hush fell over the house. The bed started to creak.

2

MALAY MAGICK

London. A summer's afternoon. Crispin Birkenhead on his way to lunch, turns down an alley he never cared much for during those six years of stamping books in the library. He brings ham sandwiches everyday but on Thursdays he hankers for a hot meal.

Following the cobblestones, his grey hair retreats like mist into smoke as his thin body is embraced by shadows cast by the two-storey terraces. The rumble of traffic is kept beyond these narrow confines and the shafts of sunlight retreat as though unwilling to fall beyond the steep rooftops. Most of these buildings had been used as offices at some time or another, all stand vacant now, their dust-covered windows, several with broken panes, like soft skin so promising and yet not without its inherent risks. His cardigan, a size too big for his thin body, twists and turns, as he glides dreamily on. The alley narrows, the shadows turn darker and colder until, eventually, the cobblestones meet a moss-covered wall.

He sighs and turns to go back the way he came, but not before his eyes catch upon a set of peeling yellow letters on ebony board. *Malay Magick.* He approaches the window, this one oddly clean, and sees three knee-high puppets, their thick eye-browed faces staring at him, their headdresses standing aloft against their foreheads, long dangling arms attached to splints, their torsos turned like frightened birds within the clasps of their faded sarongs.

From the chipped paintwork, from the dull sheen upon their bodies, they are obviously antiques. Crispin is not interested in antiques, his salary, which does not leave much over to feed a cat, cannot permit such frivolities. He turns to go but his eyes do not leave the three wooden figures. *Did they not move then?*

He is unable to take another glance for a bell chimes and a door creaks. A face emerges from the darkness—hairless, large ears with thick earlobes, black bristle on his chin and oval, deep-set eyes. No Englishman obviously.

'Come in, sir,' said the man in a deep, heavily-accented voice. 'My name is Samad.'

'Oh . . . eh, I was just looking.' Crispin steals another glance at the puppets. They do not move but, instead, stare back expectantly.

'We have nice things here.' Samad's eyes bulges out of its sockets. 'Come in, sir. Please.'

Samad's buffalo-like body follows his swivelling head into the alley, one pudgy hand holding the door open.

Crispin mutters his thanks, looks back at the alley and enters the shop. A musty smell engulfs him. He edges his way down the shadowy corridor keen to get this over and done with. Behind him the door shuts, the bell jangling his nerves as Samad's heavy footsteps trail his.

'Straight ahead, sir.'

Crispin reaches the end of the corridor and is surprised by a huge cavernous room filled with objects, piled over one another, mostly covered by dust and time. A mountain of things. Leftovers from other people's lives.

Before Crispin can turn, Samad is already there breathing by his side. He smells of sweat. Buffalo sweat.

'My collection,' Samad says with a grin, one fleshy hand sweeping out proudly at the forlorn mass.

'I see,' says Crispin. 'A lot of things you have indeed.'

'Oh, yes . . . collected over a long, long time. My mother started it and I took over. Please sir, have a look.'

These things are of no interest to Crispin, but he wanders through the room anyway making a pretence of examining some of the objects. A full-height mirror. A chest of drawers with missing handles. A valet of rosewood. Two porcelain figures of ladies with parasols sitting on a dresser. A crystal bowl. A doll's house with a broken window. A war medal. A hairbrush with strands of blonde hair still entwined. A silver locket staring from an open drawer.

'Beautiful, aren't they?' Samad's grin climbs like a lizard to his fleshy ears.

'Perhaps. But not really my cup of tea, I'm afraid.'

'A pity, sir. They are beautiful, with wonderful memories attached to them.'

'Well I must go. I'll see myself out . . . thank you for asking me in.'

Samad takes a step forward as if to block his path. 'Wait.'

One of Samad's eyes increases in size, a glutinous globe growing and pulsing. The grin is gone and in its place are white large teeth. 'I want you to bring something for me, sir. Your most prized possession, please.'

'There must be some misunderstanding, I'm afraid. I didn't realise you purchased collectibles. No, I have nothing to sell. You see, I'm really not in need of any money.'

'Ah, then let me show you something!'

'Oh no, I don't think so. There's nothing here that can possibly interest me.'

'Are you sure, sir?'

'Absolutely.'

'Just a quick look, sir. Then you can go on your way.'

'I really don't think so.'

'Sir, I can guarantee that you will not regret it. Samad knows what his customers want.'

Samad abruptly turns and without waiting for a response from his customer throws open what appears to be a wardrobe door, wedges his body through its aperture and is swallowed by darkness.

The brisk, rhythmic thumping of Samad's footsteps as he climbs the hidden flight of stairs compels the librarian to make a decision. His gut instincts tell him to flee into the alley, then down the street into the meagre June sunshine, yet Samad's fleeting indifference dissolves this sensibility. It is the allure of the mysterious object on the floor above which spurs him to pursue the buffalo-like man. A quick look, then he'll leave.

Crispin consoles himself with this notion as he slips into the wardrobe. Here the peeling walls brush their coldness against his clothes and as he climbs the creaky steps, dampness pours into his wretched bones. And wretched they are for although Crispin is forty-five he suffers from osteoporosis— an old woman's disease, he often chides himself—and he must take care or he will break his brittle bones again.

It is a suffocating climb in these dingy confines, which are only occasionally lit by narrow shafts of light from a lamp on the upper floor. As he winds his way up, Crispin is almost sure he is clutching part of a giant skeleton for the stair-rails feel unnaturally warm like bones recently hewn from living flesh. The steps narrow as they turn upon themselves and Crispin wonders how Samad is able to squeeze his buffalo-body through the coiling passageway. An image of a slithering python swallowing a struggling goat whole enters Crispin's head and he wonders if this could be the worse decision he has made in his uneventful life.

He reaches the upper level and is short of breath. Samad is stroking his chin and upon seeing his customer, the shuffles towards him, a grin alighting like a strangled bird on his face. They are in a long wood-panelled corridor where no paintings hang except for a yellowing map in a tarnished bronze frame. Crispin has only a brief moment to examine its tributaries, jungle-covered mountains and ports before Samad reaches him. It is time enough for him to realise that he does not recognise the country or region, yet its geographic scale demands that he should.

'Is this somewhere in Borneo?' Crispin asks uncertainly.

'No, sir,' Samad whispers. 'Somewhere else. No, not thousands of miles away but closer, so much closer than you think.' He quickly turns, his chunky shoulder almost knocking the map off the wall. 'Come, come follow me, sir,' he says in a booming voice. 'I have what you want. You won't regret it.'

Samad thuds down the corridor and Crispin follows. He doesn't care for the proprietor's incomprehensible ramblings. The map has to be fictional. Why doesn't Samad admit it? Or is he just a Philistine selling whatever he can at as high a price as possible?

This corridor is better lit than the one downstairs. The red carpet is badly torn in several places and the tall windows are covered in thick layers of dust so that it emits no view, only a ghostly illumination.

He stops at an open doorway. A room piled with furniture covered in haunting white sheets. Propped on the floor is a portrait of a man in a black Victorian suit whose pockmarked face is all nose and chin. The troll-like man is sneering and Crispin is again sure that this must be a fictional character for no human could possibly look so repulsive. He promptly leaves to keep pace with Samad who is now moving quickly.

The passageway turns right, then a sudden left. The sweaty odour is still present yet less pervasive and Crispin's spirit lightens when they reach a well-lit hall where a broken chandelier hangs. He will write about this odd encounter in his journal and when he retires in Blackpool as he has always planned to do and will read it beside his fireplace and, drunk with port, laugh at the memory. Later he will take a long walk on a wintry beach, devoid of soulless holidaymakers. Another ten years or so at the library. Not all that long to go.

'In here,' whispers Samad, beckoning excitedly with one hand. He removes a large key and unlocks a heavy door. It creaks open to a dimly lit room.

'So what's in here?' says Crispin, now unsure of himself.

'Exactly what you need, sir. Believe me.'

With that he gives Crispin a shove.

The librarian falls headlong into the room. He tumbles to the floor. His wrist breaks. His leg snaps in two places. Crispin hollers.

'Sorry about that, sir,' continues Samad. 'Now enjoy!'

Samad laughs and yanks the door close. The key turns. The lock clicks.

'Let me out!' Crispin yells. Hot pain-filled tears roll down his cheeks.

The only answer is the sound of heavy footsteps echoing as it recedes down the corridor.

'Please, please, please let me out!'

Crispin realises how useless his moaning is as he is struck cold by the unenviable knowledge that he is imprisoned here. Here in a room dominated by a massive four-poster bed even as he stares up uselessly at the high ceiling and its decorative baroque mouldings. The librarian knows that it is imperative that he flees this wretched place but the fact that he is unable to even stand informs him of how useless such a notion is. His wrist and his one leg are on fire sending his head spinning towards a dark chasm that is slowing opening to swallow him.

But he has to escape!

Escape from this vile predicament, this set of undesirable circumstances that smothers him in dread and . . . perhaps even disease. For this room smells old and mouldy as if corpses have been bred here to rise again only to crumble so uselessly into dust. His eyes crawl about the room, lurching then darting, searching, hoping, for some other door, some other method of egress. But heavy curtains, red and velvety, smother the windows, so all he sees are undulating shadows. He wipes tears from his eyes and, even as the darkness stiffens, his ears have pricked up to a rustling and realises, to a low thumping in the chambers of his heart, that someone else is in here with him.

From the shadows of the four-poster bed, draped with Indian cotton or perhaps Thai silk, a head lifts from the tumult of pillows to peer across the room at him. Sheets rustle like dead leaves or perhaps dead skin as its occupant slithers across it and drops soundlessly like an albino alligator to the floor.

Crouching, the figure flicks its head from side to side as though sniffing the air. When it scratches itself there is the grisly sound of sharp nails on leather. For a long moment, it just stares at the librarian, breathing heavily and occasionally snorting like a pig.

An animal, thinks Crispin, not daring to move a limb nor take a single breath. But before the thought even slinks out his head, he knows it can't be true, for he has never seen or heard of a form that moves in such a strangely fascinating manner or possesses a body as sleek as a dolphin's. Nor is the thing human for no mortal can possibly smell so pungent or have such a protracted tongue that even in the half-light it can be seen quivering below its chin or flickering between its oval eyes.

It is the idea of a being, locked in here with him, that is neither human nor animal that causes the blood to drain from his face and ice to crawl up his tortured spine. Despite the shooting pain, which causes him to gasp as if it was his last, he turns and, using his good arm, he drags himself away across the dusty timber floor. He reaches the window, beneath the velvety curtains, trying not to breathe but ends up sucking great wafts of ammonia-like stink as blind terror takes over and his mouth begins an uncontrolled babbling. This thing that is neither human nor animal follows at a distance at first, creeping low on its haunches, stopping and then quickly shuffling forward, in bursts of what can only be wanton curiosity.

As Crispin tugs at the curtain, the thing steps into a crack of daylight and the librarian, glancing back to see if he will now be killed, sees the figure clearly for the first time.

There is not a single hair on its white skin. Instead scales, the shape and size of human ears—scales of iridescent and changing colours—cover half its body. The inhuman is a shapely woman for it has two small cone-shaped breasts with black aureoles like midnight suns. But the creature is also a full-fledged man for between its sinewy legs, above the dangling scrotums, an erect and scale-wrapped penis gently sways.

Upon the oval head, eyes, composed of no more than slithers of gold, stare back intelligently. It lifts its snout-like nose and sniffs at him. Then, as if satisfied with its prey, the mouth, large and lipless, yet strangely cruel, curves into a delicate grin. Then the inhuman hermaphrodite, for that is what it is and no idea or logic can banish it away, lifts itself into a sinewy crouch and leaps.

The librarian only begins to savour its caresses when the inhuman rapes him a second time there beneath the window. With no warning of who or what kind of man Crispin is, the thrills of quivering pleasure surges up his spine and he then turns and pushes his tongue into the inhuman's lipless mouth. In a swirl of kisses and caresses, the couple, for that is what they now undoubtably are, find themselves upon the four-poster bed. From then on it is a marathon of lovemaking in its soft comforts with sheets billowing like sails around their hot bodies.

One or two hours later, the door creaks open, emitting a crack of gas-burning light.

'Your time is up, sir,' says Samad, his bulky body filling the doorway. 'If you stay any longer I'm afraid I'll have to charge you for another session with Warna.'

'Warna?'

'Its name is Warna. It means colour. I'm sure you'll agree, sir, that its name is rather apt.'

Crispin turns to Warna but the hermaphrodite has withdrawn to a corner of the bed, eyes closed, scaly iridescent legs pulled up against its chest.

'Time to go, sir,' says Samad.

Crispin hauls himself off the bed and pulls his clothes back on. Some buttons on his shirt are missing and his trousers are ripped but no matter—stars are still exploding in his head.

'And how are your bones, sir?'

'What! Goodness . . . they're perfect.' Crispin examines his wrist and leg. 'It feels like I never fell. What's going on here?'

'Warna can have that effect on clients. Some form of sexual healing, I suppose, sir. But Warna's clients—both men and women—come here not for that but for the pleasure. And

I'm sure you'll agree, sir, that Warna only delivers boundless joy. You'll still feel its heavenly caresses when you go back to stamping books in the library.'

Crispin suddenly stiffens and his body starts to shake. It is as if he has been asleep and is now awake, fully aware of his thoughts and actions. He had an exquisite dream. No, a terrible nightmare. But it wasn't real. He had fainted when he fell and dreamt it all. And if it did transpire, he was a mere observer for he surely wasn't the sick bastard putting his cock in the thing's mouth. It wasn't him straddling its firm buttocks whilst he caressed its breasts from behind. It wasn't him screaming as he ejaculated all over its leathery stomach.

And how does Samad know that he works in the library anyway?

Not believing that it could have really happened, he peeks at the bed hoping, praying that Warna won't be there, just twisted sheets and pillows—that it was just some delusion, some insane hallucination induced by the proprietor.

But the hermaphrodite is of course there, squatting against a bed post, quite, quite real, eyes cast down and quietly sobbing. But . . . but such a creature surely cannot exist. And surely, surely he did not have sex with that monstrosity!

That alien! That gargoyle! That freak!

Crispin screams and scurries out of the room. He retches and, halfway down the corridor, tries to vomit but he expels nothing but air which whiffs of ammonia. And perhaps even the dust of corpses? He darts, almost leaps down the narrow flight of stairs, not caring whether he falls and breaks more bones. He gets to the bottom and flees the shop, glancing back just once but that is enough to see the sign *Malay Magick* and the puppets, he can't believe it, they are dancing. And there is a rhythm too, a sweetly sick and sensual one, playing in his head as the wooden limbs shake and slide.

The librarian doesn't return to work. Anyway, the streetlights are burning bright so that he knows that at least five hours have passed, not one or two.

He finds his way to the tube station, then to his one-bedroom flat, slips into his single bed, turns on the television and stares at the ceiling.

* * *

Daylight. Crispin rises. Has a shower. Gets changed. Scoffs down some cereal. Takes the tube to work.

The morning is a blur. His colleagues whisper. Beneath the steel-framed windows, Crispin cannot stop staring at the dust motes that dance like fireflies in the morning sunlight. At twelve-thirty he flees down the library steps. He has forgotten to makes his sandwiches. That doesn't matter. He is walking, almost trotting down the cobblestone alley.

He rings the doorbell. Are the puppets smiling ever so mischievously now?

Samad opens the door as if expecting him.

'Another session, sir?' asks the proprietor as he leads him down the corridor.

Crispin nods, sheepishly, foolishly.

Samad, the buffalo man, has beaten him, humiliated him. Crispin wants to weep. Yet every object he has seen today is seen through new eyes. Every item burns with intensity. The streets hum like bees. The low grey clouds whisper. The artificial lights are knowing eyes that watch and wink. The people, the fleshy work-a-day mortals out there are weak, decrepit creatures.

Samad tells him the price while he opens the wardrobe-like doors. Crispin hardly hears it. Something about a portion of his income and that Samad knows his salary.

'I know everything and more,' says Samad with an ugly laugh.

Crispin will agree to any fee and so says: 'No problem. I can easily afford that.'

All he can think about is getting upstairs.

'Good,' says Samad. 'Follow me.'

Crispin climbs the stairs, he glides by the strange map and the room with the portrait, except that the troll-like man is now bare-chested and grinning. Crispin shivers. He makes a right and a left, trying hard not to think, he enters the chandeliered hall. Samad unlocks the door and lets him in.

Warna stands by the velvet curtains, legs crossed, arms folded beneath its breasts, penis flaccid against one thigh. A yearning smile plays on its lipless mouth.

Crispin is already moaning before it begins undressing him, kissing his bare body as it does so. As usual Warna does not speak. Perhaps it is incapable or perhaps it has been silenced. But there on the bed Crispin is afloat on an enchanted lake that is warm and wet and deep, so very deep . . .

All too soon, Crispin leaves two hours later. He floats down the alley, and up through the street. He feels like a balloon bobbing through perfume-filled air. It is only when he slips through the library doors does he realise how exorbitant the fee really is. But what choice does he have?

Crispin wanders past rows of books. Biology. Plants. Photography. Religion. Architecture. Computers. Biographies. Art. Sports. Film. Poetry. History. Fiction. In the reference section, he is rooted before the rows and rows of law reports where he caresses the thick old spines and gold lettering and imagines Warna stroking his member so delightfully while the creature penetrates him from behind. He pulls out a King's Bench 1932 and, taking a seat, he leaves through pages which, although dry and crinkled, are pungently delectable. Warna has written the words. These pages are filled with adulations of love just for him. He can't take the books home so he copies the rivers of text onto paper. Their secret meanings will see him through the week until he is reunited with Warna. That is all he will now do. To hell with everything else.

Within two months of being fired by the Head Librarian, Crispin's account at Barclays is empty. He has been a loyal customer for over twenty years and they refused to give him a loan. No matter. He will take his possessions to Samad. His television, clock, dining table, chairs, sofa, vacuum cleaner, stereo, bed, posters, rugs, clothes, potted plants, kitchenware, family photos, stamp collection, fridge, watches, CDs even his most precious items—a small collection of first editions—have found their way into Samad's cavernous room. When he is finally evicted, there is nothing there in the flat but a cracked mug and a moth-eaten quilt.

Without a penny or a single material thing to his name, Samad forbids the former librarian from returning.

'Most regrettable,' says the buffalo-like man, one eyebrow knowingly raised.

Crispin tries to break in that night but he swears, as he lifts a hammer to smash the shop window, he sees the three puppets pull knives from their sarongs. So, with his plans to rescue Warna thwarted, Crispin disappears into the maze of streets, weeping for Warna's wicked imprisonment and his unsatiated lust for her, all the while muttering blindly to himself and verbally threatening all those who stare at him.

Sometimes you can still see the former librarian in different garbage-strewn alleys and soiled pavements in London. Usually he is holding a bottle of Vodka and swearing or shouting or pleading for a bit of change for a cup of tea. In his mud-splattered coat, he has grown a ragged beard and wears his dirty greasy hair to his shoulders. And he smells of maggot-filled meat. For many hours he rummages through rubbish bins beside the road, especially the ones outside McDonald's—they remind him of the ham sandwiches he used to make. He pushes a Safeway shopping cart along the streets piled high with cardboard boxes and assorted treasures, his spoils from digging through other people's junk.

Perhaps he still searches for that door to the other world where inhuman hermaphrodites and troll-like people live amongst the tributaries and jungle-covered mountains. But he is mostly found seated alone in municipal libraries across the city, hour upon hour, year after year, muttering whilst copying assiduously from the law reports in a scrawly jabbering hand. This month he has pulled out the Weekly Law Reports 1974 and he is already four hundred pages through it.

Many tramps, in their foul-smelling coats, may resemble Crispin Birkenhead but if you gaze carefully into his bloodshot eyes, only in his will you see that curious yearning.

A yearning for a bit of Malay magic.

3

BLACK DEATH

The banshee of a wind howled. A rustling pool of brown leaves. Polystyrene takeaway cartons and bits of newspaper tore at his tattered boots. In a long sad wail, the wind snatched them away again down the road past the broken bottles, graffiti walls and rusted cars.

In the cold frigid air, the young man wished for his hat and scarf. It had gone nine but there was no one around except for a tramp with a scarecrow like hat searching the contents of an upturned rubbish bin. The teams of squatters in derelict buildings across the road still snored in their vomit-stained sheets with syringes and empty plastic packets strewn like used condoms on the floor. The merchants scurried in the darkness of their shops getting their wares ready for the day's trade. They sold mostly pills, knifes, guns. The children—for this was no place for children—had been taken away from this part of the city years before.

The man blew into his hands to keep them warm. A shuffling figure in a grey coat approached from the other side of the street. With long grey hair and deep wrinkles around her thick pencil-lined eyes, she shuffled up to him and scrutinised his face suspiciously.

'Mr Death?' she whispered.

'Yes,' he said. 'But it's pronounced 'deeth', like in 'teeth'.'

'Deeth? Oh, I see,' said the woman sourly. 'So you're not the Grim Reaper then?'

'No, but my friends call me Black,' he said with a small laugh. 'You know, as in Black Death.'

'Well hurray for you.' She smirked. 'Now the money . . .

Black took the wad out of his coat pocket. The wind ruffled it eagerly as if knowing what it meant to him. Except for a few coins, it was all he had.

The woman took the cash, quickly counted it before stuffing it into the jaws of a crocodile skin handbag.

'That'll do,' she said. She placed a bunch of keys into his hand. As she did so, her finger accidentally brushed his wrist. 'The place is yours for a month.'

'Thank you,' he said.

'What kind of shop is it?' she asked, removing a tissue and blowing her nose.

'A bookshop,' said Black.

'A bookshop?' The woman laughed, wiping her nostril. 'Haven't seen those around here in years.'

'Well,' said Black. 'It'll be . . .'

But the woman had already turned and left, heading for a car across the road. Hers was one of the few. Cars had abandoned this part of the city long ago.

Before the woman got to her vehicle, she fell to her knees and tumbled onto the bitumen.

Black rushed to her. Touched a coarse cheek. Rocked the small shoulder. But she lay eyes wide open to the wasted grey sky. There was no pulse. The woman was dead.

Black ran to the squat building he had just rented, unlocked it and darted in, looking for a phone. Only a clammy coldness, a thick musty smell and a featureless concrete floor, in coffin-like proportions, greeted him.

Through the dirty window his eyes caught the skeletal figure of the tramp bent over the dead woman. He dug into her pockets eagerly like a hungry animal but before Black could give chase, the man had triumphantly fled, the wad of cash flapping like a bird in his hands.

* * *

Michael Death's father was a scholar but whatever subject that cantankerous man pored over in his high-backed leather chair in that dusty gloom remained a mystery. As a boy, many years before his friends anointed him with the nickname 'Black Death', a name he found both painfully dreadful and yet secretly proud of, he would often see his grey-haired father dressed in a dark moth-eaten suit, smoking beside a stack of worn leather-bound books, a glass of cheap brandy propped beside him.

'All these books,' said his father sweeping an arm towards the laden bookshelves, 'have been in our family for generation upon generation.'

The fact that his father was actually talking vaguely in the direction of his son meant that he was drunk. Michael, who was then eight or nine, didn't mind because this was the only time his father's lips stretched upwards into the semblance of a grin. And this was the only time when his father wouldn't huff and puff or grunt and groan or curse beneath his breath.

'I have added to them in my lifetime,' said his father who, in an act of either undue excitement or ill-conceived pride, perched himself on an arm rest and gesticulated his arms like a hungry crow. 'Modestly, only modestly, of course. But they are, nonetheless, excellent books, the ones I've chosen. All I could afford with the measly trust income. Ah, if only the trustees had been honest men, think of all the books we could have acquired. Think of the proper and unharassed life we could have lived! Think of the wines and whiskeys, the excellent draughts that could have passed these lips. Ah, the good life! A life my forefather's meticulously planned for generations of Deaths to come.'

Michael's father pushed the glass aside and, yanked the brandy bottle upwards so that its bulbous bottom pointed towards the high windows and the grey clouds beyond. He took a long swig, his throat throbbing eagerly. Michael scampered across the floor and hid beneath his father's desk.

'My great grandfather, he . . . he was the one who started this collection of scholarly books.' Michael's father rocked back and forth on the armrest, one gleaming black shoe tapping silently on the cushioned seat. 'Oh, but he didn't know the kind of burden he was laying upon our family. Housing the books, adding to them. No easy task, believe me. And the expense!'

'Why . . . why do it then, father?' called Michael from beneath the desk. He spoke softly, half hoping his father wouldn't hear him.

'Who said that?' Michael's father lurched forward so that he almost toppled off the armrest. He craned his neck and gazed under the table.

'Oh, it's you boy . . . What are you doing down there? What . . . what did you say?'

'Why . . . why do you keep the collection?' said Michael, peeping his small head out.

'Keep the collection? Of course I must keep the collection. Of course I must maintain it. Not just maintain it but add to it. To enhance it. To improve it. To advance it. It is my duty. It is part of the family trust. But more than that. Much more than that. It is a family covenant! We must maintain the library. To pass it along to the next generation. It is the will of your forefathers!'

'Will I have to keep the collection too?' asked Michael, who had crawled out from beneath the desk.

'This burden flagellates me so!' cried his father. 'Have you not heard what I've been saying? Of course! Of course! Of course! Not only will you keep it, but you must enhance it, improve it, advance it! It is your duty! Do you understand?'

Michael nodded, eyes wide.

'Excellent. Because when I'm gone, when the good Lord above takes me, I want to know that the books . . . the Death collection will be yours to love! Yes, to love! Just like how I've loved it from the day it passed to me. Understand?'

'Yes, father.'

'You promise?'

'Yes, father.'

'Good!' Michael's father cackled and took another long swig at the brandy bottle. 'Otherwise you . . . you . . .'

'What, father?'

'Ah, you'll find out in due time . . . in due time. Oh, this burden, it flagellates me so!'

He mumbled something incomprehensible before slumping on the desk and began to snore.

Michael slid out. He wanted to touch his father's hair but didn't dare. Instead he ran a trembling finger upon the desk, beside an open leather bound volume, along the curving ink stains as if they were maps demarcating islands of unfathomable knowledge.

Then he tiptoed away. He glanced back at the dark shelves of books, a mountain of spiralling knowledge that towered over the forlorn figure of his sleeping father. Michael closed the heavy library doors and disappeared down the corridor which soon engulfed him like night.

* * *

What is the price of a promise? What is a promise worth?

Black thought hard but no answers crept into his head.

He shivered. It was gloomy in the cramped shop, made more sombre by dark bookshelves filled with ordered, uncompromising rows of leather-bound volumes. This previously empty space had become a cold cavern. One laden with lore and wisdom, brimming in every ancient page. Could they, like an alchemists potion, be bubbling within the covers? Secretly ready to engulf him in this half light?

Black blinked at the ledger before him and blew into his hands.

The only illumination came from the long window that ran the length of one wall. No lamps worked as the power had been cut off months, maybe years ago. In this decrepit part of the city no one paid bills and any meter reader from the utility company who dared stroll its streets would have his throat cut.

Black sat in the same high-back chair, in front of that same ink-stained desk. If it wasn't for his leather jacket, greased black hair and dark complexion, he could have been mistaken for his dead father.

The bell tinkled and a scruffy young woman with short curls and a thick blue sweater rambled in.

'Hello,' said Black as pleasantly as he could.

The woman, eyes lined in thick make up, barely glanced at him. Instead she stared up at the page-filled towers arranged in two narrow rows.

'You've got a lot of books,' she said.

'Yes,' said Black. 'Look around. If you've any questions, just ask.'

'Where did you get them?' she asked. 'You steal them?'

'Course not,' said Black. 'They belonged to my father. He died last month. So I'm selling them.'

'Need the money, do you?'

'It's a business,' said Black. 'And yes, if you must know, I do need the money.'

'Don't we all.'

Black didn't mention that his father had gambled the family fortune away. The old man had found consolation from his miserable life in the glitzy casino beneath its star-filled ceilings. He had regularly made bets whilst drunk on the free-flowing champagne.

When Black's father died the house had to be sold. The antique furniture, the old paintings that hung in the sixteen-room mansion were auctioned off. The silver, shares and jewels had been pawned long ago. There was nothing left but the contents of the library. They were the only assets his father didn't dare mortgage.

The woman pushed her way down an aisle, head craning as she read spines, shadows of the towering shelves engulfing her.

'They look expensive,' she called out. 'All leather bound and pretty old, huh?'

'They're antiquarian,' called Black. 'Interested in any particular subject? We have an extensive Occult section.'

'No, no,' called back the woman pleasantly. 'I can't read.'

'Oh.'

'I'm looking for a job,' said the woman, whose face suddenly bloomed before his, earrings swaying like spiders caught in a storm.

'I haven't one to give,' said Black.

'I don't expect much pay.'

'I can't even pay myself.'

'Then I'll work for no pay.'

'You should have come yesterday,' said Black. 'You could have helped me carry the books. You know, help me arrange them on the shelves. It was back breaking work.'

The woman tittered brightly like a tinkling piano. She touched her hair. She pouted her lips.

'I wasn't joking,' said Black.

'So, have I got the job?'

'No,' said Black.

'My name's Rhonda. I need a place to hang out. It's a bit cold here. And those books are a bit spooky, aren't they? But still . . .'

Rhonda stuck out her hand.

He shook it. It was warm and smooth.

'You can't find better, you know,' she wheezed. 'Other perks might come your way, if you treat me right, if you're nice. You know what I'm talking about . . .'

She gave him a lopsided smile.

Then, hands shaking, she clutched the desk. She groaned. Her tongue slipped out of her gaping mouth over the full red lips. Her eyes swam to the ceiling and, breath expiring, she collapsed on the concrete.

Remarkably, one hand still held the desk, clinging so tightly to its timber edge that her fingers turned pale against the dark ink stains. Then, like a dead lizard, it slid off and soundlessly fell.

* * *

Jack Smee smelt of heavy perfume which often reminded his men of rotten bananas. He draped himself in a long white fur coat and a heavy gold necklace. He sported diamond studs, one on the left earlobe, the other through a flaring nostril. His hair was dyed orange and spiked, and when he stared through the twin worlds of his frog-like designer sunglasses, Black felt that the gangster was drilling into his soul, mining for some advantage.

Jack's men in their tattooed muscles and army-issue jackets joked as they dragged Rhonda's body away. Black didn't ask where to. But smoky odour had crept in through the broken glass and a fire burnt fitfully in a dumpster across the street. Beside the blue and brown graffiti-covered walls, two grey-bearded vagabonds in long dirty coats and crumpled hats stood there like stick men, warming themselves. Occasionally they would peer into the dumpster and mutter to themselves.

'We slaughtered those morons,' said the gangster. 'They had knives. We had swords. They had chains. We had guns. They won't dare touch you. We're professionals. With Jack Smee protection is guaranteed or your money back!'

The gangster laughed so that his voice bounced upon the walls, his fists merrily thumping the desk. His teeth gleamed. His skin was radiant white. Black wondered if, like some politicians, the man wore makeup.

'I slit their leader's throat myself,' boasted Jack Smee. 'So you'll get no trouble from those sewer rats.'

'So this street is yours?'

'I own everything. This street and everything your eyes touch. And that includes you. See you soon, my friend. I like you. I like your shop. You and me, we'll do business.'

'Sure thing,' said Black. He didn't know exactly what business Jack meant but he didn't dare ask. 'You interested in books?'

The gangster roared again, throwing his head up to the paint-chipped ceiling. He ambled out, leaving the door wide open, letting the cold blow in hard. He slapped his two minders on their backs, glanced back at Black and, in his long shiny boots, shook his head and gave him a thumbs up.

Since Black's shop opened this morning no one had walked in but for the few begging for money or pushing drugs. A scar-faced teenager had even slid him a needle and syringe filled with a thick colourless fluid. Pay me later, the skeletal youth had said. But, when Jack Smee came sauntering in, these visitors vanished.

The Death Collection, so far, had not fed Black a single morsel nor would there be anything for the gangster. Black would have to be patient. He would have to ignore his cramping stomach. If he couldn't pay, Jack Smee's men might just have to smash his skull in. Black wondered if he would really mind. All of this. His father's death. Opening a shop in the only part of the city he could afford. It didn't seem such a good idea now.

To stave off the ennui and the gloom that threatened to smoother him, Black kept active. He edged along the two rows of laden shelves. He slid books in and out. Heard the soft smooth scraping of their covers. The quiet thuds of volumes opened and shut. Pages barely read, the words swimming before his eyes. But this feverish activity kept him from freezing. It kept him going. It felt colder here than outside. The dampness crept into his bones.

Someone had to come in soon. Perhaps in an hour. At four maybe. A genuine buyer. Someone who would pluck a book off the shelf. Sigh at its true value and buy it. Just one patron. Black didn't ask for much.

Towards the end of the row, from the bottom shelf, Black dragged out a volume with an embossed black cover. This one was particularly dusty and heavy, its cover beginning to shed its leather skin like a serpent. On flicking through its crusty pages, he discovered a yellowing piece of paper. At first Black thought it could only be notes left from long ago but as he unfolded it, crumbling as it was at the edges, he found it was a letter.

Eyes widening, he realised in the squinting half-light that this musty letter was written by his great-great-grandfather, Crowther Death. He had read his family history, clambering about the barren family tree whose branches hardly bore any fruit to perpetuate further generations. But still, despite its feeble fertility, the family endured. Crowther Death was a famous figure. An ancestor to be proud of—the most proficient magician in living memory.

In was well documented in Occult history that Crowther Death on a starless night faced the devil and his seven demons upon a storm-lashed beach of hideous screams and malignant flames. The magician protected himself through ancient charms and esoteric symbols and so survived. But barely.

From this ghastly encounter, Crowther Death, whose other passion was his library of ancient books collected over a lifetime, barely retained his sanity. He fired his loyal staff and had taken nightly to streets that became running sewers in heavy rain and there sought out earthly pleasures and was soon plagued by its myriad diseases. The magician was fanatical that his collection remained intact and in that dusty epistle passed the library to his eldest son, Harman Death. Harman, whether through foolishness or coercion, had covenanted in his own blood used as ink that future generations would safeguard the books.

Black stared at the words again.

For this monumental and sacred library is greater than mere mortal lives and through my very will and unbounded determination I declare thus—that the venerable Death Library shall endure in its entirety in perpetuity and the eldest sons of my illustrious family shall be its sole guardians.

The next sentence sent Black staggering across the gloomy book-cramped shop, across the expanse of cold claustrophobia, to the tottering chair, the letter trembling in his hand as if it were a blade bent on slicing his throat.

Black read the words again. He took it to the window, finger jabbing at every slashing word as though written to choreograph a knife fight. There was no mistake. The letter was quite clear.

Any descendant who refused this obligation, declared Harman Death in his long jagged hand, or who attempted to discharge himself of it or tried to break up the library would be cursed. He would become an untouchable.

Those he touched would expire.

* * *

Jack Smee had brought Black a stolen computer and miraculously had the power reconnected. The gangster knew business; he was a professional. *Selling drugs or selling women is no different from selling books,* he said. *You need a distribution network, my friend.*

Within a couple of weeks Black was wrapping volumes in brown paper tied up with string and Smee's men were carting the packages, lovingly cradling them like dead babies, to the nearest operating post office which was safely tucked away in another part of the city. Smee had set up the internet site and arranged the credit card facilities. Black got a minuscule cut. It was better than nothing. He could feed himself. He still slept in the shop in a sleeping bag which usually hid beneath the desk. *That's the best security,* Smee had told him with a chuckle. *You can scream if anyone tries to break in.*

Black didn't think his hollering would deter anyone. He had seen bleeding men running past his shop. He had heard a woman screaming in the night. He woke one morning to find a dead man at his front door. He would buy a gun as soon as he could afford to. Perhaps from the gangster. This wretched place, he knew, was corrupting his soul.

Smee brought a small heater too and, for the first time in weeks, Black no longer felt cold. He always wore gloves though. Black touched no one. Kept his distance. He let no one touch him.

Jack Smee always grinned when he sauntered in, huddled in his white fur, whispering conspiratorially about how valuable these books were. Black could feel the man's eyes sparkle greedily on that pale face behind the sunglasses. His two minders would wait outside watching the streets, the derelict buildings, hands stuffed in their army-issue jackets.

But on this visit Smee bit his lips. A frown like a small mammal creased his forehead. He played with the rings on his fingers. He picked his nose. There was even a whiff of body odour.

'There's a problem with the books,' the gangster said. 'The people who've been buying them, they're all . . . dead.'

'What?' Black whispered. 'What do you mean?'

'My contact, he said these guys got ill. Got some kind of flu, died a few days later. No one would have put the thing together but these book collectors, many of them are professionals. Doctors, lawyers, you know—people with dough. They don't accept death so readily. They investigate.'

'They found some kind of link?'

'They sure did,' said Smee. 'All of them bought books from you. The health people think your merchandise might be infected. I don't know if they are. I've been here so many times and nothing's happened to me. But I've never touched them books, have I?'

'No, you haven't. What are you going to do?'

'What do you think I'm going to do? I'm shutting this operation. Too risky for me. I'm a businessman. I got other worries. Bigger problems.'

The gangster slid out the door. His men trotted after him, their shoulders hunched, eyes still darting.

'Shit,' whispered Black. 'Shit, shit, shit . . .'

The two dead women. Now this.

He pressed his back against the desk and stared at the volumes, their leather spines like a thousand eyes gloating at him from their burdened shelves.

'What the hell have you done!' he shouted. 'You're just books, just bloody books!'

He had sold maybe two dozen. Some customers bought two or three volumes. How many had died? Ten? Fifteen? How many were killed? He could easily check in the computer. But he didn't want to. He didn't dare. These people, his poor innocent customers, they must have had families, loved ones, children.

He crumpled to his knees.

It was his fault. He should have known. The curse. He was an untouchable. So were the books.

He knew what he had to do.

*　*　*

Polystyrene takeaway cartons and shreds of newspaper tore at Black's weary boots. He had worked all afternoon. His back ached. His arms, his legs, felt like lead. Despite the cold, his face was covered in sweat.

He dropped the volumes, they spilled sorrowfully onto the hard ground. At last he had done it. Those were the last ones. They were all piled in the middle of the street. It was like a mountain of knowledge.

The books were stacked ten feet tall, their leather covers seeing the light of day, maybe for the first time. Their pages ruffled by the wind as though quickly read and, just as quickly, discarded. Who could blame this sad wailing breeze that swooped down every laneway, every nook and cranny, that dared to touch every tortured soul, every wicked being that dwelled here? It groaned its way through the city like a train wreck in slow motion.

These books were cursed. And the curse had grown potent. A couple of bodies nudged the mounting pile. Their bearded faces pale against the growing darkness. Their nostrils still dripping. Ever so slowly. Their overcoats splayed like blankets over them. Their eyes still open.

Black had shouted from the shop but he had not been quick enough to stop these two vagabonds from trying to steal the tomes. The teams of squatters in derelict buildings across the road, on seeing the crumpled figures, warily watched from a distance, from the broken windows, from the wretched rooftops, their syringes and empty plastic packets still strewn like used condoms on the floor.

Black struck a match. It lit up his grim sweaty face.

For a second, he hesitated.

Then the Death Collection burst into flames. The rising heat pushed him back. But inside, in his guts, he felt a heavy coldness. Darkness had fallen and the fire's yellow spell blazed upon the street sending shuddering shadows like hungry bats across the buildings, upon the graffiti-covered walls. The flames were huge and hungry, greedily eating up the pages, blooming charred holes into the leather covers. Ash, like a million black insects, swirled and spiralled into the dead night sky.

Was there a heaven up there? Or was it all death, destruction and utter misery?

'Believe me, it's the right thing to do.'

Startled, Black turned to see the pale figure in a fur coat. A large group of gangsters stood behind him. Perhaps ten or twelve men, some had hands on hips, neck craned up to the top of the flames.

Burning pages fell at their feet.

'It'll kill the germs,' said Jack Smee. 'Destroy the virus. Whatever it is that's infected your books.'

'Yes,' said Black. 'No one else will die now. It's all finished.'

'Too right,' said the gangster. 'You don't belong here anyway.'

There was a shout. One of Smee's men crumpled to the ground. Shadows slid out from the alleyways. Grew from the dumpsters. Lurched out of doorways. In the shuddering firelight, knives gleamed. Chains circled and rattled.

Smee's men drew weapons, shouting to each other.

'Ambush!' cried Smee.

He flicked out a gun and fired. Two attackers, who had almost reached him, twirled and fell.

Smee's men slashed with their knives, chains and nunchakus. One dropped to his knees, moaning, a knife in his blood-foaming throat, hand still holding his gun. Snarling figures danced their way through the smoke towards Smee. Clubs, knives, swords raised high.

Black cried out. A pain clawed his stomach. The attacker pulled out a dagger. Before Black could even think he had ripped off his glove and pushed his hand into the man's face striking him on one cheek.

The man staggered back. Sneezed. Spun. And collapsed.

In the trembling light thrown by the hungry flames, Black stared down at his wound. It was gone. There was nothing there but a rip in his sweater. He felt smooth flesh. There was no blood.

It couldn't be? What was wrong with him?

He didn't know what was happening.

Black tore off his other glove. He felt the walls in his mind shudder, heard it crack open. A rush of coldness engulfed him. There was no past. No future. Only this moment of hate, blood, drugs, murder surrounding him, consuming his soul. Corrupting every street, every building, every person caught in its wickedness.

He had killed, intentionally so.

Did that mean he couldn't die? What had he become?

Black didn't understand it. Didn't want to. He wanted to end it. He would plunge into hell.

He ran into the crowd of shuffling, fighting, shouting men.

There was moaning and gunfire.

Black screamed as he grasped their hands, touched their faces, their necks, even their ears. Anyone he could find. Any uncovered flesh he could lay his hands on.

Jack Smee lay twisted on the ground. His long white fur coat splattered with blood so that he looked like a dead white leopard. His dark glasses were torn off. His pale eyes, which Black saw for the first time, belonged to a sad dead young man.

'I will heal the streets,' Black cried. 'Cleanse it of all evil!'

He spun around, hands grabbing. Reaching out.

Contorted faces fell from him. Sneezing. Coughing. Arm and limbs thrown helter-skelter. He grasped anyone he could find.

'You are mine!' he bellowed. 'All mine!'

Pain exploded upon his face, his arms. His back was stabbed and shot, but still he grabbed, his strength growing with each falling figure. Knifes, guns, clubs, men fell at his feet.

He saw horror in their faces as he came for them.

Some pleaded. Some prayed.

Black didn't care.

He laughed and screamed at the same time.

Still the books brightly burnt.

The fire raged.

And Death ran amok.

4

MAN ON THE 22ND FLOOR

Once upon a miserable time there was a miserable man who lived alone in a condo on the twenty-second floor, which was as high up in the sky as he could afford.

One day, after breakfast, he found a long strand of hair in his small bathroom. It lay unperturbed on the white tiles and stared up at him in a questioning way, because the unlikely thing was curled like a question mark.

'What are you doing here?' he questioned back.

No one with long hair, in fact, no one at all, had ever visited his one-room condo. He needed to be alone most of the time, except when it got too lonely, which found him wandering down corridor after corridor after corridor after corridor in the soulless five-level shopping mall beneath the condominium tower.

He picked the offending strand up with a moist piece of toilet paper and dropped it in the bin.

The next day, he found five more.

'What's this?' he questioned again, a slight trembling in his face. 'A hair invasion?'

He disposed of the offending strands the same way. He sat down with a rock-like frown and wondered if they fell from the endlessly humming vent in his stained bathroom ceiling.

Over the next few days, he found more strands. He would wake up in the unearthly hours and see them scattered on the cracked bathroom tiles. Several of them formed odd patterns, including a disjointed fleur-de-lys and a Japanese character which re-wrote itself every time he glanced at it.

He found hairs on the window sill, under the dining table and knotted up amidst specks of dirt beside the humming fridge.

'Damn property agent . . .' he whispered.

He was in the habit of talking to himself, as people who live alone often do.

'This place is haunted and they've got no right selling it to me.'

Then one morning, he found it, hard and shiny, on his small white coffee table beside his empty cup of coffee.

'Oh God!' he exclaimed, staring at the fingernail. He quickly checked his own to see if any had fallen off. 'No, they're all here.'

The fingernail was smaller than his and of a different shape.

Another three appeared that afternoon: beside his laptop charger, on the armrest of the sofa, and on his leather watch strap.

'Shit.' he whispered. 'This is getting too much.'

His dustbin now had not only clumps of long hair but fingernails too.

Soon these were joined by teeth.

He found two of them, both molars, one nestled beside his old rubber shoe and the other shrouded by clumps of dust beneath his bed.

Just after midnight, he woke up to find four fingernails, three teeth, and a mess of hair all over him. He turned on the bedside lamp and brushed them off his midnight skin and forehead.

Where did they come from? He had no idea. Sleep had abandoned him, or him it, and so he read his Kindle on the two-seater sofa. He could hardly concentrate as the midnight words crawled off the screen and onto his fingers.

'I need to get out of here,' he whispered. 'But where, where can I go?'

He stared out of the window at the neon signs, the brightly flickering TV billboards and a moving multitude of car headlights. There was no one below, only the homeless, drug pushers, addicts, and foreign illegals who were collecting rubbish. He wouldn't last a night on the urine-smelling streets.

'I'll stay one more night,' he said, shaking his sorrowful head. 'If things don't improve, I'll check into a cheap hotel.'

That night, he dreamt that there were objects, long and short, cold and hard, in his bed, poking his flesh, hips, back, buttocks, calves and shoulders, as if they were trying to nudge him awake. Even as he tried to find sleep again, he ran his fingers along the offending objects, first this one, then that one, and felt the smoothness and familiar curve of bones!

They were scattered all over his bedding.

He was sweating, even though he could hear the air conditioner humming. This, he realized, was no dream!

He gasped and tried to get up but could not. He was fixed to the bed, stuck there because . . .

Two bony hands now gripped his wrists!

He opened his eyes and, by the moonlight coming through the window, saw two black orbs staring back!

He screamed.

The skull, its bones glinting, not quite glowing, drew closer to his face.

The smell of dead leaves and freshly turned soil clung to it, as it tilted to one side, as if wondering what had brought on such a strange reaction. It grinned, revealing several missing incisors. He tried to pull away, moaning loudly, but the bony hands gripped him tighter, painfully, by his wrists.

His blanket had been tossed aside, so that he could see the pale skeleton draped upon his body, naked except for his underpants. The skeleton's bony ribs pushed against his stomach as it held him in place, its knee bones prodding against his bare shins.

'No . . .' he groaned. 'Let me go!'

But still it held him down.

Then, he heard a scratching sound, and there crawled on the bed, a hairy creature, its pale flecks quivering. As it bounded toward him, he realized this was no animal but rather the clump of hair, fingernails, and teeth from the dustbin, now alive, active and quite horribly animated. They rolled and curled as a single entity, like a tiny rat or a large hairy cockroach.

He shivered as it drew towards him.

Then, instead of leaping at his face, they shuddered up the skeleton's spine, untangling themselves as they did so.

He stared wide-eyed as the hairs fixed themselves on the top of the grinning skull which, in turn, like magic fertilizer caused more strands of hair to not only sprout but to luxuriate in black flowing tresses.

The teeth fastened themselves into the skull's mouth with a clicking sound like cracking fingers. The fingernails had further to go as they loudly scratched their way down the arms of the skeleton to the metacarpals that held his wrists down.

'Please,' he whispered. 'No more of this . . .'

He shut his eyes and recited a prayer, but even as he spouted the gibberish, he knew that no help would come.

He unclosed his eyes. The skull stared back, bathed in glorious moonlight. Still grinning, now proudly, with a full set of teeth.

What did it know that he didn't?

Perhaps it was anticipating the pale worms which now encircled upon its pale bones. They smelt of rotting, decomposing flesh. More worms appeared, slithering out of its nostrils and mouth . . . and from the throbbing, frightful shadows of its bony anus. They moved, then stopped at certain predetermined parts of the skull and skeleton.

Then he realized, to his horror, that these were not flat worms at all, but flesh.

Moving, living flesh!

As they merged upon the skull and its bones beneath, like a jigsaw finding its solution or a Sudoku puzzle getting its fill of numbers, skin began to form.

As he watched, his horror turned to amazement.

The skull was disappearing and a face was appearing.

Not only that. But it was one he recognized.

It was . . . dear God . . . his wife!

She was gently smiling. He smelt flowers, the ones from her abundant garden she once tended so lovingly at their old bungalow. She softly laughed.

A cool breeze blew upon his face and, for a moment, he was reclining upon a boat on a gentle lake with lapping waters and chirping birds, and leaves fluttering down like kisses from low overhanging branches.

His wrists were now caressed by smooth, soft hands. Warm feet rubbed against his legs, and he felt her naked breasts sighing upon his bare chest.

'I've missed you,' she whispered.

Her voice!

How his heart ached to hear it again.

The burden of those lonely, empty months, lifted off his shoulders. 'I've missed you too,' he gasped, but before the last words were out of his throat, her lips were on his.

They made love that night. Skin upon skin. Mouth upon mouth.

Both weeping as they did so.

They woke up just after dawn, husband and wife.

And here the story should have ended with both of them living happily ever after.

But it is not to be.

Ten days after her appearance, he would wake up, as warm sunlight filtered in through the curtains, and touch her hand.

It would be stone cold.

His heart would tighten . . . for he knew she was dead.

He would stare into her face. Her small nose. Her forehead that was so often caught in a frown. He would brush strands of hair off her smooth, pale cheeks. Then he would kiss her closed eyes and her cold, cold lips.

And weep.

There was no body to bury. For during the course of the morning, her hair would shed, fingernails and teeth would drop and vanish. Her flesh would rot, her bones would fall to dust and be blown away by some other- worldly wind. This would leave him staring at a blank wall for hours.

Then, after weeks of misery, a strand of hair would appear on his bathroom floor like a question mark.

He does not need to look at it questioningly as he once did for he knows that soon he will find her fingernails and teeth and that, in a matter of days, she will appear in his bed.

This cycle of death and resurrection continued for months. He would be joyful and miserable, delighted and despairing, as she came and went.

'Why did you kill yourself?' he once asked her as they lay naked in each other's arms early one morning, the cotton blanket tossed about their feet.

For a while she stayed silent, her hair draped like forgotten dreams upon her pillow. Then she whispered, her eyes closed: 'My thoughts, they overwhelmed me. The darkness, so dreadful, always pressing into my head. Ever since he died . . . I just didn't know how to live . . .'

'Our darling boy . . .'

'Yes . . . our son . . .'

He sometimes felt like dying too. 'But you, you were getting better, weren't you?'

'Worse too. Misery filled me. I just couldn't carry on living. But I regretted slitting my wrist as I sat shivering in the corner, on that shower floor. As I felt my life slip away, I wanted to hold you so much. I didn't want to die.'

'You came back to life. But you always leave. Why?'

'I can't explain it . . .'

'It's awful for me, you always leaving. Then waiting and waiting for you to return. Never knowing how long you'll stay.'

'I don't want you to be hurt. Was it better for you living alone without me coming and going?'

'I don't know.'

One night, after weeks alone, he woke to find her skull glowing and shifting like swarms of jellyfish in the moonlight.

'This can't go on,' he whimpered. 'I want you to do it . . .'

His ragged breathing curled around the corners of the bed.

'No, it can't,' she said, her voice breaking. 'This is too much for you, isn't it?'

He turned to her. She was wondrous now: hair, teeth, flesh and skin, full formed.

He nodded.

'Are you sure this is what you want?'

'Very sure.'

He lifted his head and her hands encircled his throat.

He stared into her moon-lit face, deep into her eyes of a thousand sighs. His fingers gripped his pillow tight as his breath fought inside his lungs. Sweat burst upon his forehead.

The room closed around him and, still staring into her now tearful, loving eyes, he slipped away. And the miserable man was gone . . . floating high up, well beyond the twenty-second floor . . .

PART 2

FRAGMENTED MINDS

5

EMIL AND THE LURKING SHADOW

The gleaming green marble floor reminds me of the bathroom where I shattered Daddy's bottle of eau de cologne. Did I not then place a shard of glass upon my wrist? Can't recall. Not really.

I click my high heels upon the marble as I walked across the lobby, my footsteps echoing up to a ceiling of a hundred blinking lights. I press the magic button and the glass sliding doors whisper and smoothly open.

Exit corporate world.

Enter real world.

The sun-blazed day, I hardly saw, has left a residue upon the streets no breeze from the harbour can dissipate. The streets are submerged in darkness and the glow of the streetlights shine impotently upon the lower floors of the towering office blocks. Rock music from a pub echoes a slavish, slandering melody. I turn a corner and it fades to the distance. A sleek BMW purrs, waiting alone by the traffic light, the indicator blinking, winking—a young couple going home after dinner perhaps. Young?

'Aren't I still young?'

No way, Mon Cherie.

I look around and see nobody. But hear, then see a bus ploughing the route—three passengers sitting back bathed in a gloomy fluorescent glow. Last bus. Well past ten o'clock.

A different sound on the pavement. More surreptitious. Less distinct. Heard it before. A shadow dancing in the corner of my eye. A scraping, a ragged pounding in my head. I don't dare think . . . can it be him . . . the one following . . . lurking in the hazardous gloom. Has to be. Been following me for several nights. I've given him a name—*The Lurking Shadow*. I breathe a little faster. I turn, see nothing, just hear the sound, a hollow heartbeat upon the street.

'Get away from me,' I whisper.

I'll always be here.

'Didn't mean you, Emil.'

I know, I know.

I see Emil's face. See that last tortured glance as he walks with his only possession, a rucksack of French literature—always walking out of the door never to return. Leaving the door wide open so I see the darkened suburban houses cramped up against the street, and all I hear are distant waves sorrowfully breaking upon the rocks.

I cock my head. The Lurking Shadow again.

Two men on a hot muggy night. The uneasy student who left me and the one creeping behind. Emil's voice in my head, can deal with that—but not Lurking Shadow, too real, too dangerous. I turn away and push my pace. A bead of sweat forms upon my brow, perspiration trickles down my back, clinging to a silver chain around my neck. I wipe my brow, my face, with a Kleenex and struggle with the briefcase and handbag up a sloping pavement towards the car park. The streetlight in front is broken. I carry on regardless, plunging myself into darkness, pressing my way to the car park entrance. Blackness has a hold here. So thick it binds itself to everything. When are they going to repair the streetlight?

Never. No one will ever leave a light on for you.

'Just bloody shut up, Emil.'

I'll shut up provided you shut down.

'Go to hell!'

You'll find hell up here if you don't get into the car park soon, Mon Petite.

The car park entrance is sealed by a metallic roller blind. I take out my key card from my handbag and slide it through the slot. A tiny red light blinks, winks three times to indicate acceptance.

An angry giant wakes. A loud shuddering, a squeaking, a noisy motor whirring, hidden parts moving. The blind lifts itself from the ground.

The bottom edge is angled—long and sharp like a guillotine that has done its messy work. A McDonald's carton lays crushed beneath it, the chocolate shake spilt on the floor like blood. A twisted yellow straw points up at me. Another victim to the revolution. No cake though, Marie Antoinette, just Big Macs. The blind is now three feet off the ground and I can get into the car park if need be. If the Lurking Shadow is still following, I can stoop my body over and quickly enter.

I stoop my body and enter.
I stoop my body and enter too.
'Shut up, Emil, You're always up to no good.'
I was always up for you.
'What? Leaving the light on.'
Hah! No light is bright enough for you!
'You think you're pretty funny, don't you?'
I'm funny I'd say, Mon Cherie, but useful too, wouldn't you say?
'In what way?'
Told you to bring my baseball bat. In the car for protection.
'Not a bad idea, I must say . . . in case he follows.'
I've got an even better idea. Stop hanging about and go fetch your car!

I walk down the concrete slope towards the lifts on Basement One. The air holds a brooding stillness. Not a single car on this level—the vacant spaces numbered, stark and bare. The fluorescent lights emit a dull brightness, the artificial yellow of a smog-filled sky.

All this while, the invisible hands are whirring, the metal noisily creaking, the blind shaking as it folds into itself. Half way down the slope I know the fast-food guillotine has completed its upward course and now starts its descent. Descending in a slow cantankerous manner not envisaged by the good old Dr Guillotin who perfected his all too efficient machine on live sheep and human cadavers.

I am alone here. If the Lurking Shadow comes in now I will be meat for him—and it is at this point, no matter how hard I try to resist, that I always look back, watching the guillotine mark its slow descent downwards with a creaking like teeth chattering or fragile bones breaking.

I turn away towards the lifts before the guillotine completes its descent, taking the risk the Lurking Shadow can still slip in beneath it.

Stoop his body and silently enter.

I briskly walk to the lifts and press the button, its lights up like an eye opening. I turn and watch the roller close upon the ground. The noise dies. The giant asleep. The silence of a mortuary. Shadow could be with me, hiding behind the pillar, scurrying behind the large plastic dustbin on wheels.

'What do I do, Emil?'

Do what you usually do—run!

'What the hell do you mean?'

Always running. Like the way you ran from me.

'I never ran from you!'

You're right, you never did.

'You ran, Emil. You ran.'

I did. I did. On a cold windy night—with the waves breaking on the rocks.

'And I came after you.'

You did, Mon Cherie. You really did.

I tighten the grip on my briefcase, switch my handbag to my right shoulder. Glance at my watch. Ten thirty. What's holding up the stupid lift? The lift finally arrives with an out-of-place melodic chime reserved for swish hotels and million-dollar penthouses.

I steal a glance back at the concrete slope up towards the closed, silent guillotine, and quickly enter the lift. Cool, air-conditioned, a floor of polished marble, smooth tinted mirrors on three sides. I look older than thirty-four in my corporate jacket. My brown hair sits in a tangle just below my shoulders, a pair of silver earrings peep from beneath the mess. My make-up starting to run, ridges beneath my eyes like lines on old leaves, my face hollow, my mouth small for small kisses only. Small kisses Emil hated. He would sit back on the mattress amidst a tangle of grubby sheets, frown as if he'd had no onion in his soup (just Big Macs for you, Emil), then jump on me, retaliating with long deep kisses which left me shaking and breathless.

Breathlessly, I slip my card through the slot and press B4, the button lights for a second, then dies. The lift takes me up with the sound of compressed rushing air, the indicator flashes: B1 . . . G . . . 1 . . . 2 . . . 3 . . . 4 . . .

5 . . . 6.

'Wrong way! Wrong way!'

How do you know where you're going anyway, Mon Petite?

'Shut up. I'm going down. He's coming after me!'

You came after me. I heard you running down the road. I turned and saw your face full of tears.

'I don't want to talk about that now!'

I brush Emil aside and, in quick succession, repeatedly try to light up B4. Damn lift. Always happens. A mind of its own. With trembling hands, I slip my card through the slot again, press B4, it finally lights and stays lighted. I sigh. The eye is open—at each other we blankly stare. Did it blink then? An almost indiscernible wink?

Shit! The musical chime.

I'm on Basement One again!

The lift door opens. I scream. It echoes, rebounding off the pillars and concrete walls. Nothing. Nothing there. No one. Just dirty yellow light and heat like groping fingers upon my face. I breathe out. Going nuts.

Wait.

A white object rolls, almost floats, down the sloping pavement. It's the McDonald's drink carton, spilling chocolate shake like old blood spraying in an orgy of decapitation. With a cold certainty reserved only for those about to die, I know the object was kicked by Shadow and Shadow is in here with me.

I hear him!

Footsteps. Inside the car park. Coming down the concrete slope. Coming for me!

I press the button to close the lift doors. It stays open!

The footsteps get closer. I stagger back into the corner— my twin reflections screaming out from the mirrors like a banshee. Dear God, he's almost here, what's he going to . . .

A dark shape moves, a shadow thrown into the interior of the lift. Even as I scream, I see the glint of a dagger lifted high.

I fall to the floor, arms over my head, waiting for Shadow to leap in laughing.

The door slides shut. Thank God!

The sound of compressed air rushing, the indicator flashes—B1 . . . B2 . . . B3 . . . B4.

B4!

The doors slide open to that absurd musical chime. I get up, trembling, and step out into Basement 4, my car sits alone surrounded by pillars and numbered empty spaces. My high heels echo rapidly as I cross the expanse of hard concrete. I hear the lift going up, the rush of air.

It's going up to get him.

'Oh shit!'

Up and down like a guillotine.

'What do I do?'

Get in the car. Quickly!

'Okay, okay!'

For Christ's sake, check the back seat first!

I cup my hands on the window and peer at the back seat. No one hiding. No one lying on the floor to strangle me when I get in, just a couple of books and strewn magazines. I enter, slamming the door.

I turn the key to start the engine. It rattles! I start it again. It rattles a' bloody 'gain!

The musical chime. A bulky figure pushes out from the lift.

The Lurking Shadow! No!!

I start the engine. It clatters pathetically. 'Damn it, start now! Just bloody start! Please!'

He comes for me now, striding across the concrete expanse. Heavy footsteps. Broad shoulders. Face buried in shadows, yet I know he wears an ugly grin. And I know the dagger hides beneath the jacket, the blade eager to make minced meat of me.

I start the engine. It shudders and dies. I slam my palms on the steering wheel.

'Oh God—help me, Emil!'

Help yourself. You always help yourself. Helped yourself to me.

'Shut up, Emil!'

Shadow trots across the pavement.

Use the baseball bat!

I reach beneath the seat and bring out Emil's metal baseball bat.

Now get out of the car!

I push the car door open and step out. Shadow is striding around the car to my side.

'What do I do, Emil?' I scream.

Hit him!

'How? How?'

You damn well know how! That night with the waves crashing . . .

'Excuse me, do you need some help?'

. . .you came out racing with that baseball bat!

'I can't do it again!' Tears stream down my face.

'Hey, is there a problem?'

You damn well can!!

'Your car, okay?'

I raise the baseball bat high above my head and, with all my strength, smash it against his skull. A crunching sound. An ugly splintering.

Shadow collapses in a heap.

I reach into my handbag. Shadow moans. One eye opens. Unbelieving. Staring. Blinking. Winking. I release the catch and the razor clicks out into the smog-filled light like a long-forgotten lover. I place it against his quivering throat to close his eyes forever. Oh, those blinking, winking eyes.

Blood gushes forth onto his tie, soaking into his suit, bright crimson trickles on concrete towards his briefcase. His left leg twitches repeatedly.

Hidden in a corner, behind a pillar, Shadow's car sits patiently. Watching.

Good night, Mon Cherie.

'Good night, Emil.'

In the distance, beyond the vast expanse of concrete, beyond the towering buildings and suburban homes, I hear waves sorrowfully crashing.

6

LADIAH

'Hey Eddie,' I called out across the squash court.

Eddie turned, sweat on his face. He swung his racket over his shoulder, blinked, gave a boyish grin and said: 'Ai ya, ai ya, it's you . . .'

I figured it had been over thirty years since our schooldays and Eddie wouldn't remember. But he did. He called out my name as if it had always been there burning at the tip of his tongue. I shouldn't have been so surprised, after all, we were once best friends. Lost touch, of course, like so many school friends have and will, but it was great bumping into Eddie like that, not literally of course, for I'd be on the floor, my spectacles flying and breaking on the glass panes of the squash court.

Eddie, you see, is big—five foot eleven and strong—always had been, he was with the bodybuilding team. Some of it now turned to flab but he was still big. Me, I was puny with a dull accountant's face and only one child, not enough spermatozoa for another one, the doctor said.

A few years later, he said I had something called erectile dysfunction. Why not just say I was impotent? I took every medicine known to man. Viagra did nothing for me and Dried Tiger's Penis Powder only gave me a bad cough.

Eddie and I headed to the terrace for a drink. To our surprise we found out we only lived one street away in OUG. I told him I had a small factory manufacturing electrical components.

'I own a restaurant,' he said with a wide grin. 'You know what, between you and me, business is so good I'm printing money there!'

'Oh . . . that's great. So you're not a pharmacist?' I'd known since our schooldays that Eddie wanted to be a pharmacist like his father.

'No lah, I dropped out after a couple of years. Waste of time studying so hard, I was only doing it for the old man. No money there. Last year I bought a BMW, only one year old, 7 series. You know what BMW stands for?'

I shook my head.

'Big Money Win.'

'I thought BMW means Best Man Win.'

'Yeah, yeah, you're right. But the Best Man must first have the Big Money!' And he roared with laughter.

Eddie hadn't changed. So confident about everything.

'Hey, Eddie, why don't we go out for dinner next week.'

'Ai ya, good idea . . . come to my restaurant.'

So my wife and daughter, his wife and three boys went for dinner. Four times at his restaurant famous for its abalone soup cooked with eggs, tofu and Chinese herbs.

Eddie was printing money here all right, the place was always packed and each time he insisted it was his treat. Magnanimous and generous, that's Eddie.

I invited them to our Chinese New Year open house. He said they would try to come. *Try* usually means no, but to my surprise he waltzed into my terrace house that afternoon and gave ten-dollar *ang pows* to all the kids.

He announced that his wife, Poh Ting, and the three boys were visiting relatives. Strange, I thought, putting our open house before his family.

Eddie stayed drinking Anchor beer, chewing nuts but took no cake or the spicy chicken wings my cousin brought. Guests and family came and went but Eddie, he stayed on and on. When everyone else had left and the children in the streets had retreated behind doors, I asked him why he wasn't visiting his family with Poh Ting and the boys.

'I don't like her brother's family,' he said.

'Why's that.'

'Snobbish, you know. Think they're so grand with their Mercedes-Benzes.'

'Ah . . . don't worry, lots of Mercedes-Benzes in town these days—no big deal.' My mud-streaked Proton in the porch caught my eye. It needed a wash but I couldn't do it on New Year's Day.

Eddie turned to me and whispered. 'I took up your invite because I didn't want to stay alone at home with . . .' he glanced around, ' . . . the servant.'

Then he grinned and for the first time I saw that strange look in his eyes. So unlike Eddie—there was no confidence there, but rather a fearful yearning.

'Why's that, Eddie?'

Eddie took a long slurp at his Anchor, threw a handful of nuts into his mouth and chewed. Then he took another swig at his beer, looked at me, opened his mouth, and then I saw it, a tremor rose like a large caterpillar shunting its way up from his stomach to his face, the folds of his cheeks shook as though an earthquake was marching past.

'She's . . . she's,' he glanced around again, ' . . . doing magic on me.'

And there it was again, that *strangeness* in his eyes.

'I knew there was something not right with her when she first came to work with us.'

Eddie told me, in between the slurping of beer and the chewing of nuts, of how Ladiah, from her first day had given him looks which made him sweat on his forehead and down the back of his T-shirt. And, if by chance, they were watching TV alone, Ladiah on the floor and Eddie on the sofa, she would stretch out her legs and allow her sarong to creep up one thigh, revealing smooth, smooth flesh.

Neither Penny nor I had ever seen Ladiah. But Eddie described her as no great beauty, dark face, squinty eyes, long crinkled hair, but at twenty-four she had a shape that Eddie had not had the pleasure of knowing for many years. Now, Poh Ting was a wonderful woman but she was overweight . . . well, *fat*, to call a spade a spade . . . and having Ladiah around proved a natural distraction.

But Eddie was adamant, saying he would not have given Ladiah a second glance if it was not for the way she looked him and revealed her smooth leg all the way up those inviting thighs.

Two Sundays ago, while Ladiah was on leave, Eddie strayed into the utility room. Opposite the wall piled high with boxes which they had not opened in ten years, stood an ironing board, a set of drawers and her bed. He pulled off the thin blanket and upon the pale blue sheet, as if watching him like a vermilion eye, lay a menstrual stain. Bad thing, he thought, not knowing why. Unholy woman's magic, woman's secret power. He felt idiotic to think such a thing, but this irrational idea stayed nailed in his head.

He turned to the drawer and pulled it open to reveal red panties and bras, all neatly folded. Before he could stop himself, he found himself fingering the soft material. Something then caught his eye, a swath of yellow entangled in red underclothing. He pulled at it and let it hang in the air, not believing what he had found.

His yellow underwear.

What was it doing here?

He checked the label—sure enough it said 'Jockey'. Poh Ting had bought it at a sale two years ago, came in a multi-coloured pack of six. They were big, XL, so how could Ladiah mistake them for her own panties? And she only wore red.

'So that's why I don't want to stay home alone with her,' Eddie said, chewing the nuts a little too vigorously so that bits of their skin fell down his chin.

'What did you do with the underwear?'

'Ai ya, I didn't know what to do. I was standing in Ladiah's room with my yellow underwear dangling in my hands over a drawer full of knickers and bras, so I quickly left. Just as I shut the door, it hit me—she'd know. If I took the underwear she'd know I'd been in her room rummaging through her bras and panties. So I put it back.'

'But why? She shouldn't have taken it in the first place.'

'I know-lah. I should have taken it back. I went to her room the next Sunday but it was gone. I thought she'd found out her mistake and put the underwear back in my cupboard, so I looked but it wasn't there.'

'So what are you going to do about her?'

He looked into his glass of beer as if searching for answers within its dancing bubbles.

'I'm so ashamed,' he said.

'Why?'

'I . . . I can't take my eyes of her,' he whispered. 'She enters my dreams, dancing, naked, kissing me all over and I come, you know . . . a wet dream.'

His eyes met mine, searching for some understanding.

I nodded sympathetically.

'I have to sneak out of bed and clean myself, so Poh Ting doesn't find out.'

'But, Eddie, you didn't do anything wrong.'

'I did. In my dreams.'

'But only in your dreams.'

'Don't you think your dreams reveal your real intentions, real desires?'

I thought about it. This thin puny body of mine held little physical desires. Impotent men knew not of such things.

'I'm not sure,' I said. 'Maybe it's just your mind in turmoil sending you all kinds of images, all kinds of feelings.'

Eddie shook his head. 'Ai ya, I don't know what to do . . . she's driving me *gila*. I can't get her face out of my mind, I see her dark face, long hair, all day at the restaurant. I long to get home, not to see Poh Ting or the boys, but to see Ladiah. I spend hours in bed listening to Poh Ting snoring and I really want to, need to, go downstairs and join my servant in bed, in that dingy room. I'm so, so tired. And so scared.'

For the first time I noticed the dark rings beneath his eyes and for the third time I saw that strange look shimmering there.

'Eddie,' I whispered. 'You have to get rid of her.'

'Yes, I know . . . but how?'

I'm the type to mind my own business. So I didn't speak to Eddie until a week later. I called him at work.

'Hold on,' he said. 'Let me get the other phone.' I heard banging, loud yelling in Cantonese, a sizzling, more banging. 'Okay, it's me,' he said.

'Am I calling at the wrong time?'

'Ai ya, anytime is fine.'

'So how are things going . . . you know, Ladiah?'

'No problem now.'

'She's gone?'

'No, no—we are together now.'

'Together?'

'Ai ya, having sex lah. You see . . .'

I said nothing while Eddie babbled excitedly. He had not been able to convince Poh Ting to get rid of Ladiah. Poh Ting got furious telling Eddie he had no idea how difficult it was to get good servants these days—some went on leave never to return, some brought men into the house, some were dirty, some lazy. Ladiah was perfect.

Eddie was not ready that day to tell her how strange Ladiah was and how he couldn't get her out of his mind.

If he had only told her then, things would have turned out differently.

A few nights ago, Eddie couldn't sleep. Poh Ting was already snoring, she seemed to be sleeping so well these days. Eddie lay on the pillow thinking of Ladiah, lying in bed with her sarong tied above her breast. Once she had left her door open and he had seen her so attired for bed. Now, in his mind, he saw her with her legs splayed open—waiting for him. Her tongue rolled across her moist lips, her eyes dancing into his—it was that look in her eyes driving him wild. Her long lashes blinked, her hair flowed like a veil across her face and his stiffness pushed hard against the pyjama bottoms.

He glanced at Poh Ting, still snoring, her fat bottom facing him, one fleshy arm strangling a pillow. He slipped out of bed, his erection pointing the way. He went past the boys' room and crept downstairs.

He crossed the half-dark living room, his bare foot not making a sound on the tiles. Around him were the bits of furniture they had acquired through the past fourteen years of marriage. On the wall was a photograph of the family—a devoted wife and the fruits of his loins—his three boys, all doing well at school—tuition four times a week was paying off. His family sat smiling within the silver frame, but their eyes were questioning.

Is this what you really want?

Do you want to put all that you have at risk for your servant?

But Eddie cared not. All the jewels nor all the love in the world could stop him. He pushed on. His penis still pointing the way.

To her door. The door to that cramped utility room. The door to boundless pleasure.

It stood a crack open.

He pushed it slowly, soundlessly and entered the dark.

Ladiah's bed was pushed against one wall, half of the other wall was piled with boxes. The stuff people carry with them all their burdened lives.

On the bed lay the unmistakable shape of Ladiah. Young, slim body. Legs open. Head propped on a pillow. He approached now not knowing if she was awake or asleep. The outline of her face stood against the darkness, long hair falling around her bare shoulders.

She was breathing deeply. There was the smell of garlic, of a musty sweetness which reminded Eddie of the time when, as a twelve-year-old, he had smelt his sister's bra before it was sent for wash. It had given him a headache and an aching down below. That was the first time he had masturbated and that was the best sex he had ever had. But he was sure things were about to change.

Eddie reached to touch Ladiah's face but instead felt a hand meeting his. It softly caressed his palm, long slender fingers entwined within his. Slowly she guided his hand to an exposed breast.

Eddie gasped.

'*Mari sini,*' she whispered.

She drew him to her several times that night, the bed creaking and creaking and creaking.

Close to dawn he returned upstairs to Poh Ting who still slept so blissfully. Eddie did not feel tired, but felt vibrant, so very alive.

'Poh Ting doesn't suspect a thing,' he whispered over the phone. I thought I heard a giggle.

'But Eddie, you can't carry on like this.'

'Oh yes, yes, I can. I go downstairs every night and join Ladiah. It's so wonderful.'

'How much sleep have you been getting?'

'None!'

Again I thought I heard a giggle.

'But soon I will. When Ladiah and I are together for always.'

'What do you mean? You're going to leave Poh Ting and the boys?'

'Maybe they're going to leave me.' And then he *did* giggle.

'Eddie, listen . . . don't you think she might have put some kind of magic spell on you. You said so the other day.'

'Ai ya, I was talking *gila* things then. I want Ladiah, she's all I want.'

'What about Poh Ting and the boys?'

'What about them?'

I don't believe in magic. But I've heard stories about charms, potions, *bomohs* and the more I thought about it, the more certain I was that Eddie was under Ladiah's love spell. She was Indonesian and Indonesians knew about these things, don't they?

I closed my factory early that day and sent my four workers home. I returned to OUG and watched TV for awhile, helped my nine-year-old daughter with her homework, after which she gave me a kiss, I tucked her into bed, adjusting the fan so it didn't point straight on her face. She wanted to learn the piano, but I couldn't afford it, not until things picked up at the factory anyway.

Later that night I voiced out my fears to my wife.

'I think he's going to do something to them.'

'Like what?' she said. Penny poured me a cup of ginseng tea. She first started giving it to me six years ago, perhaps hoping it would improve our non-existent sex life. It made me more alert, that I think it did but as for downstairs, it was still a dreadfully feeble affair.

'Kill them,' I said and cradled the hot cup, wafts of steam spiralled upwards, my spectacles became misty. 'He's going to kill his family.'

Penny wiped her hands on her shorts. She had spilt tea on it. She placed her trembling cup on the table. 'What makes you think so?'

'His voice. The tone of it I suppose. Just a feeling I have. A damn scary feeling.'

'Why don't you call the police?'

'And tell them what? I've no evidence.'

'But what if something should happen?' A fat frown sat on her emaciated face. Her hair was dishevelled, she didn't even bother using contact lenses anymore. No sex, I suppose, takes the woman out of you.

I shook my head and sipped ginseng tea. Most people would have left the matter alone—none of my business, they would say. I couldn't. It was none of my business, true, but I couldn't stand by and watch Eddie kill his wife and three boys.

But I did. That's exactly what I did.

Two nights later, Eddie came stumbling through our gate. He gripped onto the metal grille like an orangutan in a zoo and yelled for me.

I unlocked it and let him in.

He sat down on the sofa, bawling his eyes out. 'Eddie, what's wrong?'

He gulped breaths of air, shaking his head from side to side.

'Tell me what happened?'

'Ai ya . . . ai ya . . .ai ya.' Tears meandered down the plains of his cheeks.

'What happened, Eddie?'

'How could it be?' He raised a large hand in the air, fingers gripping at an invisible thought. 'How could it?'

'Where are Poh Ting and the boys?'

'Poisoned,' he cried.

'How?'

'Poisoned at the restaurant. We . . . we were having dinner there. I . . . I was helping in the kitchen, then three or four tables started getting ill, stomach cramps and vomiting. I rushed Poh Ting and the boys to hospital but . . . but they never made it . . . dead, by the time I arrived.'

His tears dripped on our floor.

'Dead?'

'Yes, they were all there in the emergency ward, dying all around me, on the beds, on the floor, in the corridors. Sixteen people . . . sixteen people . . . all dead . . . all gone!' He wiped his tears with his palms and dried them on his shirt.

'My God, Eddie. My God.' It had happened. I did nothing and now not only were his family dead but others perished too.

Penny, face ashen and in a trembling voice, asked if he wanted something to drink. He shook his head and wiped his tears again.

'Eddie, can we help in some way, any way?'

'No.' He shook his head. Then he looked up at me, that strangeness in his eyes. Then I recalled he had spent two years studying pharmacy.

'Eddie, how did the poison get in the food?'

His tears stopped—as though a blistering drought had come. 'Don't know. Someone put poison in the abalone soup—it was simmering in the pot all afternoon . . . anyone could have put it in.'

Then I asked the question I dreaded to ask, but knew I had to ask it.

'And Ladiah?'

'She was helping in the kitchen all day. We were short staffed.'

'I see,' I said. Was it Eddie or Ladiah, or both of them? I didn't know. Didn't want to know. But it was murder all the same.

And I did nothing.

Two months later Eddie was dead. I couldn't bring myself to attend the funeral of Poh Ting and the three boys, but I went to Eddie's.

A large crowd had gathered at the Catholic Church. Most people said Eddie died of a broken heart. For the death of his family and so many others. They were right. The coroners report read acute myocardial infarction.

Heart attack.

Eddie didn't leave much behind and some whispered that before he died he had been spending lavishly on clothes and jewellery. Those whispers said he had a mistress but no one knew who she was.

As for Ladiah, she had disappeared the week before, went back to Indonesia and never came back.

'Don't know why,' said Eddie's elder sister, wiping a tear from beneath her dark glasses. 'Poh Ting found her very good. Did you ever meet her?'

'No,' I said, staring at the freshly turned soil. 'But I heard she was good.'

We stood in silence beneath a large tree, beneath a sky that said rain. I didn't tell Eddie's sister her unwashed bra had given her dead brother his first orgasm ever. It would not help her grief.

A few weeks later our servant went on Hari Raya leave and never came back. So unreliable servants nowadays, Penny said after waiting two weeks for her to turn up. And so expensive too.

The agency quickly found us a new one after Penny demanded our deposit back. From the first day, our new servant stared strangely at me from her dark face, her squinty eyes and whenever, by chance, we watched TV alone, she would pull up her sarong and show plenty of her young smooth legs. I could do nothing but wipe the mist from my glasses and stare.

Now Penny is a wonderful wife, but I've been impotent for years and she is her dishevelled self and, as I've said, doesn't even bother wearing her contact lenses . . . but she's been sleeping so well recently.

At night I lie in bed and think of Liza. I see her dancing naked before me with that beckoning look in her eyes and I, I am so, so stiff below. For two nights now I had to creep out of bed to clean myself.

Yesterday, as expected, I found my underpants in Liza's drawer. I left it nestled amongst her red panties and bras whose soft silky material held such musky scents, such forbidden pleasures. My thoughts return relentlessly to Penny and electricity and accidents that happen at home.

But tonight. I will go down to the utility room. And I know Liza or Ladiah, or whatever her real name is, will be waiting for me.

7

KYOTO KITCHEN

The gun sits snugly in your jacket pocket. If you see him, you'll shoot him point blank. Right between the eyes.

You tell yourself this. Over and over. Never mind the so-called fact that he was hung a year ago in Taiping prison. His body falling through the trapdoor, the sudden jerk breaking his neck or, better still, strangling him to death. You wish you'd seen his legs dancing salsa-like beneath him.

But you'd fled the sweltering traffic-locked city by then . . .

You wonder if he pissed in his pants.

You zip off your jacket, sling it over the wooden chair and sit down, quite aware of the gun and the spare magazines nestled heavily within. The restaurant is ill-lit. There are seven small tables, all empty. A small ceramic cat bounces from side to side next to the cash machine. It's painted white, has red ears with one paw raised.

Its big cold eyes burn.

You flip the laminated menu over.

Wallaby Yakiniku.

Thinly sliced wallaby pan fried with seasonal vegetables in sauce made with sake, fresh ginger and garlic.

'What you like?' asks the waitress in a light blue uniform with a brown stain on the collar. She has short messy hair which reminds you of seaweed. The mole on her forehead reminds you of a hole in the head. Her name tag says Mei. She should have another on her neck, you decide. The one that says *Made in China*.

'Chicken Katsu,' you say. It is, after all, five dollars cheaper. 'And Japanese tea.'

She scribbles the order, wrinkles her nose and saunters away.

You haven't shaved or had a shower for days. You slept last night in these same clothes on the sofa, the television blaring its way through old soaps, adverts, news breaks and game shows.

Or was that the night before?

Outside the window, across the one-way street, is a supermarket and an ATM machine. Beside it, is a second-hand clothes store with an over-weight, middle-aged blonde woman arranging multicoloured dresses on a metal rack outside. A man with spectacles, wearing a dark blue beanie walks a black poodle. An assortment of people wander by beneath lumbering grey clouds.

Your reflection in the glass is ugly: crumpled jumper, dirty brown hair, sunken face, hooded eyes. You drop a couple of pills into your palm and dry swallow them. You tap the empty bottle on the table.

A car rolls by, an industrial beat and an acidic voice spewing from its open windows.

Rap is crap. That's what Jenny used to say, her blue eyes lighting up.

'Watch your mouth,' you'd reply. 'Just say it's rubbish, okay?'

But now you know the undeniable truth.

Everything is crap.

It's chilly and you regret taking your jacket off. The furniture is dark brown and there's a framed poster of Mount Fuji on a wood-panelled wall. It's faded and so are the two red lanterns hanging above your head. There's a stale smell of garlic and beer. This restaurant is exhausted like an old woman who refuses to get out of bed.

Mei appears with a pot and tea cup. A Japanese pop song crackles from hidden speakers. The woman's voice is desolate and off-key. You tug a paper napkin from a metal dispenser, then pluck a pair of chopsticks from a plastic container. Your elbow bumps against the gun's barrel.

Yes, it's there. You feel safe with it. It keeps you company beneath the mattress as you lie awake at night in the bedsit, your thoughts churning.

Becky. Jenny.

They're whispering in your head. You're whispering back:

If I see Gazali, I'll shoot him dead between the eyes. That's what you tell them. Over and over. You really will, even if your bullet just flies at fleeting shadows.

You've seen him spying from office windows, then vanishing like tinted smoke. Glimpsed his moustache behind the chanting Hare Krishna woman passing out leaflets. Caught him mingling in his khaki uniform at a corner outside a department store, then disappearing just as the green man appears and pedestrians hurry across the ever busy bitumen.

Once you'd even seen him across the aisle at JB Hi-Fi pretending to look at CDs. He had his beret and a smirk on his face. But when you looked up again, heart pounding, he was gone.

You've never believed in ghosts. But what you saw on YouTube changed your mind. Often, you'd find yourself, hunched over a screen in the city library. You glanced at the row of craning necks, like sheep to the slaughter, worshiping the machine. They, like you, need to surf. Go anywhere, just so you don't have to think.

As usual, you googled: *Jalan Duri Murder*.

Jalan Duri . . . Thorn Street.

Sure enough, out jumped the search results. The first two were the English language newspaper articles which you'd read countless times. You knew them by heart. Then there was the blog about how the house was now vacant, unsaleable and unrentable. Everyone knew about what had happened and no one dared live there. You had read that one too. It was riddled with spelling mistakes. But then there it was.

Something new.

A YouTube video.

Entitled *Jalan Duri Mystery Lights*. You stared at it, biting your lips, feeling in need of a double shot of Jim Beam. You put on the headphones and clicked. At first there was only a black screen, the sound of shuffling and someone mumbling. Then the house, in a shaky night shot, slowly came into focus.

A modern Californian-style bungalow.

That's what the agent said when she rented it out to you. Her business card read Elaine Choo, Reapfield Properties, Kuala Lumpur.

'Everything's new inside,' chirped Elaine that afternoon beneath the searing sun beside parked cars and neighbouring front gates. 'It's just been painted and it's close to the shops and restaurants. There's a small swimming pool at the back. I'm sure your family will like it.'

They did, especially your wife, Claire.

In the night-shot video, the two-storey bungalow with its rendered walls, its tiled roof and arched windows, was surrounded by hazy spherical lights. There were five of them, pulsing and steadily circling above the swimming pool.

It could have easily been a hoax. Still, your heart was beating rapidly in your chest like a caged bird. You struggled to breathe as you clicked back to the search results.

Then you noticed the second video. It was called *Jalan Duri Ghosts*.

'Chicken Katsu,' says Mei as she slips the meal in a red lacquered Bento box before you. 'Everything okay?'

'Fine, fine,' you mumble.

The sweet savoury smell turns your stomach queasy. The pale egg draped over the crumbed dead meat is like brain tissue oozing out. You sip some tea to calm yourself.

You close your eyes and the second YouTube video plays in your head. It's always repeating over and over, ever since the day you saw it.

The digital read-out says 2.21 a.m.

The image, saturated in yellow, is shaky. It pans to the left, over the top of the familiar iron gate, before darting to the right. Then it halts at a dormer window upstairs. The window to your family room. A light inside glows. Staring out are the three unmistakable figures.

Three dark, lonely figures.

Each shorter than the next, reminding you of Babushka dolls. Each fitting neatly into the other.

Becky. Jenny.

The tallest is the Filipino maid, Maria.

The camera zooms out. The grainy image slides down, trembles on the road, then pans up along the iron grilles, before focusing on the large padlock and chain. Then it jerks upwards.

Hands tighten against your throat. Your heart pounds like a hammer in your chest. He is there. Always there. His cheeks pushing sickeningly against the grilles, twisting his head one way then the other as though he was trying to escape through it, or to decapitate himself.

There's no doubt who he is. His moustache. His cropped greased hair.

Gazali.

Hello, Tuan.

'You bastard!'

That was what you screamed in that library the first time you saw it.

Heads spun at you.

Then you smashed a fist into the keyboard. That was when the stumpy librarian escorted you out of your seat, pass the hall with its flapping community notices and out the automatic sliding door into the cold air.

'I'm sorry, sir,' she said in her curly brown hair and loose green sweater beneath that purple sky. 'We can't have you in here.'

'That's okay,' you stammered. 'I'm sorry about the keyboard.'

Stumbling away beneath rustling trees, you then spied, lit by a dim pool of light from a streetlamp, a figure wearing a beret beside a butcher's, watching you. You had seen him often enough in your nightmares, glimpsed him in shops and crowded streets, but here he was, standing so erect, shoulders back, as though proud to be your acquaintance.

Which is why you now carry a gun and two spare magazines.

The Chicken Katsu is getting cold. It sits like a severed hand on sticky rice. The thick brown sauce is coagulated blood. There's a miserable slice of tomato interlaced with cucumber to resemble a flower. But this flower can only be made of cancer cells.

You never enjoyed Japanese food, Claire and you, not until you worked in KL. Life was pretty good. Your girls were happy. Becky nine. Jenny twelve. They were at the international school and they had made new friends.

But after what happened, Claire withdrew into the unreachable depths of herself. And why wouldn't she? You had returned to the city where you were born. The idea was for a fresh start.

But silence built upon silence, until it was screaming at you both. You no longer had sex. No longer ate together. You only stared at the TV and chased beer with Jim Beam, too drunk to walk out the door let alone go to work. Then one day you found her handwritten note. It said: *I have to go. Life together is too hard. Sorry.*

It is all too easy to pick that moment when life collapsed all around you. It was at a lunch-time function at one of KL's five-star hotels when Claire's mobile rang.

It was the police.

The inspector wouldn't say what it was about but he insisted you both had to go to the station immediately. So you quickly drove your Volvo into the congested city centre and parked illegally at the station's front gate. As both your footsteps rang upon the external metal stairs to the inspector's office, you felt the sense of dread grow with each step.

The office was hot and cramped. A printer whirred. There were several ancient-looking computers, an air conditioner coughed and rattled. There were two men there. One was busy writing at his desk.

The other man got up, buttoning his dark blue jacket as he did so. He had a chubby face and the pocks on his cheeks seemed to crawl like large ants.

'We've received a phone call,' he said, eyeing you up and down. 'Your neighbour, I think he's from Iran, he phoned and said that your security guard has stolen your car.'

'That must be Claire's car!'

Claire drove a small Honda which she used to go to the neighbourhood shops or to visit friends.

'Why would he take my car?' Claire gasped. She clutched her red handbag protectively against her stomach. 'Maybe he didn't steal it. Maybe it was some kind of emergency.'

Then she cried out, 'The children!'

'This security guard,' said the Inspector, scratching his neck. 'He left your gate, also your front door, wide open.'

'What? What the heck are we doing here then!'

'Don't worry,' said the Inspector. 'Our men are already there.'

You sped through the Saturday afternoon traffic with dreadful thoughts churning through your head. Claire called the school and everyone she knew but no one could tell where the girls were.

When you got home, the electric gates stood wide open. Three police cars were scrummed at the front gate and uniformed men loitered in the driveway. One was taking photos. A couple yakked on mobiles. One was smoking and flicking ash into the swimming pool.

They couldn't find Becky or Jenny. Maria was missing.

They wouldn't even let you into the house.

The bungalow with its red tiled roof and arched windows stared with mistrusting eyes. You stood in the garden, a tightness gripping your chest. You felt like collapsing and held Claire's shoulder for support.

Then you staggered back into the blistering street, pass the police vehicles, and leant upon the car's hood, breathing hard, the sun pounding your head, sweat trickling down your back.

Your mobile began to ring as news of their disappearance spread through the city. Everyone was trying to be helpful, everyone offered their . . .

Hello, Tuan.

You look up and jerk back. There is Gazali, with his thick moustache, sitting in the restaurant in front of you. He's in his beret and khaki uniform. There are dark stains on one sleeve.

His eyes dart at your empty pill bottle. He scrutinises you for a second before glancing at your bento box as if he's working out its contents.

Then he grins at you.

Morning, Tuan.

It's after twelve but who cares whether it's morning or afternoon in the realm of the dead? Perhaps, you think, he's still on KL time. That was his habitual greeting each morning before you slid into your car, before your driver eased you out into the leafy bungalow-filled streets. Gazali would salute, press a button and the electric gates would swing shut.

You'd been there nine months, when it happened.

Eating Japanese, Tuan?

His voice is soft and ingratiating and seems to hum its way through his thin chest like a lawn mower. There's a whiff of cigarettes and body odour.

You slowly reach for the gun in your jacket, your eyes never leaving his. Sweat trickles behind your ear.

You don't care if he's real or not. He's been following you, haunting you ever since you saw that YouTube video, but you've never seen him this close. Yes, you now know, ghosts exist and you're going to shoot this one . . .

I have something to tell you, Tuan. Something important.

You withdraw your arm. You will wait and see what he has to say.

'What?' you whisper. 'What's so important?'

It's this, Tuan. Either you're insane, I'm insane or we both are.

You realise he's only in your head. Gazali spoke some English, halting and broken most of the time, but here he is speaking fluently, although still with his Malay accent. Yet, right now, the difference between what is real and what is not doesn't seem so far apart.

'What do you mean, I'm insane? You're the mad bastard . . .'

No, no, Tuan. Sure, I did what I did . . .

'You did what you did? You killed my maid then you . . .'

It was love, Tuan. But Maria rejected me. So I sat there in the guard house, knocking my head against the wall, pinching my stomach until it hurt so much. All just to forget her.

'I don't care about your sob story, you murderer!'

All you have to do is find me and hold me . . . .and kiss my tear-filled eyes. That's what I said to her, Tuan, but she wouldn't listen. Then, that afternoon, when she was hanging out the clothes, I came from behind and put my hands around her throat.

Oh, she was so soft, so small. And her skin, so warm. I pushed my face into her hair. It smelt so sweet, so pure. I squeezed her throat tightly with my fingers, with all my love. Maria's necklace, her crucifix became entangled in my fingers as if trying to protect her. But, by Allah, I still squeezed and squeezed, until we were both kneeling on the grass. We had become the truest of lovers.

'You bastard . . . you mad bastard!'

Your hands are trembling. But he's close and you know your shot won't miss. His eyes grow wide, they're chasms into madness. You'll let him talk for a moment as you fight to clear your mind.

In the end, we were both lying on the grass beneath the hanging laundry. I held onto her beneath its shade, whispering in her small ears. Oh, our bodies fitted so perfectly together. The sun was hot and high above us. Then came a gust of wind and the wet clothes were flapping, dancing for us. It was beautiful, believe me, Tuan. Then I looked up and saw your girls staring at me from the window upstairs . . .

'You . . . you were supposed to protect them . . .'

They fought hard, Tuan. Your elder girl, she cut my arm with a knife.

You jerk at the sound of sudden footsteps. It's Mei, balancing a plastic bowl on a tray. She slides the bowl on the table.

'Miso soup,' she says. She frowns at you but there's a glint of fear in her eyes. 'It comes with the Chicken Katsu.'

You say nothing and she hurries away.

You slap the bowl. It crashes.

The puddle of soup, bits of dark green nori and tofu scatter on the wooden floor.

I'm very thirsty, Tuan. What a waste. The Miso looked good. I've never had Japanese. Not once in my life . . .

Yes, the first time I saw Maria was when I went to ask for a glass of water. She was mopping the floor in a pale yellow dress. I could see the look on her face. It was so intense that it seemed that the ceiling fan's blades were slicing up her very thoughts. I felt a brilliant light pouring into my heart.

'I don't want to know about it. You said you had something important to tell you.'

Ah, Tuan. You see, after I killed them, I knew I had to get away. But I had to get rid of the bodies. So I prised open the manhole and threw their bodies into the septic tank. It smelt awful in there. Maria went in first, then your daughters . . . the elder one first.

You thrust the barrel against his forehead. Your finger tightening against the trigger.

'I don't care if you're real or not,' you snarl. 'But I'm going to shoot you!'

Wait, Tuan. Let me tell you what I came here to tell you.

'What is it, you bastard?'

Your daughters. They're, they're with you. They follow wherever I go . . .

'Bullshit!'

How can ghosts haunt other ghosts, Tuan? I just want peace now. I want . . .

His eyeballs slide horribly towards the window and he raises his arm, his index finger trembling.

Standing limply on the pavement, their foreheads almost touching the glass, are two thin pale-faced girls.

One is taller than the other. They both have shoulder-length brown hair. You recognise them straight away.

Becky. Jenny.

They're dressed in the same clothes as you last saw them that morning. Becky is wearing a white cotton dress. Jenny, who had caught the soccer craze since the World Cup, is wearing the outfit for the Brazilian team.

They stare at you, their eyes expressionless.

'Becky, Jenny,' you whisper. 'You can't be real . . .'

Your girls are covered in muck. Their locks of brown hair dangle wetly upon their foreheads. Dark splotches run down their cheeks like leeches and soil their drenched clothes.

With a death-like thud, Becky slaps her palm on the glass. It leaves a black splotch. Misshapen it is, like a map of some demonic island. Her hand is filthy. Her nails dirty. Her mouth slowly opens and closes, like a limp suffocating fish, as if she is trying to tell you something. Her eyes are pleading . . .

Becky, your daughter who is eight, who was eight, she would be ten now, has small tears welling in her eyes. Tears which you want to kiss away. Jenny, your older girl, your first born—her face a hundred times sadder than you've ever seen—reaches one limp hand towards you, her fingers curling, slowly uncurling . . .

Oh, dear God!

Sobbing, you stagger from your seat and stumble past the empty tables, almost bumping into Mei who is holding a rag at her chest. The two red lanterns hanging above the window are like blood-stained heads in nooses.

And the ceramic cat. It no longer moves.

You fling open the restaurant door and lurch outside.

Cold air hits your face.

A red scooter whooshes past.

Irrasshaimase! Mei calls out. Welcome.

Or you think that's what she calls out. Why would she say that anyway?

Is it a welcome to madness?

Your two daughters turn, heads swivelling. Their limp bodies shuddering towards you. Their eyes are dead. Dark water pools about their bare feet.

They have whispered to you through your days. You see their weeping faces in the night, but now, they're here . . .

Their hands reaching for you.

'Becky! Jenny!'

'Yes, daddy,' they call back in a dead monotone.

You don't care if they're dead or alive.

'I'm here, my darlings. I love you!'

They stop right in front of you. Awful raw sewerage wafts from their limp bodies.

Becky touches you on the chest.

You gasp and step back.

'Daddy . . .'

Her touch is horribly cold.

A woman screams. It's the blonde woman across the road, frozen next to the clothes rack.

You look down and realise the gun is swaying in your hands.

Heavy, solid, loaded.

You turn to your two girls. But they're gone.

There's just the empty pavement. Not even the dark puddles remain.

Where are they?

You search through the restaurant's window. There's your table, the bento box, the pot of tea and the empty pill bottle. But your girls aren't there.

There's Mei, staring at you, her body quite still. Her lips are twisted and the rag is pulled tightly in both hands like a rope. She's a mannequin in a psychotic establishment. The lantern-like heads in their nooses sway from side to side. They are chuckling at you.

Then you notice the wooden signboard above the front door.

Kyoto Kitchen.

It's painted in thick black brush strokes.

You twirl around. A gawking crowd has formed across the street. Their fingers point. Their eyes fearful.

'Becky! Jenny!' you holler. 'Where are you?'

Then you see him darting across the road.

Gazali!

Fleeing like the murderer, like the coward he truly is.

You had hired him to protect your family, instead he murdered them. Killed your daughters. Your darling daughters. Destroyed your reason for living.

'Gazali!' you bellow.

He stops before he gets to the opposite pavement.

Gazali turns. His beret is clutched tightly in his hands as if he is trying to rip it apart. His cropped greased hair glimmers in a shaft of sunlight. His drooping moustache bounces almost imperceptible.

But you see everything.

The two elderly women beside him. The blonde woman with one hand supporting herself on the clothes rack. A man with an army jacket. A teenage boy carrying a Target plastic bag. An Asian woman with a pram.

They're all glaring at you as if you're the criminal. Even the baby with a pink bib and pacifier has small burning eyes. They're staring like idiots. Mouths stupidly open.

Gazali calls out to you. His voice echoing above a four-wheel-drive trundling past.

All you have to do is find me and hold me . . . and kiss my tear-filled eyes. That's what I said to Maria, Tuan. If only she came to me . . .

'Where are they, Gazali! Where have you taken your girls?'

Gone, Tuan. Gone for good. I'm free now!

'This is bullshit!' you scream.

You raise the gun.

A van screeches. Someone screams.

There's the sound of a plane overhead.

A car honks twice. Grinding music blares from it.

'Rap is crap,' you whisper.

No, Tuan!

You squeeze the trigger. You shoot Gazali. Right at his chest.

But he's no longer there. The blonde woman clutches her stomach and collapses into the clothes rack.

'Where the hell is he?' you yell. 'The bloody murderer!'

The crowd screams. Some flee into the supermarket. Most get in each other's way. Gazali, the coward, is hiding amongst them. You know he is.

You shoot again. And again. And again.

The pram overturns. There's the sound of breaking glass. Blood splatters the wall like graffiti.

Bodies collapse.

You're running amok. You know you are.

But the feeling is delirious.

And, dear God, for once you're laughing!

Yes, really, truly laughing.

You stumble across the street and, standing amongst the bloodied bodies, you look for him.

He isn't there!

Perhaps he's run into the supermarket.

You grin and reload your gun.

The automatic doors slide open and the screaming truly begins.

8

THE BLACK BRIDGE

Snow.

From the hills that surround the town it indifferently drifts. Upon bare soil and barren rocks, upon the base of trees, it sweeps. From my window this morning, the trees were grey, feathery and clinging like ghostly hands to the low clouds but now, in the wintry breath of evening, they are like conquering warriors marching down shadowy slopes.

My boots, hard and heavy, follow empty pavements. A car, a van, a bus, occasionally passes through our slushy streets. There is hardly a sound except for the *click, click, click* from the pedestrian crossing.

I've walked here all my life. I know every crack in the pavement, every blemish on the shop walls, every angle of the stooping buildings, every flutter of the *koinobori*, the carp-shaped wind-socks that now colourfully flutter high up over the gorge to mark the change of season. Hundreds there are, strung up on lines, but one has fallen far below and is stuck between two jagged rocks, one end flapping like a useless flag as the river tries to drag it away.

I've never left this place, this hot spring town where tourists flock like hungry gulls during the holiday season. There are better jobs elsewhere but I choose to remain a janitor at the high school. That's all I've been these thirty-eight years. I'll retire next month. They've kept me well past retirement age as I do a pleasing job. Now I have to go though as I'm too old.

Old Hiroki. I've been called that for as long as I remember.

But once, I was young. Bristling with life. Handsome too. Skin smooth and glowing like moonlight on my face. Muscles taut upon my body instead of this flesh wasting away. And these tired old bones, barely holding this thin decrepit body together!

Today I take my usual stroll past the tourist information centre, the road wending its way up to the Hotel Morino Uto, whose windows are endless eyes, then down the slope past the imposing concrete façade of the View Hotel, along the small pretty red bridge, then back around past the empty park, the stunted apartment blocks and up to the main road, across the Black Bridge, the public foot bath, then right past the convenience store, then I'm home.

Home is one room, a small kitchen and a tiny bathroom. There's room for a bed, a chair, desk and no more.

Not even for memories.

But that's a downright lie, for they sometimes rise like corpses from the grave. They lie beside me, breathing coldly, fetidly against my neck, as I stare from my damp pillow into a silent unearthly darkness. We all have our memories, bitter or precious, don't we?

I am seventy-three and cough a lot, especially at night. Perhaps it's to chase the dead away. Doctor Ogawa says it's the cigarettes. Maybe. But I can't blame those happy sticks for my aching hips, nor the piercing pain in my knees when I stroll too much, especially in a bitter chill. But, ah, once I had arms, fingers, so strong, strong enough to pull a nylon rope so very tight!

Yes, I've lived here all my life.

I've told you that before. But we old people, we repeat ourselves, don't we? I've visited the big city many times over the years. But it's too busy, too many people, all in a hurry. This town, its streets, its surrounding hills, it clutches me tightly. A dance partner that never let go. My boots tap its pavements, resonating in my eardrums. Each echo demanding another, a ceaseless rhythm it is. So I walk.

Yes, there's the Black Bridge too. Must tell you about that. Long it is, its metal rails like prison grilles binding me.

To Myko.

To that time, the season when the fish too swam the sky. To that Sunday evening stroll, just as the sun was sinking into the hills and street lights flickered on.

Her parents had to visit a sick relative in the city, so I carted over a tattered cardboard box of bottles to her narrow wooden house beside a stream. We drank maybe four, five cocktails each, chatting all afternoon. My plans to study engineering. This boring town. Our lousy parents. Even the bad smell of their tatami mats. We laughed and sometimes kissed when she allowed me to, followed by a grin on her face as she pushed me off. I liked the birthmark on her cheek which she reckoned was ugly. But, shaped like an undiscovered island, it made her who she was, a unique girl who loved to sketch imaginary couples ballroom dancing. Later, wanting to get something to eat, we stalked out into the cold, crispy air with a purple sky quivering above as if we were the only two people on earth.

I'm not sure how it began. But as we trudged through town, my legs felt heavy and the air swam thickly as her words began to bite. She wore her black, thigh-high boots which made a clunking, scraping noise on the pavement. They made her two inches taller than me so that when she peered down intensely into my face, I felt I had no will of my own.

'I don't want any more lies,' she hissed.

'I'm not lying.'

'You are. I know you are. You better come clean, Hiroki.'

I bit my lip and eyed the snow-covered hills bitterly.

'No more lies, okay?'

She was jealous of a girl I knew in high school. I cannot even remember her name, this girl who was slightly plump, but with bright, intelligent eyes. Myko was suspicious of that friendship. She thought it something more. And perhaps there was, but nothing beyond a kiss behind the toilet block.

'Believe me, I'm not lying.'

'I know you are. I just know it!'

Our voices were raised by the time we got to the Black Bridge, so named because of the thick metal guardrails than ran along its long span. The sun had fallen behind the hills and the streetlights struggled against a rising darkness.

As we crossed the bridge, Myko, wearing a thin yellow wool sweater and red leather miniskirt, never feeling cold even in the depths of winter, craned her head from side to side as if she had a stiff neck, then started shoving at my shoulders, flinging my hand away as I tried to calm her. She jabbed a finger hard against my chest and pushed hard as if it was jelly.

I gulped.

Her breath stank of sour rum.

She shoved me to one side, staggered to the rail and started to climb it.

'Tell me the damn truth!'

'Don't be crazy, Myko! That's dangerous. Come down!'

'You love her, don't you? You're just playing with me!'

'Come down! Please!'

But instead, she climbed onto the next rail. She peered over the side, down towards the gorge, a hundred feet below.

'Tell me the truth now. You're screwing her, aren't you? Tell me the truth of I'll jump!'

'Don't, Myko! Please!'

I gasped.

She had now climbed to the top rail but one, her body swaying, her skirt flapping, one hand grasping the black metal, the other gesturing at me, whether to come or go or curse at me, I wasn't sure.

She was a fledging tree in a wild breeze . . .

'So you tell me! Or I'll jump! I mean it!'

'Please don't, Myko!'

'Tell me about the two of you!'

Then her expression changed into one of surprise, or perhaps realisation, for the birthmark on her cheek jolted, her mouth fell open as if she was singing a soundless song and her head spun away, hair twirling black in an ever white stillness, as she lost her balance. Her pleading eyes met mine just before her fingers parted from the rail and her body slid over.

I sprang towards Myko but before I could reach her, she tumbled into blackness. The last thing I saw were her boots, thigh-high and shiny in the hard yellow glow of the bridge lights. My stomach struck the rails and my fingers just managed to touch the slippery leather before it jerked away. She had bought those second hand at the outlet shop just a month ago. I peered over the edge but saw only darkness. There was no splash. Just the sound of rushing water and the wind like needles piercing my face.

That was a long ago. Many years have marched by.

All this time I lived alone.

I've never been with anyone since.

Never married. No children.

A lonely life, you could say. Perhaps even a desolate existence.

But it's not that way. Really.

I have my work at school, even though that will soon be gone. Still, I have my small home and the sound of my boots. And I can walk every day, not just on weekends and holidays. I'll have time to fully appreciate the flapping of the *koinobori* too, in their long colourful lines, fluttering freely over the river. The snow. The clouds. The trees on the surrounding hills.

All this, fills my life.

I pass the brightly-lit Family Mart but don't go in. I know every aisle, every item on the shelves, even their price tags. The pot noodles, pickles, teas, juices, cakes, bread, soba and mochi balls. The mochi balls, they are my favourite. But not today for my stomach is tight. My head heavy. Perhaps my heart too.

I light a cigarette and stroll on.

I carry on walking because there's nothing else. I could have been thinking a thousand things. Or nothing. Sometimes I feel as though these thoughts don't belong to me. As if they belong to that old janitor man from the high school and I'm somebody else. Someone yet to unveil himself. Someone entitled to live another life. I wonder what it would have been like if I did go to college or if Myko and I didn't take that fateful walk. We could be sipping tea now in a small house on a hillside by a babbling stream, browsing through her sketch book of ballroom dancing couples.

But no, I'm living this life. And it's me. This decrepit old man. Struggling with memories. Visited nightly by corpses. They yearn to tell me things. I know it from their eager whispering.

Last night, I dreamt that a red fish emerged from my ceiling. It trashed upon my bed, its paper skin crackling on my blanket, its mouth wide open, swallowing me into a world of watery dreams. Then it regurgitated me and out I fell into a wintry sky of nightmarish blackness and a crowd of naked corpses, ropes around their necks, stared up, big-eyed, from the gorge below, arms open wide.

I wend up a slope, past a squat four-storey apartment block, bicycles parked neatly at the front, sighing to myself. I turn a corner and my breath falls out my throat. I've been too deep in thought and not prepared myself. Crows leap from the bitumen, black rising from black, wings beating hard like thunderclaps in my ears, taking to the frigid air as if they too dread my company.

It's the Black Bridge.

Of course, it is.

Long. Wide. Waiting.

A fog enshrouds it like a white cloak and I can't see the other side. It curls in thick drifts along the rails, fingering towards me.

Crows cry, echoing a quiver in my skull.

The asphalt is covered in half-melting snow, most of it piled up on each side.

I start to cross. Each time I do so, my uneasiness grows even as I bury the memories by softly whistling to myself. That same sorry tune I've been whistling for decades. I keep expecting to see Myko but all I've ever seen are other pedestrians, a vehicle or two and the screeching crows.

But today is different for, up ahead, the fog clears like veils drawn aside and a cold drizzle kisses my face.

I blink, wipe my glasses with the bottom of my thick sweater and stare.

A thin figure stands, leaning against the rails. Perhaps a hundred metres away.

She's tall. In red mini-skirt and thigh-high boots.

I gasp . . . my own boots clatter as I stumble . . . towards her.

There are other almost imperceptible noises, naked slushy footsteps hurrying. It's the corpses. I can even smell their decay. They holler, mouths open, teeth clattering in their skulls, joints creaking, voices shrill, whether urging or warning me, I don't know—but my only thoughts are for Myko.

Her one pale hand rises to clutch the air, fingers, which seem abnormally long, are gesturing, demanding I hurry. As I approach, she flicks back her shoulder-length hair and begins her climb.

Yes, I've seen this before, so often in my dreams, before I wake up and find the dead snuggled like ancient lovers beside me. But now, it's almost real.

Alive and breathing.

She's still a distance away but I see her eyes, hard like icicles ready to pierce my heart.

'So you tell me, Hiroki! Or I'll jump! I mean it!'

'Please don't!'

'Tell me about the two of you!'

The words burn my brain

'No, Myko,' I whisper. 'There was nothing. No, no . . .'

My boots drum hard in my ears. I'm running. Running to her. She is swaying on the rails. A sapling being uprooted in a raging storm.

'Myko!'

But it's too late. Her mouth opens. Her head spins. One hand reaches out at me.

And, in a flash of twirling hair, she's gone.

There's only the noise of rushing water below.

Moaning, I collapse to my knees. The road is cold, hard, wet. Smells of dirt and petrol. My breath heaves, forming wisps before my eyes.

'Myko! Why? Why?'

I loved her. And I still love her!

I run my fingers through my thin, damp hair, fingernails biting into my skull. I blink at the swirling fog. Its dreadful whiteness tightens around me, chilling my bones, shivering this cold, tired heart.

Then, before me, the fog clears.

I don't believe it!

Through my smeared, rain-speckled glasses, I see her again!

Standing on the rails, just ten feet away. Behind her, the sun is setting and the sky is a pulsing purple. There are crows and clouds. The black dots cry mournfully as they circle the fluttering lines of the *koinobori*.

Myko stares at me with large unblinking eyes. I remember that same thin wool yellow sweater she now wears. My fingers stroking her hair that curls about her small shoulders. My tongue on her birthmark, then my mouth upon her soft lips. Her small face trembling with emotion.

'Why don't you tell them what really happened, Hiroki?'

I raise my pleading hands toward her. The wind has risen and my cheeks shiver. My heart is pounding but the sound seems to echo from far over the white hills.

'What . . . what are you talking about?'

'You know.'

I shake my head. 'No, no, I don't!'

She steps up to the third rail. The one on which she lost her balance a moment ago and fell into the gorge. Why does she keep repeating the same thing over and over?

'Come down, Myko!'

'Why should I?'

'It's dangerous. You'll fall from there!'

'No, I won't.'

'You fell, you fell . . . come down now!'

'I didn't fall, Hiroki. I didn't fall. Don't you remember?'

'No, I don't want to!'

'You need to remember. Stand up!'

I rise to my feet. Pain pierces my knees. My legs tremble.
I'm not sure if it's the cold or fear.

'Come here, Hiroki. Remember.'

I shake my head, blinking rapidly, biting my lip. Not
wanting to.

She stares down at me. Pity in her eyes.

Then they turn hard. Icicles piercing my heart.

Her lips are tight. Her eyes angry.

'Tell me about the two of you, Hiroki!'

'No . . .'

'I know you are screwing her, you bastard!'

Blood shoots up my chest, burning through my cheek. I
try to control it but it sears through my limbs, into my liver,
straight through my head.

'That's not true, Myko! Not bloody true!'

'You're a liar! You're screwing her. I know!'

My face burns. My fingers are claws.

I leap at her.

I try to stop myself, but I can't. In a single movement, so
swift, it's only an angry blur but I see my hand, yes, my hand,
attached to this spindly arm of mine, push her shoulder and . . .

She's gone!

I rush to the rail. My stomach hitting it hard. I'm still
screaming, or sobbing, I'm not sure which, even as I peer
over.

There's nothing but darkness.

I moan, grabbing the rails to stop myself from collapsing. My mouth is open but no words come out. I turn back towards the bridge, double over, claw at my face, wanting to rip my eyes out. My glasses, so useless now, clatter to the asphalt.

'Myko, Myko . . . I did it. It was me . . .'

I wipe rolling tears with my sleeve.

'I've been lying to myself all these years. Lying, when I knew the truth all along.'

I shake my head, breathing hard, as if this can erase a memory unveiled. Before my shivering face, my breath swirls its contempt.

'I'm so sorry, Myko. So very sorry.'

I turn and place one boot on the first rail. I climb to the third.

The shadows of the hills, the houses, the purple sky seem so close. Pressing in against me. Whispering that this is the right thing to do.

I stare down the dark chasm.

Smell of leaves from trees. Flowers in the air.

There, through the fog, I glimpse a blurred image of Myko below. Slowly, even without my spectacles, the image sharpens and I see her lying face up in the river, her body wedged between two rocks, the water splashing about the long boots. Her red mini skirt is unnaturally bright, the only colourful thing in the mist.

Is this me? A tree in the wind, on a foggy mountain surrounded by snow? I sway, I tremble. Feel myself uprooting. I think of Myko and what I did to her. And what I must now do . . .

Footsteps on the bridge.

Two youths. Voices raised.

Their silhouettes emerge through the white.

It can't be. But it is!

Faces glowing . . .

Myko and . . . myself!

We're of high school age. Our voices sharp, arguing. Fog curling about our shoes.

Ghosts!

I look down at the gorge. Myko, her body, is gone!

Of course she is. Because she is now approaching, crossing the bridge with me beside her. My fingers are slippery on the cold rails, clutching harder as they approach. Young, bright and full of hope that's soon to be snatched away.

Then I realise they're wearing school uniforms and are not arguing but are instead laughing. He's holding a phone that's playing J-pop.

The boy sees me, a figure perched on the rails, turns the music off, eyes me for a moment before approaching.

'Hey, is that you Old Hiroki?'

Yes, it's me. Of course it's me.

'What are you doing climbing up there?' the girl calls. 'It's dangerous. You might fall.'

'Come down, please,' the boy says.

He steps towards me, grips my shoulder and carefully helps me down. His hands are strong and sure upon my frail body.

'What are you doing here?' he asks.

I shake my head.

What can this old man tell them?

'It's wet and cold out here, sir.' The girl picks up my spectacles from the wet asphalt. She places them gently into my crinkled hands. 'You dropped this. You should go home.'

'Yes, yes,' I say, wiping off a smear of snow and putting them back on. 'Home . . .'

'You're retiring next week, aren't you?' The girl smiles. She looks nothing like Myko. No birthmark. Hair cut short like a boy's. 'We're making mochi balls for you. I hope you'll like them.'

'Mochi balls? My favourite. Yes, yes . . . leaving school . . .'

'Can we help you home?' The boy looks as though he means it.

I shake my head.

'Okay, see you then, old Hiroki.'

'Take care, sir.' The girl makes a small bow.

Take care too. Both of you.

They stroll away, hand in hand, the fog enshrouding them as they cross the bridge and they disappear like restless spirits.

But I know I'm the ghost.

It's just me, the crying crows, the shadowy flutters of the *koinobori* and this black lonesome bridge. Around us, the snow on the hills melt at the base of trees even as the sky darkens and the moon rises, big and bright.

For awhile, I just stand shivering in its glow, hot tears streaming down my shrivelled cheeks.

I wipe them away. Light a cigarette.

I glance back to see distant shadows, numerous stick-like figures in the fog, skulking at the opposite end the bridge, teeth clattering in their skulls. But they soon recede into the white, their joints creaking as they withdraw. I turn away from their vengeful nightmares . . .

After a while, my boots echo in my head.

Going home now.

To my one room and these memories.

I pull off my boots and place them in the corner by the front door.

I use the toilet. Wash my hands. Turn up the heater. I amble over to the window and draw the blinds down, keeping out the moon-lit night.

I pull a yellowing copy of the Asahi Shimbun from the clutter of my small desk. I re-read the opinion piece on a serial killer, active for seventeen years but never caught. 'The Bridge Strangler' had asphyxiated his victims, men and women, on lonely bridges. Another paper called him the 'Koinobori Killer' because the murders took place at the start of that season.

I can't say which name I prefer.

Nor am I sure why I keep such a newsprint.

But what of the Black Bridge?

There where I can cross the rails and fall, fluttering freely.

An old fish swimming the sky.

I place my head on my pillow. Close my eyes and shiver as I push away the other memories.

From outside, beyond the trees in the snow-covered hills, comes a strangled whispering.

Of my cold, cold corpses.

PART 3
DARK TECHNOLOGY

9

HAWKER MAN AND I

With a long sharp knife, the man in a yellow singlet expertly sliced the papaya and slotted them into individual plastic bags. He placed these succulent treasures into the clear display case. With a piece of white cloth, he wiped the wooden chopping board and slotted it away.

Then, past his sleek dyed-blonde hair, he eyed me.

You might think that it sent a shiver through my spine. But it didn't. If truth be told, and I'm going to tell the whole truth here, I was thrilled.

In black trousers and slippers, the hawker casually leaned against the metal bench-top which was no more than four feet long and three across and there, beneath the rickety red-blue umbrella, he faked a yawn. He was good looking, not in that Leonardo DiCaprio kind of way but more like that cute guy at Guardian Pharmacy.

He then wiped the condensation off the soybean water container. It sloshed there all white waiting for thirsty customers. But patrons there were none as it was late.

I decided that there was no point waiting there at the side of the road. The bus was bloody late again. I couldn't call my brother as he was out of town. I slid my phone back into my handbag. The Hawker Man stared again. This time, he was grinning.

Suddenly, it struck me. I recognised him!

But where?

Didn't I send him a greeting on WeChat and he had replied 'Hi gorgeous'? I was almost sure of it.

The only reason I sent him a greeting, other than him being cute, was his tagline: *deus ex machina*. I didn't know what it meant but it sounded interesting.

Sometimes you do stupid things, don't you?

He had then sent a series of messages wanting to meet me but I ignored them and then blocked him. This was not more than a week ago.

Was he stalking me? How did he find me anyway?

I looked around to see if there was anyone else about, but there was no one. There were only streetlights and the blazing headlights of cars shooting past.

I should have been scared. But I wasn't. Not really.

I was not pretty. No ravishing beauty. I was all beef noodles and Fanta Orange and was on my way into Jho Low territory if I wasn't careful. I wore glasses as contacts would redden my eyes. The girls at secretarial school joked about my scruffy ponytail. They were all so pretty. So feminine. They got driven home by boyfriends. One was having an affair with a rich businessman.

There was no point waiting for the bus, so I trudged back to the mall. The hawker was adjusting the handlebars of his motorcycle, the one attached to his stall. Its seat was ripped and held together by blue tape. He looked up and winked. I thought I heard him say something.

I hurried away, climbing up the six tiled steps to the mall, glad to be out of sight of him. It just had to be coincidence that we had met on WeChat.

Entering the building, the automatic sliding doors swishing open, I glanced back towards the main road to see his metal contraption, its large spoked wheels and its tattered umbrella looming in shadows pierced by shards of brightness from speeding cars. The Hawker Man stood in front of it, hands on his hips as if he was modelling for me.

I would go back to KFC and ask the boss for a lift home. He had done that a couple of times before. After hours of word-processing tuition at the secretarial school plus a four-hour shift serving fried chicken and asking 'Spicy or Original?', I was exhausted. It was a thirty-minute bus ride to get here and would take almost an hour to get back to the house I shared with three girls. And they didn't like me much either.

I wasn't scared that the hawker seller was interested in me. He probably didn't even know we had met on WeChat, with its billion active users, and the fact that someone actually liked me gave me a small thrill.

I was glad to be in the mall's glaring lights. It felt much safer. But all the businesses were shut and there was no one around. There wasn't even a hint of air conditioned air now. The metal roller doors were pulled over each entrance to the once welcoming shops.

Going past a hairdresser's, a reflection darted in a mirrored post like a slimy lizard. There was no mistaking it.

A figure behind me. Hands in pockets about twenty feet away beside the empty information counter.

The Hawker Man.

I was sure of it.

I clutched my handbag, quickly turned down the corridor and froze in my tracks.

KFC was closed!

No! Can't be!

My boss wasn't there. Where the heck was he? He would usually spend another twenty minutes after the workers had left, listing cleaning jobs for the next day. But the metal shutters were pulled down, shutting me out.

I had no choice but to grab it or catch a cab. It would be expensive but right now I would pay anything to get away from here.

Then I heard whistling. Cold sweat climbed on the back of my neck.

Slowly, I turned.

Shit!

The Hawker Man stood leaning casually on a wall beside McDonalds in his yellow singlet. He swaggered towards me as if he owned the mall, or perhaps even the world. His belt buckle, with a big metal 'H', shimmered beneath the fluorescents.

'Hello, gorgeous,' he said. He seemed taller. Older. His lips sneered. 'I saw you looking at me. Why didn't you reply on WeChat?'

Damn!

He *was* stalking me!

He reached behind him. I thought there would be a weapon. The fruit-chopping knife. A gun. Instead he flicked out a white piece of cloth. The one he used to wipe the condensation off his soybean container.

I smelt body odour and garlic.

'Please go away,' I said. I gripped my hand to stop it from trembling. 'What . . . what do you want?'

'What do I want? Don't you know, gorgeous? When you send someone a greeting online, it can only mean one thing.'

'You're mistaken. I don't know you. Go away please.'

'Of course you know me. You're a sexy girl. I like those with glasses. I like those with big bottoms. And you thought I couldn't track your location? So easy these days, if you know how, dearie.'

He stepped towards me, tightly gripping the ends of the white cloth in both hands. He raised his muscular arms and the cloth surged towards my throat.

I turned and ran. I tried to scream but nothing came, just a dismal frog-like croak. He chased me down the corridor, his slippers slapping the floor behind me.

Past the shops I flew. Shoe shop. Cosmetic shop. Electrical shop. Phone shop. Convenience store. Pharmacy. All closed. No sign of a customer or a shop assistant anywhere.

I turned the corner past the toy shop with the children's rides in front. Barney. Wiggles. Cars. Minions.

Then I saw two security guards lounging by a corner and my heart soared. They wore green uniforms and berets with red feathers. They stood chatting at a side entrance.

I called for help. The guards turned, their faces perplexed.

'Help!' I yelled. 'He's trying to rape me!'

Their faces jerked up. Panic in their expressions. They scurried towards me, eyes darting, faces uncertain.

'There! There!' I pointed. 'See him, behind me? He's down that way!'

One guard, the taller one, stared into my face as if trying to work out if I was mad.

'Relax,' the other guard said. 'We'll take care of you.'

'That man, he followed me here. I don't know why. Then he started to . . .'

The taller guard turned and sauntered down the corridor towards the Hawker Man.

He called out, 'Hey there! Hey there! Don't cause trouble here.'

The two spoke for a few seconds.

Then his body jerked. He screeched. It echoed like shattered glass from the corridor.

He was on his knees beside the Hawker Man, his beret on the ground, one feather dislodged and fluttering on the tiled floor. He seemed so small, so helpless. The hawker was behind him, his white cloth around the guard's face, blinding him. His head jerked up to grin at me. Then with a swift wrench, he broke the guard's neck.

The man slid like a sack to the floor.

The other guard barked a curse. His body trembled as he stood beside me. He stared wide-eyed at the grinning man twirling his white cloth at the end of the corridor. A drop of sweat trickled down the guard's cheek. He took a deep breath and released his truncheon from his canvas belt. He lifted the weapon and, yelling out, ran at the killer.

As the guard reached him, the Hawker Man smirked as he took a side step and spun him around. He did it smoothly, effortlessly, as if he had practised the move for years. The guard lost his balance, his head struck the metal shutter of one of the shops. He fell to the floor with a cry, his truncheon rattling on the floor as it slipped from his hand.

Then, with a loud crack, the hawker drove his naked heel into the guard's throat. He chuckled and slipped his foot back into his slipper. The guard's body shook, then stopped except for his one hand, a dead hand whose fingers continued tapping the floor.

'So easy when you know how!' the hawker called out to me. 'You have any more friends you want me to kill, dearie?'

He stepped about the two dead bodies, eyeing them as if admiring his work. He slung the white cloth on one shoulder and reached for his back pocket and brought out a shiny black comb. He slicked back his hair, glancing at his reflection in a mirrored post as he did so.

I turned and sprinted down the corridor on my right.

He shot down a parallel corridor after me.

My heart pounded in my head as I heard him running.

I fled for the mall entrance but his thin shadow slid across it first. The hawker must have taken a shortcut to block my escape. With nowhere to go, I turned back and leapt up an escalator, my ponytail flying as my shoes clattered on the metal steps up to the first floor.

This one usually went down, full of contented shoppers. But not now. It was empty and deadly still.

I stopped at the top and looked down, barely able to breathe, staring over the parapet to the ground floor below. I was expecting him to chase me but he didn't.

There was no sign of him.

Where the hell is he?

Maybe he decided to leave? Maybe he was afraid of getting caught. Maybe it was safe. Maybe I could go home after all. Everything had become one *Big Maybe*.

Breath spilled from my throat. I wanted to go home. Not to that shared house in the city but back to my village. The village where I grew up where I knew all our neighbours. No traffic. No malls. Only chickens, ducks, bicycles and puddles after the rain. And no murdering hawker hunting me in an empty shopping mall.

Then I heard it.

Whistling.

Followed by the sound of slapping slippers.

They slowly echoed up to me. Getting louder. But still I couldn't see him. I peered down as the whistling got louder still. Then, sure enough, the yellow singlet came into view directly below me. The white cloth gripped in one hand.

My legs trembled. Sweat dripped down my cheeks.

He jerked his head up.

'So there you are, gorgeous,' he called, spinning his cloth like a lasso in the air. He was no cowboy. But a mad, mad killer.

'No!' I gasped.

'You know, I was so surprised when you messaged me. I thought we could go on romantic dates together. Be happy. Have children. Have a wonderful life. Grow old together. But you just ignored my messages. Then you bloody blocked me!'

'I'm sorry,' I called back. 'So, so sorry!'

'Sorry solves nothing. Sorry no fucking cure! I'm going to . . .'

Something beeped. And continued beeping. He turned from me, looked down, rummaged in his pocket and jerked out a phone. It looked like a Huawei. He shook his head irritably as he typed a message.

I was about to flee when I saw them. Behind me, two supermarket trolleys stood outside a closed DIY shop.

Can I do it?

I ran up to one of them, grabbed the red handle bar and rolled the trolley across to the parapet. Then with all my strength and to my surprise, managed to lift the metal thing up to the level of my breasts and flung it over the top.

I watched it spin in the air, falling in all its shopping glory. Then it slammed right into the head of Hawker Man.

He screamed and fell as the trolley clattered loudly across the floor on its side, rubber wheels spinning uselessly.

He lay splayed on his stomach, his head on one side, eyes blinking, mouth opening and closing as if he was having trouble breathing, his Huawei still in his hand. Blood leaked from his head, puddling darkly on the floor.

He turned onto his back. His T-shirt stained with blood. His mouth opening, closing. He stared right up at me, eyes burning into mine. Although his face was twisted in pain, a grin slid up his face.

I hurried back for the second shopping trolley.

This one was hard to push as its misaligned wheels tried to veer the thing off in a different direction.

Again, I managed to lift it up and dropped it over the top.

It plummeted straight down, right into his unmoving body.

I expected the trolley to make a crashing sound. But it didn't. Instead it was almost as it the thing was made of some other material for it didn't bounce off but instead was stuck, held fast by his body. Then it began to shake and rattle, and as the hawker's arms and legs shot out in a spasm, the trolley somehow seemed to be *absorbed* into his body. He was now embedded in the metal mesh!

I stared unbelieving, not wanting to think of how that could have happened. The only thing I knew was that I had to flee and so I ran down the escalator.

Halfway down, I realised I had left my handbag on the floor. It didn't matter. There was hardly any money in it. Only my phone. The one with the stupid WeChat app, the one with a billion active users. The one that got me into all this trouble.

I glanced at the tangle of man and shopping trolley, but the only movement now was one wheel spinning in the air beside one twisted shoulder. I couldn't understand how the hawker could be part of the metal thing. As if man and machine were fused together.

I continued racing down to the ground floor and then, without glancing back, shot down a corridor towards the main entrance.

Just past the information counter, my feet struck an object and I crashed to the floor. My glasses leapt off my face. Pain gripped my arm. With cold tiles upon my cheek, I saw that a mop, of all stupid things, had tripped me up. A blue bucket rolled away as if it couldn't stand the sight of me. A cleaner must have left them and gone home. Or had he or she encountered Hawker Man who now lay bleeding profusely in some corner of the mall?

I cursed my carelessness, reached for my glasses, wiped them with the bottom of my blouse and put them back on. As I struggled to get up, I heard a shuffling.

Scraping metal.

I glanced back down the corridor. It was blurred but I saw it: *movement*.

No!

I tried to get up, but pain shot up my leg.

My ankle. I must have twisted it when I fell.

Breathing hard, I struggled to my knees and managed to haul myself up.

The thing, whatever it was, was halfway down the corridor. There came the sound of metallic scraping on the floor and the sound of slippered feet as they shuffled forward, breathing low and loud as it did so.

I watched wide-eyed as it approached, closing in, my legs unable to move as if paralysed by this horrible sight of man and embedded machine, or perhaps *vice versa*, that grew more loathsome as it approached.

I could see now that metal mesh, bright and shiny, was firmly fused into a human body creating a chimera of madness.

Above it, the fluorescent lights flickered as if in protest at this loathsome sight.

The shopping trolley was tangled in arms and legs. It pierced face, chest, stomach and thighs like speared fish. Its mesh caught into clothes and skin, surrounding the human organism, protecting it like armour. I could even see the blood-stained white cloth, the one he twirled in the air, within this insane contraption. The plastic child seat from the shopping cart was fused into one thigh while the broken mesh, the splintered ones, were spikes, weapons protruding from the body. The red handle bar poked through his skull in an almost perfect horizontal.

In this marriage of man and metal, he had become more than a monster. He became an abomination, something that should not be allowed to exist. He, *it*, whatever it now was staggered towards me, mouth wide open, and with eyes that said he was no longer human.

'No!' I cried. 'Noooooo!'

But, even as it shuffled toward me, I realised I still had one advantage. The hawker was burdened by the trolley he bore. His armour of metal mesh, his weapon of spikes, got in the way. He had difficulty walking and lurched forward like a metal tortoise.

The sound of scraping metal. The slap of slippered feet.

I can still get away!

I hobbled toward the mall's entrance and the automatic doors slid open. There was the sound of traffic and the humid night air and even though I smelt car fumes, it was a blessed relief. I held onto the shiny bannister and hopped my way down the six steps toward the road.

Cars shot by, headlights blazing. I would be safe here. I could stop a car. People would help me.

But as I got to the bottom step, I heard it.

A creaking. A sort of groaning.

As if some noisy thing needed a good oiling.

A dark shape moved. It wheeled its way towards me, the metal bench top clattering, as it creaked across the pavement. Then it stopped ten feet away. This box-like contraption attached to a riderless motorbike. Soybean water sloshed white in that big plastic container sitting on the metal bench.

Coldness shot up my spine.

I shuddered.

The hawker stall moved by itself?

A thought struck me.

The internet of things.

But it was no computing device. It couldn't send and receive data like a smart fridge or a smart air conditioner.

No. It was more than that.

Like the abomination in the mall, scraping its way down the corridor, this wheeled menace, for that was what it was, had a kind of *consciousness*.

That it's alive!

I stood there frozen.

The hawker stall seemed to eye me beneath its red blue umbrella, its wheels still creaking as if it was getting ready to run me down.

This is madness!

Then I heard another sound. Automatic doors sliding open.

No!

Not wanting to, but knowing that I had to, I spun round.

There he was. Shopping trolley man.

By leaning back and putting his weight on the metal mesh, he was propelling himself forward on one leg. Beneath him two trolley wheels spun, rolling him out of the mall to the top of the steps.

It was like a monstrous skateboard. Or a car-wrecked pram. It would have been comical if it wasn't so gruesome.

With teeth barred on his ghastly head, the handle bar poking through it, the thing thudded down the first step. Then the second step. I smelt blood, metal and burnt rubber. His white cloth now hung from the top of the metal mesh like a flag. But this was no surrender, for the cotton was soaked red with blood. Red was for anger. Red was for death.

'I'll get you now, big-bottom girl,' he said in a strange, almost metallic voice. 'See what you've done to me.'

'No . . .' I moaned.

'There's nowhere you can run to,' it echoed. 'You're all mine, dearie!'

A warm wetness soaked my jeans.

'Eh . . .' I gasped.

Then something struck me from behind.

I yelled, fell and hit my head on the pavement.

Dazed, I looked up from the brown pavers to see soybean water sloshing in its plastic container and one wheel of the hawker stall beside my head. It was creaking beside my ear as if pleased by what it had done.

But I had no time to think of what it might do for coming towards me, bouncing on two wheels down each step came the shopping trolley man, rattling away as he did so.

This madness, metal, flesh and mesh, lurched toward me. His arms outstretched, fingers opening and closing, as if getting ready to embrace me.

I was trapped between the two: this abomination and a hawker stall that had come to life. Everything now came together in a loathsome slow motion.

Shopping trolley man was saying something in that metallic voice as he came, step by step, closer and closer, smelling of burnt rubber. I couldn't understand him. Couldn't understand anything.

I tried to get up. But the hawker stall nudged my shoulder from behind and I fell again.

'No!' I sobbed helplessly on the ground. 'Get away from me!'

Warm tears spilled down my cheeks.

The mesh of man and metal was now almost on top of me, looming like a half-constructed tower block, surrounded by cranes and scaffolding.

'Wanna have fun, dearie?' it said with a grin. Eyes not on me but staring upwards so all I could see were the whites of his eyes.

Then, like a slow landslide, he toppled himself on top of me.

I screamed.

The metal mesh, the sharp broken ones, poked my ribs, my small breasts, now piercing them as he fell into me. I cried in pain. Blood slid down my neck and stomach. His lips gnawed hungrily at mine.

Then I felt it.

Heat, blinding heat, surged through me. My body trembled. My insides went cold even as they stiffened. My hand that was striking the ground repeatedly became hard even as I saw metal fusing into it. My thighs, my stomach were now fused with the metal mesh.

The shopping trolleys wheels, all four of them, spun rapidly, as if in delirious excitement. In reply or perhaps in approval, the two large spoked wheels of the hawker stall creaked as the thing and the attached motorbike shot backwards.

As a burst of light exploded in my head, I realised that man, metal and *woman* were now fused into some new abomination, some other new insanity that shouldn't even be thought of, let alone allowed to exist.

We are the shopping trolley couple!

Even a I realised this insane almost ridiculous notion, I felt my mind slipping, blanking out, as it was yanked away, as it melded into the consciousness of this new loathsome entity.

The hawker stall wheeled forward, wheels creaking, umbrella quivering in an almost sexual way.

I knew what it wanted. It was as if my mind was already joined to its consciousness. It yearned to couple with us into some other abomination made of flesh, bones, metal mesh, rubber wheels, metal cladding, red blue umbrella, a motorbike with a seat all ripped and held together by blue tape, cut papayas and a plastic container filled with soybean milk. An unspeakable contraption would wheel itself into the night, well out-of-sight into some arcane world where such madness truly belongs.

As for me, the old me anyway, I knew I would never WeChat again.

10

THE APP

Sam's new Samsung Galaxy ST changed his life. He'd had many other smartphones before, replacing them every year, but this one was different. It was brilliant for it moved between apps seamlessly, managing messages and contacts incredibly intuitively, doing stuff super quick too and with a seductive elegance.

It looked snazzy cradled in his hand, like a pretty girl draped upon his arm. This was good for he hadn't dated a girl in years. He thought his head was too scrawny for his body, nor did he like his bulging nose. So attracting the opposite sex was tough.

He'd been exploring the Samsung's myriad features for several days when one evening, after watching several steamy YouTube videos, he noticed an app that wasn't there before. He certainly didn't remember downloading the thing.

It had an odd name: *You Lite.*

What was it doing here? He tried deleting it but the thing just seemed to hang on to its ephemeral existence. As it was getting late, he went to bed without thinking anymore about it.

The next day, he took the 7.42 a.m. train to work. As usual the carriage was filled with harried commuters. Most were engrossed in their smartphones, either texting, playing games, Facebooking, reading ebooks or listening to music. A few just stared blankly into the tight spaces between each person.

Sam was lucky to get a seat. With time on his hands, he decided to check out the obdurate app. He tapped it. There was a pause, then up came the welcome screen and, to his surprise, he was looking at a grinning photo of himself. That was really curious. Could the app have taken a photo of him without him knowing? Yet he didn't recognise the background and he was wearing a white T-shirt that read *You Lite*. Very strange. Perhaps it just did some clever photo editing there.

Beneath his photo, a caption read: *Your Ultimate App.*

Yeah, he'd heard of such claims before. He didn't even know what this one was supposed to do. Well, at least it was free. For the moment anyway. It would probably, like many free apps, try for his credit card details after the end of the trial period.

Sam tapped the 'Go' icon. Immediately, on a luminescent red background, leapt the words in brilliant white: *How are you today, Sam?*

Fine, he typed back.

How did the app know his name? Maybe it went into his mobile's Settings and found it there.

That's good, what are you doing today? came the reply.

Sam wondered if this app was like that old ELIZA computer program, which processed natural language. Users were often tricked into thinking they were interacting with another person. The *You Lite* app was likely an updated and highly sophisticated version of it.

Off to work, he typed, wondering how it would respond.

App: *That's good, but rather boring, don't you think?*

An unexpected reply. Perhaps it used some sort of random phrase generator.

Yeah, but I've got a pretty assistant, he entered with a grin.

App: *What's her name?*

Sam: *Louise.*

Is she single?

Boyfriend.

Bad news, Sam. Have you heard of BMW?

No.

Best Man Wins. Do you like her a lot or just a bit?

A lot.

When you get to work, take a photo of her.

You Lite was certainly the oddest app he'd ever come across. Sam forgot all about it until after lunch. He had just been speaking to a client about some bonds that had just become available on the secondary market when Louise bent over at her desk across from him and begun to adjust the strap on her shoes. She had short brown hair and silky legs that glowed into his eyes.

He whipped out his Samsung Galaxy ST and took a shot. It made a loud click.

Damn!

'Did you just take a photo of me?' said Louise, looking up at him with her grey eyes, her head at an inquisitive but rather attractive angle.

'Oh no,' quipped Sam, thinking fast. 'Of course not. I wouldn't want to shatter the lens on my new mobile. I was just testing out a new app.'

'Oh, I see,' she said with a smile. 'I thought the company was looking for a new model. You know for our adverts.'

Sam liked her good humour. He liked her face too. Her smooth skin. Those long eye lashes. She had a slight frame and smallish breasts. He'd often do nothing but think of her. She was in her early twenties and he was twenty-seven. They'd make a nice couple.

Except that she had a boyfriend. His name was John and he was in construction. He'd met him a couple of times. He was tall, full of himself and talked endlessly about cars and boats.

Just then Brian, his immediate boss and Senior Vice-President, strolled past yakking on his mobile. He had slick black hair, round metal glasses, red braces and an annoying bow tie. He gave them a quick but disapproving glance.

'Oh yeah,' Sam said in a loud voice. 'I've got this report for you to look at.'

He passed Louise a file and turned back to his computer.

Whilst on the platform waiting for his train back home, Sam felt his mobile twitch in his trouser pocket.

It was *You Lite*.

She's pretty, was the message.

Yeah, he typed back.

App: *I mean it. She's a 10.*

Sam: *I know.*

You should ask her on a date.

Boyfriend.

BMW.

I'm not that good.

They'll break up tonight.

You're kidding.

Ask her out tomorrow, Sammy.

He slipped the mobile into his pocket. He didn't like being called Sammy. He had to admit that this app was brilliant. It was as if he was texting a real person. He knew that computers were incredibly powerful and could store huge amounts of information. Several years back, a computer called Watson had even beat the reigning champions in a popular quiz show. *You Lite* was probably accessing a similarly powerful server somewhere but its ability to pretend to converse with him without a single mistake was amazing.

The train was delayed and Sam got home late. He sluggishly climbed up the two flights of concrete stairs to his apartment, microwaved a Chicken Oriental, cracked open a beer and ate mindlessly in front of the television. He took off his suit, showered and went to bed.

* * *

'Will you have dinner with me tonight?'

Louise looked up at him from her desk, her eyes registering surprise.

Sam's throat went dry.

Why did I do that? He thought. *She's going to say no!*

But that was unlikely. She would use some typical excuse: a netball game, movies with friends, maybe dinner with her parents. *Some other time perhaps, Sam,* she'll say. So no hurt feelings. It kept office relationships cordial.

He decided that it was a stupid thing to do to listen to the app. Why should she want to go out with him when she had John? John with his cars and boats. But he had seen her earlier, blowing her nose into a tissue. He knew she'd been crying. So the foolish notion came to as he ate his sushi roll: *if not now, then when?*

He could see her thinking. Her long eyelashes trembling beneath the fluorescent lights.

Then she said it and he could hardly believe it.

'Sure,' she said. 'Thanks for asking.'

'Great, Louise. That's wonderful.'

'I don't know if I'll be good company though. John and I broke up last night. But it'll be nice to go out.'

'I'm sorry to hear that. I didn't know. What sort of food do you like?'

'How about Korean? You know, that one round the corner?'

At dinner, Louise said that she was Facebooking on the bus back home, when up popped a photo of John with another girl. They were in each other's arms, naked on a red leather sofa. The girl was holding a whip. All her friends had seen it. John had remonstrated, saying it was a fake photograph but she refused to believe him. Sam was delighted with this news. He sympathised with her and tried being as caring as he could. They agreed to dinner again in a couple of days. This time they'd go to the Italian around the corner.

Sam grinned all the way on his train-ride home. Not even his fellow-passengers, its shaking carriage or the irritating hissing of its doors opening and closing bothered him. He held onto that warm glow in his head. So this was what happiness felt like. He slipped into bed, blissful thoughts slipping in and out of his brain.

During the night, his Samsung beeped.

What the hell!

He knew he had turned the damn thing off. It had jerked him out of deep sleep.

It carried on beeping, each one getting louder, until he grabbed it, almost knocking it to the carpet.

He expected to see the alarm clock app which he must have mistakenly set but, no, it was *You Lite*.

It had a message, flashing on the shiny red background: *You forgot to say thank you.*

He typed in, *thks*. Then collapsed into bed.

The next day, he forgot all about it.

* * *

At the Italian restaurant, they ordered a bottle of white, mains and desert. They chatted, joked and laughed. Sam was surprised at how well they got on. Later, they strolled arm-in-arm through the now quieter streets, illuminated dimly by decorative street lights. They passed a cathedral lit dazzlingly against the night sky. Autumn leaves covered the pavement and they kicked them around playfully as they walked, the fallen foliage rustling and nestling against their shoes.

Whilst waiting with Louise at her bus stop, the two kissed. Sam didn't know how it happened. It just did, without thinking.

The best things happen this way, he thought.

And, by far, this was the best thing that ever happened to him. The two embraced as the humming traffic echoed from some other place, as the lights from the surrounding buildings winked, as the brownish-red leaves trembled in their bare branches as if not daring to fall.

Sam and Louise were lost to the city and the world.

For the next few days, the two of them saw each other every evening after work. It would usually end up with her spending the night at his flat or him staying over at hers. They didn't tell anyone at the office that they were seeing each other except that Sam thought that his boss, Brian, had grown suspicious.

Intimacy is hard to hide.

At dinner at Subway several nights later, whilst Louise was on Facebook, he felt his mobile twitch in his pocket. He pulled it out. It was *You Lite*. He'd forgotten about the app for the past few days.

App: *Brian does suspect.*

Sam: *Suspect what?*

You and Louise.

Shit.

A career buster.

I know.

Watch for my email.

'Everything okay, Sam?'

Louise was staring at him.

'Oh, it's fine,' he said.

'You just looked so worried.'

'Oh no, it's nothing. It's just this app doing strange things.'

'I've got one like that. It's a silly game that keeps freezing every time I get near the high score.'

Sam forced a laugh. He was worried about his job. Without it, he couldn't even afford the rent of his cheap flat.

They finished their drinks and spent the night at Sam's.

The next day, they took the train to work. Louise would usually slip into the office first and he would follow five to ten minutes later. By now, the two of them had started discussing moving in together.

After his nine o'clock meeting that morning, Sam checked his emails. And there it was, as promised: one from *You Lite*.

There was no message but several attachments.

It revealed that several risky bonds from a Chilean company which Brian had sold to clients had gone bust. Instead of giving them the bad news and losing their business, he had been paying them coupons using the bank's money.

Then his mobile beeped. It was the app.

Go to the President.

Why?

Recommend that the bank take over these bonds.

Huh?

Read my 2nd email.

He had missed that one as it was buried amongst the torrent of spam. This email had an attachment analysing the company. It predicted that it would, within days, be taken over by a global mining corporation and that new shares would be issued to current bondholders. The share values would rocket because new technologies made these mines highly profitable.

Sam took the analysis, which he presented as his own, to the President. At a late night meeting, the company's senior management agreed with Sam, bought over the bonds, and the bank made millions.

'This is bullshit!' snarled Brian, his eyes blazing behind his round glasses. 'I know you did none of that research. You're not qualified nor are you bloody clever enough to do it.'

Brian's face twitched with anger. He had just found out that he'd been fired only to be replaced by Sam.

'You're finished, Brian,' said Sam. 'I hope you've packed up. I'm moving into your office tomorrow.'

'I don't know who the hell's been helping you. I'm going to find out where those reports came from. I have contacts with analysts. I'm going to expose your relationship with Louise too. You're not going to get away with this!'

'Time to go, Brian. Looks like security's here to kick you out. And I've always hated that stupid bow tie and braces of yours.'

Brian stormed back into his office before the grim-faced security guard could get to him. The guard followed him in to watch him pack his personal things. Minutes later, he escorted Brian out of the building.

Just then *You Lite* beeped.

Don't worry about him.

Brian sped off in his white Porsche his mind whirling. He didn't know where he was going. He barely saw the other cars, the pedestrians and buildings. They were but an aching blur in his head. He decided that it was going to get even no matter what it took. The angrier he got, the faster he drove.

Just as he got onto the highway, Brian realised how stupid it was to be so incensed. Whatever had happened, had happened. He might not be able to get another job in finance but there was other work he could do. He could even start his own business. He certainly wasn't short of funds.

But he'd get even with Sam first. The bastard must have gotten help from outside. He had to be dealt with. Finding out where the analysis came from was Brian's top priority. No one was allowed to cross him and get away with it.

He felt his breath quicken at the thought of Sam. He pushed hard on the accelerator.

Just as he was navigating the turn, his iPhone burst out screeching.

It was so loud, it sounded like a jet engine in the confines of his car. Instinctively, Brian brought both hands to his ears.

The Porsche spun out of the control.

'Nooooooo!' he screamed.

But the sound was so loud, he couldn't even hear himself.

The car smashed through the barrier and ploughed into the rocks below. Brian was dead well before the car exploded.

* * *

Over the next two weeks, Sam spent an increasing amount of his time hunched over his smartphone. He spent hours every day with *You Lite*. Louise complained but being a self-confessed Facebook addict, she resigned herself to updating her status even more often.

He had installed an updated version of the app. It included a speech recognition mode so he no longer had to type his messages to *You Lite*. He just had to say them and the app would write back its reply. It made things a lot more convenient.

'I bought the apartment,' he said.

App: *Glad you took my advice.*

'You sure it's a good investment?'

Good location. Great design.

'Just collected my new BMW.'

Best Man Wins, Sammy.

Sam chuckled.

He didn't mind being called 'Sammy' now.

He no longer wondered about his app, gift horses and all that. It had done wonders. Nor did he dare to think about how it managed to do these incredible things. He was certain now that it wasn't just software in a smartphone. And if it was linked to anything, it wouldn't be to a powerful server sitting in a building somewhere, but it had to be connected to something.

Or someone.

That thought sent dark shadows spiralling in his mind. So he always pushed it aside. But it left a coldness in his gut.

He had to focus on the positive. *You Lite* had given him Brian's job. Although it was a pity that Brian, who must have been so upset at being fired, had killed himself. The app also recommended share purchases and Sam, together with his best clients, had made several killings. His app was a dream come true. So there was no need to ask how or why, was there?

You Lite was his best friend. It gave him all kinds of advice: which team would win the game, which clients would give him trouble, which horse to bet on and even which tie to wear to a meeting. He had fired a clerk because the app said that she was not up to the job.

Sam and Louse now dined at the best restaurants. They had designer furniture, accessories and clothes. They were now invited to the best parties and openings. They'd been on a luxury 7-day cruise. They lived in a brand new apartment that overlooked the city's skyline.

All was perfect in Sam's world . . .

Except for the dreams.

Sam had the same dream every night.

It began about a month after they moved into their new apartment. In it, his Samsung would beep louder and louder. He would fumble for it and the message from *You Lite* was always the same.

Now you are mine!

He would jerk up in bed, breathing hard, sweat on his forehead.

Louise would be sleeping soundly beside him so he knew his mobile hadn't actually gone off. He always checked, just in case, and it would only be the same black lifeless screen staring back into his eyes.

The Bose clock radio would usually say it was one or two in the morning. The city lights would shine dimly through the blinds into their bedroom. The Versace lampshades, the Persian rug, the ten thousand dollar watercolour Louise fell in love with, seemed to mock him in the half light.

Tonight though, his throat burnt, so he quietly crept to the kitchen. His head throbbed, his stomach was coldly knotted, his limbs quivered and he needed three glasses of water to slake his scorching throat.

How could he feel so terrible when life was so good?

He stood alone trembling before the sparkling white counter top, amongst its shiny Miele appliances Louise was so proud of, and vomited.

Sam spent the rest of the night hunched over a toilet bowl.

'What's wrong, baby?'

It was Louise wearing a big frown and a new white nightie. Her hair was dishevelled.

'Nothing, darling,' he moaned.

She touched his shoulder. 'You must have a bad tummy bug. You haven't been well this past week have you?'

'I'm okay,' he said. 'Just leave me alone, okay? I'll be fine.'

'Sure, but tell me if you need anything.'

'Okay,' he grunted before vomiting again.

Sam staggered from the toilet bowl, washed his face and stared at his haggard face in the mirror. He hardly recognised himself. He was pale, thin and his eyes were pink. He leaned his forehead tiredly on the glass. He felt so ill, he almost wept.

When it was bright outside, Louise made him some coffee and toast, which he didn't touch, and went to work without him. He promised he would see a doctor. She texted him several times that morning to see how he was. He replied that he was fine even though his vision now began to swim.

The doctor didn't think that much was wrong with him. Perhaps a touch of the flu and exhaustion. *You Lite* thought that too, so it was probably a correct assessment. He got back to the apartment just after twelve, made a lemon and honey drink, took the prescribed pills, switched his mobile to silent and went to bed.

He dozed off.

A loud beeping shook him out of bed.

It was *You Lite*.

He fumbled for it to turn it off.

The luminescent red on its screen glared into his eyes.

Rise and shine, Sammy.

'Why in God's name did you wake me up?'

I can think of all kinds of reasons.

'You're a bloody . . .'

Here's one . . . now you are mine!

The text was there: white and quite unmistakable.

Now you are mine!

'What the hell!' he cried.

This was no dream. This was real.

Why was You Lite doing this?

Then the realisation struck him hard.

His app, his so-called best friend, was not what he thought it was. Yes, it brought him a life he could only dream of. Riches, a great job, a beautiful girlfriend, a fantastic apartment and that new-model BMW.

But *You Lite* was doing something else. It was making him sick. So terribly ill that he felt that his soul had been crushed. Or was it his vanquished soul that had caused this illness?

He didn't know. He didn't care.

Right now, all he knew was that the app had to go. It would never come back into his life no matter what promises it offered.

He stumbed to the window.

He slid it open.

The sound of traffic and a cool breeze rushed at him.

He shoved the mobile out of the window.

It would be a long drop. Down twenty-eight floors to the pavement below. The Samsung could shatter to a thousand pieces and *You Lite* with it. It could go to its demented hell of ones and zeroes. It was a double crossing fiend. The word 'frenemy' came to him and he wanted to laugh.

'Goodbye, you bastard!' he cried.

And laugh he did.

At last, at last, he would get rid of it. He would be free.

He would get healthy again and, together with Louise, they'd have a wonderful life. He would never need the advantage of this app. He'd do everything by his own wit.

'Goodbye forever, you bugger!'

But his fingers, they wouldn't work.

They couldn't release the mobile.

'Let it go!' he gasped. 'Let the damn thing fall!'

But still his stubborn fingers held onto the infernal thing.

Then, very slowly . . .

his hand turned!

The red screen like a raging demon was facing him.

The thing was so bright it hurt his eyes. He couldn't turn his head away for his neck muscles wouldn't respond. The screen's intensity grew so bright that it pierced right into his brain.

He staggered back. His arm extended before him.

For a brief second, he saw himself wearing a white T-shirt with the words *You Lite* printed on it. He was winking and giving himself the thumbs up.

Then the red screen exploded in his head.

Now you are mine!

Sam stepped back, screaming.

He tried to get away from it, this evil thing in his mobile. But he couldn't because he was holding it. He crashed into a lampshade, knocked over the painting and tripped onto the rug.

'Let me go!' he yelled. 'Please!'

Now you are mine!

The words filled his brain, over and over.

Now you are mine!

The deep voice, its endless echo brought a void into his head. He felt his soul being sucked into it.

'Now you are mine!'

The damnable phrase, repeated over and over, pulled him further and further away. Into a cold, shiny place where he felt only numbness.

Just as blackness swamped him, Sam realised that words were leaping from his own tongue.

Then he blanked out.

* * *

When Sam woke up, he didn't know where he was.

He tried turning his body, but couldn't. His hands wouldn't move, nor would his arms or feet. No part of his body would respond.

He felt nothing either. He was neither hot nor cold. There were no physical sensations. Not even the movement of air in his lungs.

Although he couldn't turn his head, he could make out the familiar shapes of the stainless steel oven, the tall fridge, the curvaceous designer taps, even the polished blue kettle. He realised that he was lying on the kitchen bench and the lights from the sleek pendant lamp above, the one they had only recently installed, only confirmed it.

Again, he tried getting up but still his body was frozen to this spot.

Instead of panicking, he tried to think clearly. Why couldn't he move? Perhaps it was some form of sleep paralysis. But what was he doing on the kitchen bench anyway? Did he sleep walk here?

Then he heard footsteps. Followed by whistling.

They grew louder.

A shadow crossed his vision.

Whoever it was then stepped back, opened the fridge and pulled out a carton of milk

Sam blinked.

He gasped, but no sound came. He couldn't believe it.

He was looking at himself!

He was dressed in jeans and a red polo shirt with his hair neatly combed.

But no, this couldn't be him. This had to be some imposter.

Then the figure turned and glanced at Sam.

'Ah, it's you,' said the imposter. 'You're up. You've been asleep all day. Well, you've been ill, haven't you, my friend?'

'What the hell!' cried Sam.

But nothing came out of his mouth.

'Ah,' said the imposter, sticking his face forward. 'You're quite right to be upset.'

'Who are you?' Sam said but again no words came out.

The imposter laughed. 'Don't you recognise your own best friend, Sammy?'

No, he couldn't believe it!

This just couldn't be.

'I do like all these new clothes you've bought, especially those designer suits. Love the apartment too. What? Don't have anything to say, Sammy?'

But the horrible truth was staring Sam right in the face. The damn thing was wearing his clothes and talking to him.

You Lite.

The imposter was You Lite!

You Lite reached for Sam and suddenly Sam felt himself lifted in the air. It made him giddy. He wanted to vomit but nothing came.

This imposter that was once an app safely locked away in a smartphone was grinning. But it was not safe even there. No, the thing was especially dangerous then, for it had seemed so harmless. Now it was grinning cruelly.

It should have made the blood rush to Sam's head. But Sam felt none of it. He could feel no part, nothing of his body. But he felt anger and hate enter his brain.

And then Sam caught a reflection in the stainless steel oven.

He thought he would see himself and his double, confronting each other face to face. But what he saw was insane.

There was just the imposter alone, holding a Samsung Galaxy.

He was talking to the thing.

'Time to sleep, Sammy,' said *You Lite*. 'Louise should be home soon. I'm really looking forward to that. She's a lovely girl. I've wanted her from the time you snapped that photo of her. I'll take her out for dinner. Maybe we'll go to that Korean restaurant where we had our first date.'

You Lite chuckled.

'Well, it really is my first date with your girl, isn't it? I may switch you on, so you can see it all. I'll leave you on mute, of course. Can't have any interruptions at our romantic dinner!'

You Lite did a little spin in the kitchen. It was a horrible movement that made Sam nauseous.

The imposter laughed.

This had to be a dream. But Sam knew this was no dream. He knew what had happened. His life was now a living nightmare.

You Lite whistled as he strolled into the bedroom.

'Oh, I'm going to enjoy your life, Sammy, especially your gorgeous Louise. As I always said, and you should remember it: BMW, Sammy, BMW.'

Then the app clicked a button.

Everything had turned black for Sam.

You Lite's life in flesh and blood had now just begun.

11

BLACK HONDA JAZZ

The blue Suzuki Swift.

His footsteps tapped across the basement car park, towards it.

He was the Old Uncle's bodyguard. Keeping his boss safe often meant sitting alone in dark restaurants or brightly-lit cafes, cracking his knuckles, getting bored.

He had other duties too.

The 'extras', he called it.

To put it simply, he killed for his boss. He silenced business rivals and blabbering ex-lovers.

He liked killing women. It was hilarious, watching them beg. Some of them even promised sex but he never indulged.

The last one he put away had pissed herself, her urine trickling in streams down her pale thighs. In disgust, he kicked her in the head and her skull cracked upon the rim of the bath. She was dead but he slit her throat anyway, the thick blood soaking her white nightie.

He squeezed into the car and glanced at his Rolex. It was after ten. The watch was a gift from his boss in gratitude for that last job. The cow had chosen the wrong man to blackmail. Stupid bitch.

He was invaluable to the Old Uncle. That's why he let him stay in his condo rent free, one of many properties the tycoon owned in the city.

Pity he didn't pay for his supply of women too. It was his one vice, for he didn't drink, smoke, gamble or do drugs.

Women.

Couldn't live with them or without them . . .

So went the all-too-true cliche.

He had slapped one this morning. She scurried away weeping to the bathroom but he didn't mind. Eventually she would have to come out to take the punishment. But luckily for the bitch, he had to get to work, so he let her go.

He switched on the ignition and the Suzuki purred to life. He hated the car. It cramped his big body. Felt like he was in a coffin. He wanted something big, powerful, but the vehicle was inconspicuous and could be parked in dark narrow lanes. So useful when he had to do 'the extras'.

As he eased the vehicle forward, an echoing screech made his head swivel. A black Honda Jazz sped along the concrete columns, towards him.

'Must be in a hurry,' he muttered, hitting the brakes.

The Honda shot past him, sped down the driveway and, making a sharp turn, almost struck a wall. It zipped down the lane behind him but the driver may as well have been headless as his rearview vision was blocked by a parked pick-up truck.

He loved pick-ups, especially the monsters. He wished the Old Uncle let him drive one so that he could bully cars off the roads. He hated being a big man in a small car.

The Honda screeched again some distance away.

Idiot must be in a hurry.

He shook his head. Stress kills.

Bullets and blades too.

He grinned.

The knife slicing into the woman's warm throat was one fine memory. The pressure of the sharp blade cutting into her tight flesh and the thick blood that spilled on his hand, dripping down his arm onto his good-luck Buddha tattoo, brought a stirring in his loins. He had dipped one finger into her gurgling throat and sampled her blood.

Warm and tangy.

As he eased the car out again, a horn-blast jolted him back, his head struck the headrest. A black shape like a big bat swooped in front of him, the Honda almost colliding with the front of his Suzuki.

'Shit!' he cried. 'Double shit!'

The Honda screeched around the corner and again shot down the back lane. He turned and, glancing past the pick-up truck, saw a flow of long hair and big sunglasses.

Crazy bitch!

He waited for her to zip past him again. He glanced down the driveway, beyond the concrete pillars, aluminium air ducts and dirty white walls, but only saw bumpers of parked cars poking out, all held captive by time and endless dust of churning wheels.

Where's the bitch now?

Looking for a parking spot? Or was this her private racing track? You never knew with these crazies.

What she needs most is a hole in the head.

He would gladly oblige. But he wanted to see her grovel first, bawling her eyes out, offering him sex, like all the other women did. What she needed most was a royal buggering before he sliced off her breasts.

He chuckled.

Out of curiosity, he waited but still there was no sign of the Honda.

He turned up the rap number, the electronic voice snarling through the speakers:

Me, a billionaire gangsta,
You, a low-life prankster . . .

For the third time, he eased the car out of its parking spot.

As he cruised down a ramp, a blinding light burst from his rearview mirror.

'Damn!' he gasped as he covered his eyes with one hand.

Through his stubby fingers, he saw headlights on high-beam. The sheer power of it made his head throb. These headlights had to have been custom fitted.

The vehicle tailing him was close—*too damn close*—almost kissing his bumper.

He cursed and swung sharply at the bottom of the ramp, the familiar B2 sign, the black and white exit arrow, blurred as he shot past.

He glanced back.

The bloody Honda Jazz!

Blood rushed to his head.

Breathing hard, he pushed on the brakes, slowing the car to a crawl.

'Stupid bitch,' he growled. 'I'll get you!'

The Honda honked.

He refused to speed up.

'I'm gonna smash your car in. Shoot your tyres up. That'll teach you a lesson!'

Except he couldn't. He stopped himself from yanking out the metal club he kept beneath the front seat.

Must think straight.

Can't cause a commotion here. Not at his condo building. It was home. The police were sure to get involved.

So instead, he allowed his Suzuki to crawl like a wounded animal past the parked cars whilst the ventilation ducts, like curious eyes, watched.

The Honda honked again. Then it nudged against his bumper and his chest jerked against the tightened seat belt.

'Fuck!'

He jammed on the brakes, slid down the window and gave the woman the finger.

The Honda switched off its headlights, reversed, moved back and stopped. Then it flashed its headlights. Four times.

He pushed open the car door and got out. The air was stale and hot. He was about to grab his bat to smash the woman's car when his phone whistled a melody.

The Old Uncle.

'Hello, boss,' he gushed.

'Get here quick. I need to head out.'

'Yes, yes, boss. I'll be there faster than fast.'

'Good. That damn Mercedes out of the workshop yet?'

Through the windshield of the Honda, the sunglasses-wearing bitch grinned, tossed her hair back and shook her head as if she pitied him, one manicured fingernail making small mocking circles beside her skull.

Making fun of him? Egging him on? He would bloody get her.

He swallowed.

'Yes . . . yes, boss. The driver, he collected it yesterday.'

'The BMW air con needs bloody fixing too.'

'Sure, boss. I'll tell him.'

'I've got many things to do today. Don't be fucking late.'

'Okay, boss.'

The Old Uncle ended the call.

He sighed.

He could just see the Old Uncle and his bristling grey beard perched on his rosewood stool in shorts and slippers, barking orders at his servant. One jewelled finger would be flicking through his iPad as he sipped local coffee.

No, he couldn't do it. Couldn't smash up the bitch's car.

He squeezed himself back into his Suzuki. The Old Uncle shunned publicity and if he heard what had happened he would . . .

Tyres screeched.

Before he could turn around, the Honda hurled past his car, almost hitting the open door. It sped along several empty parking spots and disappeared down the ramp.

'Shit! Double shit!'

He slammed the door shut.

'I'm going to get you!'

Then he remembered the Old Uncle. Saw his eyes blazing in the corner of his mind.

Don't be fucking late.

He took a deep breath. He realised that he'd been gripping the steering wheel too hard. He took his hands off and wiped them over his face.

He forced himself to drive slowly down the slope.

'Don't know who you are crazy bitch. But I'm not going to waste time on you.'

The sign at the bottom read B3. He turned, following the black and white exit arrow.

Then he made another left.

'You're lucky mad woman indeed. Old Uncle needs to go out. Bet he's got some bitch on heat waiting for him.'

He sniggered and turned up the rap number:

Me, a billionaire gangsta,
You, a low-life prankster,
Gonna show you my member . . .

But it was cut short by a bang that sent his car hurtling.

His head jolted and his body shuddered.

The Suzuki veered and slammed into a concrete pillar. His body yanked hard against the seat belt as the airbag burst and ballooned against his face.

Everything went black.

* * *

He opened his eyes to see white. At first he thought that he was playing in snow. Then he realised his nose was pressed up hard against the airbag's nylon fabric.

'Shit . . .' he moaned. 'Double shit . . .'

He wondered if he had blacked out, but he wasn't sure. He swallowed and figured that this was a real bad-luck day.

Very bad indeed.

Then, as if to emphasise the point, the door flew open. A figure stood there, legs apart like a shapely gunslinger.

He blinked. Blinked again.

The woman!

The one from the Honda Jazz.

Tall, wearing a black leather jacket, matching pants and long thigh-high boots.

She leaned over him and he caught his reflection in the big lenses of her sunglasses. He looked dazed and a little bit . . . scared?

No way! Can't be!

It was always the other way around. He made others tremble. Made them piss in their panties.

With a click, she undid his seat belt, grabbed him under the armpits and dragged him out.

The bitch was strong. Damn bloody strong.

He fell hard on the oil-stained concrete driveway and grunted, one foot still hanging like a discarded leg of lamb in the car.

'Got my lover boy at last!'

Her voice was deep and tough. Husky too which he found somewhat sexy.

But it didn't feel that way. Not now as he lay sprawled on the hard, cold concrete floor that smelt of diesel and car fumes. He looked up at her but instead two fluorescent lamps met his eyes, one rapidly blinking.

His head hurt. His neck ached. There was a ringing, like some awful diva singing soprano, in his ears.

Then she bent over him. Took her sunglasses off and he saw her eyes.

They were brown . . . no, green. He couldn't be sure.

Must be the knock on my head. Can't focus!

Those eyes though. They seemed to burn right through him, as if they knew everything he'd done.

'Now you're mine,' she whispered.

Even in his concussed state, he felt drawn towards her face, her perfectly shaped nose, those curling eyelashes, tight lips, smooth skin, framed by a mass of luxurious light brown hair.

'What . . . why did you . . .? Did Old Uncle send you?'

She laughed. It was deep and strong and echoed around his head.

'Who . . . who did?'

'You don't want to know, believe me, lover boy.'

He felt a jab in his thigh. He turned in time to see her remove a syringe, put the cap back on the needle, and slip it into the pocket of her leather jacket.

She grinned.

It was a sneering sort of smile, perhaps one a vet would have before putting a dog to sleep.

He tried getting up but his body wouldn't move.

She grabbed him around the armpits and dragged him away from his vehicle and across the driveway. For the second time, he was impressed with her strength.

Then, without even needing to catch her breath, she hauled him into her car, squeezing his large body onto the back passenger seats.

He tried to struggle but his limbs refused to move.

It's the damn injection . . .

Whatever drug she used, it caused instant paralysis.

The space at the back of the Jazz was even tighter than at the front of his Suzuki. His neck was bent awkwardly. The ceiling brushed his hair. The moulded plastic interior pressed in on him. He hated being a big man in a small car. Especially a prisoner crammed like a useless child in the rear seats.

Once his legs were stiffly bent into the car, she slammed the door shut. It reverberated in his skull, confirming that he was her prisoner. Then she went around the side and got into the driver's seat.

She turned to him.

'Time to get you comfortable. It's going to be a long, long ride. Oh wait, lover boy . . .'

She squeezed her body in between the two front seats and made her way to the back. How she could do that so easily, he wasn't sure. For she was no small woman either. She wore a tight black blouse beneath her jacket and, despite a trembling in his guts and a feeling of utter helplessness, he could not only notice but also, in some corner of his mind, appreciate her pale ample cleavage. As she clambered over him as if they were in a wrestling, pressing her knees into his thighs, her elbows into his chest, he could smell her perfume.

Chanel No. 5?

Whatever it was, he liked it a lot.

For an insane second, he wondered if this was so bad getting kidnapped by a gorgeous sexy woman. She could do all kinds of kinky things to him. But then reality told him that this was bad, very, very bad.

The good-luck Buddha tattoo on his forearm eyed him.

You got that right. But sorry, can't help you, my friend.

The Enlightened One whispered.

Don't you know that life is about suffering?

He was jolted from his thoughts by a snap, followed by three more sharp clicks. The woman squeezed back to the driver's seat, pushing one boot into his stomach as she did so, then giving him that flash of a veterinarian killing smile before she turned on the ignition.

She flicked on the music. A soppy love song. Sickly sweet. This Whitney Houston number made him want to vomit.

He fought back by humming the rap tune:

Me, a billionaire gangsta,
You, a low-life pranksta,
Gonna show you my member,
Rip you asunder . . .

But it was no use. The fucking greatest-love-of-all swamped his brain.

Then he realised that bitch had handcuffed his hands to each of the car door handles.

Shit. Shit . . . Double shit!

His legs were splayed, each foot bound by a black plastic strap to the door handles too. He didn't know when she had done this. Perhaps when he was admiring her cleavage and smelling her Chanel. A lot of things happen to men when they're not noticing . . . especially when they're being distracted by a pretty woman.

The thought surprised him. He was no deep thinker and right now he had to figure out an escape.

The woman slipped her sunglasses back on. The designer logo flashed at him. She adjusted the rearview mirror. Then she leisurely painted on some bright-red lipstick, before slipping the lipstick back into a red leather clutch bag placed beside her on the passenger seat.

'Must always look good, lover boy,' she chimed, glancing back. 'No matter what the circumstances, don't you think?'

He didn't know what to think. He felt stupid sitting on the back seat like a freshly caught goat.

Then she switched on the ignition and the Honda purred to life. The engine sounded strange, like mangled voices echoing from a cave.

It had to be the bump on his head. A concussion perhaps.

The car shot off, leaving his damaged Suzuki, like a slaughtered animal, behind. He suddenly missed it. They had done lots together. Though he hated the thing, it was almost an extension of himself.

The Honda jerked a sharp left and slid down the ramp. Through the tinted window, he glimpsed the B4 sign as the car made another shuddering turn.

This, he knew, was the exit level. It led to the main road, followed by the expressway to the city.

There was always a guard at the boom gate, where the electronic card was swiped. The brawny guard, who had a big grin, usually stepped forward to greet the drivers and was bound to see him handcuffed at the back.

Damn bitch has no brains!

His heart soared.

The guard would stop the car or at least alert the police. Armed with the licence number, the police would easily find the Honda. He didn't care whether he came under their scrutiny now or not. He would move to another condo. Lay low for a while.

What mattered now was to get out. No matter what.

The Honda would make a left, then a right and they would be at the boom gates.

He would shout out at the guard. But could he do it with the drug coursing through his body?

'Wh . . . wh .. where ah . . . are yo .. you taking me?'

Good!

I can still speak!

'Never you mind,' the woman sang back. 'But I can tell you it's somewhere far, far away.'

'I . . . I . . . I'm go . . . gonna kill . . . you!'

The bitch laughed.

'Like you killed the others, lover boy? You're a real expert now, aren't you?'

He fell silent. How the hell did she know?

'Enjoyed it too, huh?'

And how did she know where to find him? Who the heck did she work for? Was the Old Uncle trying to get rid of him?

It didn't matter. He would yell as loud as he could when he saw the guard. That would put an end to her plan.

But instead of turning right which led to the exit, the Honda Jazz made a left.

A left?

There's no bloody left turn!

There should have been a wall there.

One with a paint-chipped *Residents / Reserved Parking* sign on it.

And yet the car *did* make the turn. There was no wall in sight.

The Honda sped past pillars, aluminium ducts and dusty fluorescent lights. He had seen none of this before. It was as if this section of the carpark had always been there. But there was one thing different.

There're no other cars!

All the parking bays were empty.

The bitch opened the car windows, each one sliding down. 'Need some fresh air, lover boy?'

The air was bad. Hot and smelling of petrol.

'Wh . . . where are we . . .?'

'You'll find out!'

She turned and shot down a ramp.

A ramp?

This was the lowest floor in the building. No ramp, no lower floor, should exist.

Bloody nuts!

And yet the car drove down to a new lower level. This part of the basement parking was still as old as the rest of the carpark with its dirty walls, fluorescent lamps, oil-stained concrete flooring and misshapen air-conducting.

Perhaps even older.

There were still no cars. Not a single vehicle parked here. It was a cold empty desert.

A sign, 'B5', flashed by.

The love songs, this one was George Michael, continued to play horribly on. Careless or careful whispers, he didn't care for any of it.

'Wh . . . where . . . are we go . . . going? Please?'

The woman chortled.

It echoed like a hungry cat mewing in his head and sent a shudder through him.

The Honda sped around the basement and, he couldn't believe it, slid down another ramp.

B6 flashed by.

Sweat beaded his forehead. Not just from fear, but from the heat.

He tugged at the handcuffs. Pulled on his tied legs but there was no give. He was strong but he couldn't escape. Even if he did, what was he going to do? Strangle the woman and have the car crash into a concrete column? That was better though than being her prisoner. Caught in this spinning, descending madness.

The lucky Buddha shook its head at him in despair as the car shot down yet another ramp. No good luck symbols nor talismans could save him now.

He was thrown about the backseat as the Honda zipped around the empty car park before shooting down another level.

How many crazy levels are there?

Still the car went round and round, down ramp after ramp.

Faster and faster the Honda zipped, screeching on each turn.

Hot wind rushed in through the windows.

Each level hotter than the next.

B9, B10, B11, the signs read.

His armpits were soaked. His fingers dripped. Sweat poured down his forehead into his eyes and curled into his mouth.

The Honda still sped around and down the levels it shot. The car was now a furnace.

His head shook. His body quaked. His heart trembled.

'Wh . . . where . . .?'

But the bitch just laughed as she eyed him in the rearview mirror.

'Please, where . . . are we . . . going?'

'Can't you guess?'

For a second, instead of her pretty face, he glimpsed a skull with a head full of fiery hair. Pale, hideous, smirking.

He jerked back, hitting his head on the headrest.

Then it was the woman's face again. She threw her hair back with one hand and carried on racing around the car park.

He smelt blood. A nose bleed. It made red blotches on his shirt.

She turned up the music. The horrible love songs hurt his ears. Then to his horror, he realised that Amy Winehouse was dead too. All of them were!

Was this car his coffin?

Still the car shrieked as it sped, bumping and swerving as it it was out of control.

No damn car can go this fast and not crash!

At every turn, he thought the car would skid and hit one of the pillars, but it just kept going.

The signs *B12, B13, B14, B15, B16, B17* flashed by.

His face was burning. Sweat poured down his forehead. His body was drenched in it. He fought to breathe.

The walls leapt at him. The florescent lights quivered and sometimes became snakes. The oil-stained driveways went endless on and on . . .

He glimpsed figures too.

Dark shadows skulking behind concrete posts, their red-green eyes leering at him. Their limbs long. Reptilian. There were more and more of them as they the car shot down each level. But when he tried to look for them they melted into the concrete.

Sometimes he saw flames, licking wildly up the walls.

All in my head. Has to be!

Still the car continued to screech, getting louder like a screaming banshee. Swerving and hurtling its way onwards. Hot wind continued to blast in through the windows.

On and on went the love songs. Dead singers all of them. Louder and louder, hurting his ears. It was as if the wind and the music were one.

B18, B19, B20, B21, B22, B23, B24 . . .

Down and down they went.

B25, B26, B27, B28, B29, B30, B31, B32, B33 . . .

Deeper and deeper.

The numbers became a blur.

He didn't think he'd be seeing the Old Uncle on this bad luck day.

He wanted to laugh and cry at the same time.

'I know who you are!' he shrilled.

The bitch lifted her head and chortled.

The car sped faster still.

At an incredible, impossible speed.

Further and further they plunged, the woman shrieking in delight and him screaming, tears streaming and drying upon his cheeks.

No, he wouldn't be seeing the Old Uncle today.

Another Uncle waited for him.

In the flaming bowels of hell.

12

MR SKULL

An internet sensation he had to be.

Brian was, after all, frustrated with life as a cafe manager, tired of two-timing as a Grab driver and mostly exhausted from being the official photographer for his girlfriend's endless FB poses. Ying, understandably, wanted to be an internet sensation too.

Come to think of it, he didn't know anyone who didn't. After all, why slog all day at work when there's money in just uploading stuff? And he'd be famous!

His videos on YouTube just didn't work because, in retrospect, no one wanted to see his reviews of the best fish ball noodle soup stalls in town. So he thought he could find fame on Instagram by taking shots of an object in different locations. In his case, he chose a soft toy. Others had done it before with good results.

People like cute.

So he found Mr Skull.

Mr Skull was a skeleton soft toy with a big head with an even wider smile. It was cuter than cute, chubby, ridiculously floppy with a matt black background and a skeleton body in a glow-in-the-dark white.

Mr Skull's first outing was at a shopping mall.

At lunch with Ying, Brian sat the soft toy on the sushi conveyor belt, snapped the photos and retrieved the floppy thing before it was out of reach. Then it was Mr Skull eating a California roll, drinking ice-cold Japanese tea and saying hello to the pimple-faced waitress. With so many Instagram likes, the result was, as they say, just awesome.

From then on, Mr Skull made many an appearance. It galavanted wherever Brian went. It played the piano at a hotel lobby, sunbathed on the beach, frolicked at Sunway Putra Mall, ate banana leaf rice and even sat on the toilet seat at his rented room located behind a row of grubby shophouses. Brian took all the pics, cropping, filtering, enhancing, and improving his skills as he did so. Brian was no doubt on his way to becoming an internet sensation.

Except this honeymoon with Mr Skull didn't last. One day, whilst taking a photo of the soft toy on a stack of books at MPH, Brian staggered back, bumping into a book shelf of self-help books and almost dropped his phone.

'Monkey fuck,' he said under his breath. 'Something's wrong.'

He stared wide-eyed at the image. Mr Skull's arms would normally flop by his side unless he had placed them on an object for support, perhaps on a souvenir item or a tissue box. But in the photo, the soft toy's floppy right arm was slightly raised as if it was about to reach out for something.

'How did that happen?' he said. 'Impossible . . .'

A trick of the light perhaps?

He took his glasses off and wiped the lenses with the bottom of his T-shirt. Then he stared hard at the screen and that's when he saw it. A thin dark shadow just behind Mr Skull's head. It was as if there was a presence there, an evil one.

Why the heck did he think that?

He jerked back and stared up at the soft toy, which suddenly didn't look cute anymore. But Mr Skull's arms were flopped by his side and there was no shadow. All was bright from the book shop's fluorescent lighting. The soft toy stared back ever so innocently at him.

No shadow.

Nothing extraordinary happened for the next couple of days and Brian pushed the anomaly to the back of his mind. He was back in his room, directly behind a busy laundry shop, liking photos on Instagram, whilst lying in bed in his boxers staring at the paint-chipped wall when he happened to glance at Mr Skull. The soft toy was propped on an old Ikea shelf which was fine. The only problem was that its left arm was draped over the top of a Hard Rock cafe mug and its head was turned so that it was looking directly at Brian.

'No . . .' he whispered.

He didn't recall placing Mr Skull in that position. He had come home from a cafe, pulled the soft toy out of his backpack and tossed it on the shelf. He was almost sure that the toy was on its side, lying down.

'Why are you sitting up?' he ejaculated, as he sat up in bed, one bolster falling to the tiled floor.

Looking at you.

'What!'

He thought he heard it whisper. In a sort of squeaky bell-like voice.

Now looking at you, looking at me.

'Bullshit, man!'

Brian stood up. He was ready to grab the table lamp to fling it at Mr Skull. He was expecting the soft toy to start moving. But it didn't. It just sat there on the shelf looking at him as if he was a curiosity. Perhaps a sexual monstrosity found on the dark web, for what was happening was dangerously dark.

Was he losing his mind?

That was the first thing that popped into Brian's head.

He didn't think sleep would claim him that night so he took two sleeping pills, pushed Mr Skull into a cheap plastic drawer on top of his underpants, and flicked off the lights. Except he left the bathroom one on. The small musty bathroom with a cracked mirror and broken shower head.

Brian shivered beneath his cotton blanket. He wished Ying was cuddling him in bed instead of living with her parents. He wished she wasn't cheating on him. He wished he had tons of money and never having to work. But mostly, he wished he never bought Mr Skull. Never heard of Instagram. Never went surfing on this thing called the Internet.

He did sleep. He had no nightmares.

Instead he dreamt he was in a cafe. There was something wrong with it though. What was it? He then realised what it was. He had his handphone on the table and occasionally fiddling with it. But there were no other phones. No tablets, laptops or mobiles on other tables. No one tapping away or scrolling the screen. People were talking quietly, giving each other full attention or glancing around, meeting the eyes of strangers.

Was this the 1990s?

Man, he didn't even know when people started being addicted to smart phones but he did realise one awful truth: people were hopelessly addicted. And, like him, they had no idea of this addiction.

'We have our heads buried in technology!' he gasped.

Then he woke up.

It was dark. What had happened to the light in the bathroom?

He quickly glanced at the shelf.

And he almost screamed.

For there, bones glowing in the dark, was Mr Skull again. His luminescent skeleton-head looking right at him.

Shit!

He had left the soft toy in the drawer.

How the hell did it get back up there?

Its legs were dangling off the shelf. Every so often, they would slightly sway back and forth. Brian gulped and felt his chest trembling. It was as if Mr Skull was sitting on a park bench in Cameron Highlands, breathing the fresh air, admiring the view.

Then, the arm. It moved.

Slowly upward. And it gave him a wave.

A bloody wave.

Brian was about to jump out of bed when he heard it's voice.

You think too much, Brian.

'Huh?'

Even in your dreams, you think too much. Of course, we've got our heads buried in technology. We're addicted to it.

'You're not bloody talking. Bugger it, man! This is a dream. A nightmare!'

If you say so. You humans are addicted to everything. All you guys need is the bait. Something that'll press the right buttons. As for me . . .

'You? What the monkey-fuck are you? You're just a stupid toy I bought.'

A toy? No, I'm no toy. I'm your Instagram sensation . . .come to life!

'Bullshit! This is just a dream.'

Every photo you took of me has given me life. Every shot giving me a bit of soul . . .

'That's dog shit . . .'

You humans don't realise the opposite though. Every photo taken of you steals away a bit of your life. Yeah, selfies too! Take too many shots and one day you'll just drop dead. Just like that. So go on . . . take more photos of yourselves, you vain idiots!

'I don't believe you. How many photos . . .'

Oh, many, so very many in a short burst of time. People have already died. Haven't you noticed all the unexplained deaths?

'I don't know! I haven't been keeping up with . . .'

The news? It's all fake now. Everything is fake. Fake food. Fake faces. Fake boobs. Fake religion. Fake politicians.

'And you're a fake monkey-fucking toy!'

Hahahaha! Yes, but I'm no toy now. You've given me life . . .

'One photo too many, huh? And they die?'

Yes, for sure. You're smart, Brian.

'Thanks. But pull my cock all you like. I still think this is a dream.'

Okay then, let's just keep talking until you wake up.

'Sure, if that's what you want.'

Yes, I like talking. I've never talked before. It's such fun. You're such a good listener too. Can I tell you a story?

'No.'

It's a ghost story. One of those Tunku Halim ones.

'Never heard of him. It's all dog shit . . ..'

I'll tell it to you anyway. Once upon a miserable time there was a . . .

But Brian's eyes had already closed and he was snoring.

* * *

The next thing he heard was the beeping of his phone alarm. This dingy room which he called home was bright with sunlight and he heard the shouts from the usual Tae Kwon Do lesson from the community hall across the small carpark. A hawker stall creaked its way past his window, the bulky silhouette and umbrella was an undulating darkness against his drawn curtains.

Perhaps this was the *mee goreng* stall that was always beside the Petron station or did it, after midnight, sell knifes and shabu to wandering children on bicycles?

And where the hell was Mr Skull?

He looked up expecting to see the doll on the shelf. But no, it was gone. He leapt over to his plastic drawer and pulled it open but the soft toy wasn't there amongst his underpants.

Where the monkey-fuck is it? Did I really talk to the doll last night?

He had no time to search for Mr Skull. Instead he hurried to the toilet, did his business, showered, got changed, ate some left over pau from the fridge, grabbed his backpack and was hurrying out the door past the old shophouses and snarling backed up traffic for the MRT.

He got off the train at Plaza Connaught, hurried over to the office, said hello to his colleagues, made a 3-in-1 coffee and was soon perched at his cubicle. All that time, he only had one thing on his mind.

Where, where, where are you Mr Skull?

He pulled his laptop from his backpack and

. . .*there it is!*

Sitting so innocently as usual amongst his stuff.

He wiped the sweat off his forehead with a tissue.

'How . . . how did you get here?'

Instead of giving Mr Skull his usual spot propped ever so cutely beside his fake pot plant, Brian left it in the backpack, zipping the bag up harder than he had meant to. He didn't want to see the damn toy.

He could hardly focus that day. He kept checking to see if Mr Skull was in the backpack, half expecting the doll to have wandered off down to the coffee shops for some *teh tarik* or snacks at 7-Eleven. But no, the floppy thing stayed put.

'Good, good,' Brian whispered, relief like a cool stream flowing through him. 'Don't move, man. Never move.'

His thoughts were ablaze though. Mr Skull had come to life. This was freakish as freakish can be. But it was what the doll had said that set his mind on fire.

The thing had come to life because of the hundreds of photos he'd taken of it and uploaded.

It said that the reverse is true for humans.

He couldn't stop thinking about Ying. His mind burning vengeful circles in his brain.

She was obsessed with herself. Wanting more and more photos of herself posted on social media. That was all she talked about. Life was one endless photo opportunity.

'But do I want to photograph you to death?'

Was it even possible?

He recalled how some aborigines refused to have their photos taken. They thought it would steal their soul. That though was dog shit madness. It had to be.

He had picked up his phone and was staring at her latest FB photos.

She thought him stupid. But he knew. He'd known for weeks. She was planning to leave him.

He felt a trembling ache in his guts. He couldn't bear to be without beautiful Ying. Didn't want anyone else having her.

She'll be mine forever.

He only had to take photos. Hundreds upon hundreds of them. And upload them.

'But were you lying?' He had unzipped the backpack and stared at the soft toy. 'Is it all dog shit?'

But Mr Skull just sat there silently, leaning against an empty water bottle. A non-committal smile on its face.

'It doesn't matter. Maybe she'll die. Maybe she won't. I'll leave this up to God.'

Or perhaps the devil.

The latter notion sent such a cold trembling in his chest, that he jerked up in his seat.

He hadn't been to church for three weeks and his fellow church-goers were feverishly reminding him to go. But he didn't much care about church or God or anything else.

He was going to do it!

* * *

And did it he did.

Although dubious as to Brian's motives at first, Ying's enthusiasm got the better of her and so that Agong's birthday long weekend became a photo shoot extravaganza. Whereas he would normally grudgingly take twenty or more shots at one location, he now excitedly took two or three hundred. He had upgraded the memory card in his phone for the task. Even bought space in the cloud.

Face bright, eyes twinkling, limbs feverish with excitement Ying glided from one pose to the next:

Squatting.

Pouting. Grinning.

Tongue stuck out. Fingers gesturing.

Heart signs. Peace signs. Gangsta poses. Funny faces!

She'd become supermodel extraordinaire: chin over shoulder, leaning over, exposing the pale décolletage of her breasts, her long well-shaped legs gleaming white beneath the hot sun. Her vanity, her creative posing, knew no bounds.

'Sure I look cute?' she asked.

'Of course, Ah-Ying,' he replied.

'Don't look fat?'

'No way. So very slim.'

'You need to stand further away lah.'

'Okay, okay.'

'And hold your phone higher!'

'Sure . . .'

They took the MRT and LRT across KL to all the sights, playing tourists, for don't they say that it takes a tourist to discover your own country? They even got lost a couple of times, but Brian tried to assuage Ying with the idea that you need to get lost before you're found. But she would have none of his pseudo-spiritual bullshit.

'Not much time left for photos!'

'We'll go to Dataran Merdeka. We can stay there till late!'

'Yes, good idea! Great place for photos!'

When the shoot was finally over, Brian's back, arms and hands, especially his thumbs, were sore. It had been a long weekend of non-stop photos. Ying didn't want to go back to his room. She said she was tired. He expected that. She never liked his place anyway. She found it too grubby, which it undoubtedly was.

'Bet she's going to see her new man,' he whispered to his pillow when he got home. 'Disloyal monkey-fucking bitch!'

He regretted the words as soon as they exited his mouth for he loved her. He wished Mr Skull was with him for he needed someone to talk to. But he had left it on the MRT days before. A female foreign worker had called out, pointing to the soft toy tossed on the seat as he exited the train, but Brian just shrugged and walked out, relief washing through him as he ambled away down the crowded platform. Perhaps some child would find Mr Skull but hopefully the cleaner would have thrown the thing away or, better still, incinerate it.

As for Ying, it was time to upload her photos. He knew her password. She used it on all her social media sites. The more people who saw them, the better, he figured.

The more deadly.

It was late. He didn't know how long it would take to upload the photos. There were more than a thousand of them, he was sure.

He made himself a 3-in-1, sat on his bed and began the uploads . . .

* * *

The next day, he was yawning all the way on the MRT on his way to work. He chatted with his colleagues, made coffee and, with a big yawn, sat at his cubicle. He was called into several meetings and didn't get to send Ying a message until lunch time. He began to worry when she didn't answer.

Worry?

Shouldn't he be happy? Didn't he want her dead?

But she couldn't be dead. No way. The photo thing couldn't have worked. It was so far-fetched. So monkey-fucking crazy.

Perhaps she was just ill.

He called her later that afternoon but she didn't pick up. He was so worried that as soon as he got off work, he took a taxi to her house in Kepong. He knew something was wrong when he saw a small crowd at the front gate. There were a few familiar faces: a cousin, an aunt, an old school friend.

The sun blazed into his eyes as he crossed the street. Could it have worked? Was his Ai-Ying, dead? Why the hell did he do it?

Why? Why? Why?

He was crazy. Foolish.

As he entered the crowded semi-D of hushed voices and frowning faces, her dishevelled mother, wearing a loose house dress, grabbed his arm so tightly that it hurt.

'She didn't wake up,' she gasped, eyes swelling with tears. 'She was so happy when she got home last night.'

He nodded and clutched her small shoulders, not knowing what to say. What could he say?

I murdered your daughter.

'Oh, Brian. She was always so healthy. The doctors don't know why this happened!'

He stumbled over to the coffin which was placed at the far end of the lounge, his feet barely able to move. Ying's father, thin, frail and muttering, leading him, his thin trembling hand upon Brian's back.

Dressed in her most expensive dress, Ying's eyes were closed. Neither smiling nor frowning and almost at peace.

Her final pose for the cameras.

He glanced back at the other visitors.

Did anyone take a photo?

He sighed. No, of course not.

It wasn't the done thing. Not yet anyway.

Facebook status?

Dead. Very dead. Murdered.

Brian didn't dare touch her. Not even a stroking finger on her sleeve or her cheek. She would be cold. Her organs, her blood chilled, whilst outside the sun blazed an angry heat upon the cars and roof of the houses.

Brian wanted to fall on his knees, one hand clutching onto the gleaming, timber coffin, and weep rivers. But instead he stood in one corner beside the broken electric organ Ying used to play as a kid and wondered where the hell Mr Skull was.

* * *

Two days after Ying's funeral, Brian lay in bed shivering in his Uniqlo boxer shorts, antibiotics streaming in his blood. From the community hall, came the distant shouts of the usual Saturday Tae Kwon Do lesson.

He groaned and wondered if it was time for another dose of paracetamol. His skin was cold and clammy.

A rotting corpse.

Like Ai-Ying all dressed up in her coffin.

He lay upon his damp pillow, the memories circling his skull like crows, their feathered wings ready to suffocate him. He closed his eyes and must have for a moment fallen asleep, for when he opened them again, he saw it.

The staring eyes. The wide smile of the soft toy.

Mr Skull.

Legs dangling, swaying nonchalantly beneath the shelf, throwing shadows like truncheons upon the paint-chipped wall.

He pulled a bolster to his chest.

'What . . . what the monkey-fuck are you doing here?'

Saying '*apa khabar*,' of course!

'Apa fucking *khabar*?'

A Malay family took me in after you left me on the train. That's how I learnt Malay. So, you *tak sihat?*

'Why . . . why have you come back?'

I had to. You gave me the gift of life. Our bond can never be broken.

'You shouldn't have told me about the damn photos.'

Ah, the photos. So *bodoh* of you. Took so many of them, didn't you? Stole your girlfriend's soul . . .

'I didn't know it would work.'

Oh, it does work . . . If you truly believe it.

'But I didn't believe it . . .'

Deep in your guts you did. Now listen . . .

'What?'

You took Ying's soul. But because you love her this means to you she must return.

Mr Skull raised a hand towards the bathroom.

The bathroom door creaked. A rotten coffin opening.

A chill slithered up his neck.

Something pale moved behind the door, a wavering shadow within his small miserable bathroom with its cracked mirror and broken shower head.

What the hell is it?

The door slowly creaked. Something stepped out of the bathroom.

The figure, dressed in white, had long, dripping hair.

Even though her face was pale, deadly white, and half hidden by hair, he recognised her.

My Ah-Ying!

She drew towards him in a dripping long white dress.

His heart thumped. Cold sweat dripped from his forehead.

Still closer she drifted, head jerking from side to side. Feet leaving murky puddles like blood on the tiled floor.

As she reached the bed, she opened her mouth.

Brian was about to scream, expecting fangs to lunge at his neck.

But no . . . they were just normal teeth.

What the monkey fuck?

She lay down beside him on the bed, sighing, body away from his. Her bottom cold and wet against his thigh. Cold, because she was long dead. He was about to say something when her phone appeared in her hand.

It clicked as she took a selfie. Then a shot of them both, perhaps for old times' sake. She edited the photos, brightened them up, removed blemishes, added lipstick. Made it her profile pic.

He craned his neck to see what she was doing now.

Scrolling through Facebook!

Looking at posts and news items.

Scrolling, liking, sharing . . . and even commenting!

She sighed again.

Was it for the past or the future?

He didn't want to know.

Or a life remembered on social media?

No, that was too weird.

As for Mr Skull, he was now sitting at the end of the bed in a Yoga half-lotus position, its fat skeletal head nodding.

From the glare outside came more Tae Kwon Do shouts, followed by the sound of crunching car wheels and the looming silhouette of the hawker stall creaking away to its designated corner for the day's business.

To sell knives and *shabu* to children.

Brian shivered.

As soon as Ying was bored with her phone, she would probably turn and strangle him. Simple revenge. An inexorable truth. Perhaps she would grow fangs and bite out his throat. She used to love horror movies.

He didn't want to die. No antibiotics could save him now. He made a stupid mistake and now he was going to pay.

He sobbed the verse . . .

'I will fear no evil, for thou art with me . . .'

. . . but forgot how the rest of it went. Something about the shadow of death . . .

He should have gone to church more often.

Mr Skull was chattering away.

But Brian could hardly hear any of it. The toy talked dog shit anyway.

Another thought rushed at him . . .

As you feed your ego, so you kill your soul.

He didn't have time to contemplate its meaning for suddenly Ying shifted her body.

But . . . he knew its meaning, . . .yes, knew it only too well.

Or did he? Either he was wiser or more foolish than he thought.

As she turned to him, a dark mist swept over his eyes. He saw only its swirling blackness but he no longer felt Ying's weight on the mattress.

Then the mist cleared.

He bolted upright.

Mr Skull sat grinning at him.

Meet Mrs Skull, he sniggered.

The new soft toy, a head shorter than Mr Skull, not as chubby and with pinkish lips, sat cross-legged beside her husband.

There was something familiar in the soft toy's expression.

'Is . . . is that you, Ying?'

The soft toy smiled and lifted a hand in greeting.

Yes, it's me, Brian. Thank you.

'You're . . . thanking me?'

Your thoughts set me free. As you feed your ego, so you kill your soul. So true.

'I didn't want to kill you . . .'

Never mind about that. You're right, you know, our heads are buried in technology. I didn't want to be a ghost lying beside you on the bed playing with my phone anymore. Now I'm free!

'Free?'

Yes, free to be with Mr Skull, my husband.

'But . . . but I love you.'

I love you too, but only as a friend. Love between a soft toy and a human just won't work.

'It sometimes does . . .'

Maybe. But you killed me. The human me.

'Sorry . . .'

That's okay. I prefer being this way.

Mr Skull took his wife's hand. *Come my dear, let's go. Then it turned to Brian, eyebrows raised. Can we leave? Is that okay?*

Brian nodded. 'I'll even open the door for you.'

He slid out of bed, thinking that the room would spin. But he felt perfectly fine, even refreshed, as if he'd never been ill.

He opened the door, which creaked open to the bright sunshine, the parked vehicles and a hazy sky. Children in white uniforms were streaming out of the Tae Kwon Do lesson. Birds chirped in the trees. A hot wind touched his face.

He turned to say something, but the bed was empty and Mr and Mrs Skull were gone.

PART 4
GRAVEYARD VOICES

13

44 CEMETERY ROAD

Janice died a week ago.

With this thought, I dragged myself from bed. I smiled grimly into the mirror and dropped my toothbrush back into its ceramic cup, fluorescent paste still hanging off its bristles. I grabbed my walking stick and the front door of our small cottage swung shut, thudding like a coffin lid behind me.

It was just past six. Well before light. Before windows are lit and children are hustled off to school. Before sunlight glares between rooftops and cars speed noisily through roads. At six o'clock, darkness still reigns.

Before Janice died, I stayed in bed for as long as I could, enjoying lying against her soft sagging breasts, a wisp of her white hair upon my brow. Eyes half closed, I would watch the crimson hue outside, like a flame, raze across our low iron fence.

Oh, that morning, how she breathed softly upon my cheek whispering her secret. Her fingers held the pillow as though she were a child clinging to the remnants of a fairytale dream. With eyes closed she looked younger than her seventy-three years. That faint smile gave no hint of death.

Since the funeral, I have not dared stay in bed a minute longer. The sheets are cold and there is too much space on Janice's side. There she had read. There she had knitted. There she had been.

'Winter has come,' I whispered to a streetlamp and its mosquitoes danced and flickered in an incandescent orange glow. 'Will I die today. Or live again?'

At the roundabout, I turned left. Trying to keep my back straight, as if this would solidify me against what waited ahead. I shuffled past the dark playing field. Beside the swings and slides, a skateboard bowl had been dug out. After school and during holidays, the place was bursting with teenagers balancing like demons on mini-chariots. Even in the dark, the bowl trembled with energy. Ah, the relentless joys of youth.

What did Janice whisper on the day she died?

'I have a secret, my love.'

'What secret?' I propped myself on the pillow and stared into her grey eyes.

'Meet me. In seven days.' Her lips quivered and I could tell whatever this was disturbed her badly.

'Why? What are you talking about, Janice? I see you everyday.'

'In a week,' she whispered. 'At the ruins in the forest.'

'How come? What's this all about?' My wife was behaving so strangely. So incredibly odd.

'Just promise,' she said, taking my hand, hers coldly trembling. 'Just promise.'

'All right, all right. If it's such a big deal. But why . . . .'

'A week from now, my love. At the ruins. At dawn. No later.'

'Oh, do tell, Janice. What the hell is this all about?'

And then she whispered a craziness that made my old heart shudder.

As I passed the scattered buildings of the nursing home, I saw most of the lights were already on. We old foggies get up early. Perhaps we know we have squandered our youth, even our middle age, and now in our twilight years we know time is precious. That our remaining life need meaning so when Death comes pounding on our door we can look him squarely in the eye and know we're ready. And to you, feminist, Death, I'm afraid, is a man.

I have one regret. Janice and I did not have children. We thought of adopting, perhaps a child from Africa or Asia. We had even contacted a few agencies. But we had second thoughts. Would we be able to give the child enough of our love? In the end, Janice left it to me and I had my doubts. Janice was more disappointed than I thought she would be. Sometimes when we went shopping, I would find her in the baby shop, staring whimsically at shiny new cots draped in pretty fabric.

By now I had reached the end of the road. A dead end except I knew, hidden behind a clump of bushes and a tired-looking sign, was a dirt track that cut through the forest. I stood before it, breathing hard, not to catch my breath, although at my age this would only be normal, but because I was sure I felt a cold hand stroking my spine.

'You can't believe this nonsense, Janice,' I had snarled that morning. 'This is madness.'

But she didn't answer. She just turned away.

Half bewildered, half angry, I stormed out of bed into the study. Her secret, it was the most ridiculous thing I had ever heard. I couldn't concentrate on the biography for her words darted like irritating wasps in my head.

I put the book aside and when I crept back to the bedroom, I found her lying sprawled out on the twisted sheets, window wide open, lace curtains billowing like tortured sails in the wind. Her eyes stared icily at the ceiling, lips curled into a dreadful grin. I cried out and held my dead wife, trembling in the shafts of sunlight whilst her body grew colder and colder in my arms.

The ambulance men said there was nothing they could do. The coroner could not find the cause of death. A mystery disease perhaps. Did the bruises on her throat have anything to do with it? What bruises? I hadn't seen them before. They showed me, hidden beneath her hair, black marks on her neck. The doctor wasn't sure what made them. Nobody could be sure of anything. So many mystery illnesses nowadays.

Wiping wetness from my cheeks, I started up the track. The silhouettes of houses fell back and shadows of trees encircled me like vengeful ogres. Wild grasses swept by my boots. Frogs whooped and a lonesome bird called an incessant warning. I took my time with the steep climb, shoving my walking stick into the dark earth to heave my stooping body forward. My legs ached. My hips sore. Had I taken my arthritis pills this morning? I couldn't remember.

A rustling in the bushes. I almost cried out. It could have been a dog or some wild animal. Too dark to see. Or was it something more sinister? My heart was beating fast. No use dying of a heart attack. Not now. When I was so close. I breathed in deeply to calm myself but instead the smell of dead things and faeces filled my nostrils. I bend over, clutched my hat and heaved up whatever was left of last night's dinner. It was mostly liquid. Pathetic really.

I picked myself up and steadied my old body, bile burning in my throat. I glanced at my watch. My trembling hand making it hard to tell the time. An anniversary gift from Janice so many years ago. Not quite sure which one though. But we were on holiday somewhere by a sunlit beach. Was it in this country or not I couldn't be sure.

'Oh, Janice,' I said. 'Our life has become a huge blur.'

One thing I still know though: this dirt track had a name. It was called Cemetery Road because it led to a small cemetery on the hill deep in the forest. Only one of four roads in this once thriving village. A village that existed two hundred years ago. But after the forest fires which destroyed half the homes, things turned bad. Folks moved to the big town, abandoning their broken-down timber houses. Making any kind of living here was hard.

In the last few decades though, as the big city relentlessly sprawled northwards, people returned with their cars and mortgages. In this new suburb they built their roads, houses and shops. As for Cemetery Road, it lay buried in the forest reserve, a mere track for hikers leading past the ruins of a mansion.

I plodded uphill, breathing hard, my old bones stiff and aching. Although chilly, my bald head beneath my hat was hot and my hands had grown sweaty. Dawn crept its way up through the leaves and branches.

Just before I reached the graveyard, the entrance leered over me, its lopsided post threatening to crush my skull. I stepped back startled. I had arrived all too quickly. No, I didn't need to remove the strangling foliage to know the numbers carved into the mossy stone.

'I've arrived, Janice,' I whispered.

44 Cemetery Road.

As a child, we had gone into the ruins on a dare but barely made it up the gravel path. The place scared us, even more than the cemetery next door. Zack, the pluckiest of our group, claimed he had seen strange lights, like candles flickering in the windows and shadows, gliding to and fro as though restlessly waiting. I didn't believe this nonsense. But there were stories about this sad place. Stories whispered only after a couple of whiskies.

Who knows if they were true. But history there was. Eamon Fitzgerald had come from Perthshire, Scotland. He worked as a kitchen hand before striking it rich in the gold fields. He bought the only land available then, twenty acres next to the cemetery, and there built the biggest and only stone house in the village.

After Eamon died, his son George made several extensions to the home. When George found out his wife Vera was having an affair with the gardener he cleaved her head with an axe and threw her down the well. He died in prison before he was hung and with no offspring, the mansion was left empty. Then came the forest fires and the village was soon abandoned.

I pushed open the rusty gate which creaked out a guttural warning. Whether for me or someone or something else I wasn't sure. My shoes crunched upon the gravel buried by wild grass. Otherwise, it was silent here. Too awfully silent. No birdsong. No frogs whooping. And colder, too. Icy and damp it was. A trembling grew in my bones.

If I was to turn back, now was the time. To retreat through the gate and scurry down the track. Past the nursing home and playing field. My warm cottage behind the low iron fence would be waiting. I would make some tea, pick up a book or flick on the telly. The morning programmes could sometimes be interesting. But the years . . . they would ravage me. And I had promised Janice. Yes, I had promised her. That was my excuse. I knew better though. And so I heard my footsteps drag my old bones up the old driveway.

Dawn filtered through the foliage. I could take no solace from that. For now, I could see a thick mist hung like a dismal cloak through the thick trees ahead, where the garden had been reclaimed by forest. The skeletal remains of rose bushes stripped by winter clawed their way to the stone ruins. I shuffled past the fallen remains of a pergola overgrown by creepers.

I groped at the timber post and part of it crumbled into dust. Age, it does such things.

Birth and death is the normal cycle of life. But Janice had other thoughts . . .

'I met someone yesterday,' she whispered. 'At the ruins.'

I knew Janice often went by the old mansion on her hikes and meeting other hikers was not unusual.

'Oh, who was it?'

'No one we know,' said Janice. 'It was a lady dressed in white. She gave me something.'

'Oh, what was it?'

'Everlasting life.'

'Ever . . . what?'

'Everlasting life. When I see you in seven days, I'll pass this precious gift to you.'

'What the hell are you talking about, Janice! This is crazy!'

'Is it crazy to want to live forever? It'll be you and me, young again, and living 'til the end of time!'

Young again? Until the end of time?

That was why I stood here trembling, at this dreadful desolate place, at this appointed hour.

Here to confront her madness! Or was it mine?

I pushed my way past the groping branches into what once was the main part of the garden. I felt a tingling on my neck, as though someone was watching me. My eyes darted about but I saw no one, just overgrown bushes and white drifts of mists like malevolent ghosts. I drew my coat tighter against my body and my breath hung in the air. I cautiously crept down one of the broken footpaths.

A bulky shadow loomed ahead of me. Was it a vicious creature waiting? No. Just a fountain with a fallen pedestal. Murky water, brown and oily, stagnated there, giving off a foul odour that grabbed at my guts. I clutched my mouth to stop myself from vomiting again. It wasn't the smell that made me want to retch. It was fear.

Suddenly I was surrounded. Trapped! I spun around and gasped. Figures encircled me, their faces lunging forward. I was about to flee when I realised that the threatening figures were but sculptures.

Through the heavy mist the stone shadows stood like sentinels. Sad grey faces peered through foliage. An ear, an eye, an elbow, a foot, protruded from the bushes. A lion with one claw. A rat in its mouth.

'Janice,' I whispered, holding back my tears. 'What insanity awaits here? Why have I come?'

As if in reply there was a queer sound. Like someone laughing.

I looked up to see a figure in a white dress dart before me.

'What the . . . ' I gasped.

I stumbled backwards from the fountain and knocked into something hard. I screamed.

A face peered right into mine. A stone face.

In its hands it held a jug of wine. A Greek-like sculpture with flowing robes. Discoloured and chipped by time and the beating of the sun and the drumming of rain.

I glanced around me but she was gone.

'Where is she?' I whispered. 'What am I doing here?' 'For me, my love,' a familiar voice said. 'For me.'

I turned and gasped.

It was Janice. But not the Janice who had laid in my bed, a wisp of white hair on my cheek, soft sagging breasts on my chest. Not the Janice who knitted and did the crossword puzzles and made endless cups of tea.

This was the Janice I married fifty years ago.

Radiant and alight with energy. A red dress flowed about her slim body. Her hair blonde and shining even in the dim light. Her skin glowing like moonlight.

Oh, how young, how so alive, she looked!

'Surprised?' Janice said. 'I told you I'd be here waiting.'

'Yes, but . . .'

'Everything I've told you is true. Everlasting youth, my love. That's what I've promised you.'

Before I could ask her one of a thousand questions, Janice took my hand.

Her hand was freezing. I tried to yank mine away. She gripped my fingers harder.

'Come, my love. Come with me.'

Walking briskly ahead, she pulled me through the entangling trees, past its watching sculptures, to the fallen masonry walls. I dropped my walking stick but she didn't heed my protests and kept pulling me. My legs had trouble keeping up with her lithe dancing movements and I stumbled twice.

Up the once-grand entrance steps she drew me. The building had lost most of its roof and, beyond the crumbling brick structures, gloomy clouds like giant ghosts swept by.

We entered what must have once been the kitchen. The rusty remains of a stove slumped like a dead thing in one corner. The floor was roughly tiled and covered in bits of broken wood. In another corner were some broken ceramics, a fork and a metal cup.

'Let's wait here, my love.'

'Janice,' I said. 'How . . . What . . .'

'Shhhhh . . .' she said and put a finger to my lips. The appendage felt icy. And since when did Janice paint her fingernails? Almost never. But her's were now painted red and the fingernails were long like claws.

Then I noticed her eyes. Now I could see them properly. How unlike the rest of her they were. Not young and vibrant like the rest of her body. Her eyes seemed unnatural. Older than those of my departed wife. Older than old.

They were dead.

'Don't ask questions, my love,' she said. 'You'll soon meet my new friend.'

By now the sun had risen but because it was kept hidden by layers of swirling clouds we were in a world of neither light nor dark. As for the mist, it encircled our limbs, gripping us with a damp coldness.

Janice didn't seem to mind for she grinned at me expectantly, her lips bright red.

'Thank you, Janice.'

I turned to see who spoke and there standing behind me was the woman dressed in white. My throat went dry.

'Hello,' I stammered.

Despite my fear, I couldn't help noticing how stunning the woman was. Raven hair cascaded down in flowing curls. Around her neck she wore a gold locket of a strange design. But what I noticed most were her eyes, dark and penetrating as though she could see into the depths of my soul. But, like Janice's eyes, they appeared to be dead.

'Nice to make your acquaintance,' she said in a low voice. 'I've heard a lot about you. My name is Vera. Do you know why we've brought you here?'

'For everlasting life,' I said. 'So that I don't ever grow old. So that time can go to hell and Janice and I can live together forever.'

'That's right!' laughed the woman. 'Time can go to hell. I like that. You know what you want, old man, don't you? But do you know how I'll achieve it?'

'Yes,' I said, drawing in a quick breath. 'I saw the bruises on Janice's neck. You're a . . . a vampire. You're immortal. Anyone you kill will also turn into a vampire. I know the legend. I've read about it. Am I right?'

'A legend is only a legend,' said Vera. 'Like all things in this world, parts of it are true. These vampire myths remain hidden in the human subconscious. All cultures have vampire legends. That should provide a hint that we are real. But humankind has forgotten us. Consigning us to mere stories and teenage movies. So much the better. We are safer than ever before.'

'So you are a vampire!' I drew in a deep breath. My conclusions, insane though they were, were correct. My hands began to shake. 'Will . . . will you give me everlasting life? Will you make me young again? I want to be with Janice 'til the end of time.'

The woman laughed. 'You are indeed persistent for an old man.'

'He's always been like this,' said Janice, smiling at me. 'Ever since we met. I love him dearly.'

'Thank you for bringing your husband to see me,' said Vera, stepping towards Janice. 'I'll be forever grateful.'

Vera embraced my wife. Janice stiffened and her arms flew up flailing at the air. She tried to fight against Vera but couldn't. Vera stepped back and Janice collapsed to the ground.

I stood frozen in horror. In the half-light I could see Janice's neck had been ripped out.

Vera turned.

Then I saw her for what she was. There was a wound in the side of her head covered in black blood. Then it vanished and she was beautiful again.

'What the hell have you done!' I yelled. 'You've killed my wife!'

'I've done what I've always planned to do,' said Vera, wiping the blood from her mouth with a white handkerchief.

She stepped slowly towards me, eyes shining bright.

Her mouth opened impossibly wide to reveal fangs. Long and sharp.

'Why?' I cried, stumbling back, pulling myself along one wall. 'Why did you kill her?'

'Kill her? She was already dead. She was the undead. Just like I am. How cursed I am to wander aimlessly through time. Cursed to feed off animals in the wild or to take the occasional child, the homeless tramp or wandering backpacker. Never letting on that a vampire dwells among you pathetic humans. I used your dear wife to bring you to me.'

'Me? Why me? What do you want with me?'

Vera continued stalking me. I had retreated into the remains of another room. From its sprawling dimensions I guessed it was a grand living or dining room. At my feet the broken masonry of a fireplace were scattered over white marble. Through the French windows the dark shadows of the forest beckoned.

'You are the last descendant of George Fitzgerald. When my husband split my skull with an axe and threw me down the well, I yearned for revenge. I killed him in his cell and promised to slay all his descendants. Then came the fires and the mob to hunt me down. So I fled and stayed away for so many years. But I've always remembered to return to finish the work. You are the last descendant of George Fitzgerald!'

'You're wrong! I'm not a Fitzgerald. George Fitzgerald had no children.'

'No legitimate ones. Your grandfather was George's son. His mother was the maid. She was dismissed when he found out she was carrying his child. So you see, you have come home at last. This is the house of your ancestors!'

'No!' I cried. 'This can't be real.'

Vera glided towards me, arms reaching out, tongue licking her bright red lips. She grinned, 'Revenge, after so many years, how sweet it feels.'

I tripped and fell painfully on my back.

'No!' I groaned. 'Please . . .'

She stood over me, chest heaving, running a finger down her long curly hair. 'I wonder how much blood is in that thin old body of yours.'

Just as her fangs flew to my throat I heard a terrible ripping, a shrieking that filled the dawn.

The ground trembled.

The vampire fell back, hands clutching at the walls for balance, hair thrown across her vile face.

'What's this!' she moaned. 'What's happening!'

With my last vestiges of energy, I got up and threw myself out of the house and back into the forest. I ran, hobbled, fell and ran again. I heard the vampire cursing behind me, giving chase.

Still I forced my legs to move. I must have come out the wrong way for the trees suddenly opened up, and instead of the track I was confronted with white gravestones. But something terrible was happening here.

The ground was shaking. Clumps of earth were thrown high in the air as if the place was being hit by artillery fire. If only that were true for the reality was far more terrible . . .

Bodies in half rotten clothes pushed themselves out of their graves. Worming their way out, clawing at the soil. Eyes wide and eager.

I turned to flee but Vera stood behind me, blocking my path. She was not grinning though. Her body shook, her face wild.

'No!' she cried. 'This is impossible!'

'We have come for you, creature of evil,' a dreadful voice echoed. 'Harlot of the devil, we will destroy you!'

I spun and beheld a hideous figure, rotting flesh draped off its chest. A grey organ pulsed horribly within. It raised its thin arm. A crooked finger pointed accusingly at the vampire.

Eyes, large and bloody, stared angrily from a skull-like head from which a few strands of hair hung. Upon its arms and legs were patches of shining white, bones showing through. Swatches of cloth, once fine clothes, still clung to the figure.

'You do remember us, don't you, darling Vera?' it growled. 'Now it's our turn.'

It clenched its hands into bleeding fists.

Behind it, several other figures, all rotting beings, groped their way forward, moaning and groaning their curses as they surrounded Vera.

'Return to your graves!' cried the vampire. 'You are all dead! I killed you centuries ago!'

'Yes!' cried the figure. 'We are indeed dead. But we are alive again to rip you off this living breathing earth.'

Before the vampire could reply, the figures fell upon her. I ran for the forest.

I heard a terrible shrieking and thumping.

And finally the ripping of flesh.

I knew as I fell moaning upon the track that the figure that spoke was George Fitzgerald. My ancestor. Did he come to protect me or did he wait through the centuries for his own revenge?

By the time I stumbled down Cemetery Road, the forest was awash in sunlight. Birds chirped in the trees. A yellow butterfly drifted innocently by. I could feel a warmth creeping back into my bones.

What had happened up there at the ruins? I didn't want to think about it. There would never be any answers.

I stepped out of the forest into the bright morning of suburbia. Up the road I trudged, already missing my walking stick which I would never retrieve. My body ached painfully. Vehicles sped about. Children being hustled to school. I shuffled past the old folks' home. A man in a bright yellow T-shirt was watering the rose garden.

Beside the playing field a car stopped, its lady driver asked if I needed help.

'I'm fine,' I said. 'Couldn't be better.'

'Are you sure?' She looked like a doctor or a vet. Maybe a psychiatrist.

'Perfectly fine.'

A little girl in a pink dress waved from a child seat. I grinned at her. She could have been my granddaughter.

'Thank you for caring,' I said to her mother. 'This can be a lonely road.'

I carried on. I could see my house now. A small cottage with an iron fence. There Janice and I had lived. There I will make my cups of tea.

There I will past the time. There I will eventually die.

14

GRAVEDIGGER'S KISS

I had not seen Lucas for a few days. It was his habit, as was mine, to stop at the Jolly Axeman religiously every evening for a pint. Even whilst nursing a bad cold, the old gravedigger would be at the corner by the window, his sandpapery voice quietly rasping in the pub's smoky haze. We did no more than exchange pleasantries on these occasions for we gravitated towards different groups. Naturally, he mixed with fellow tradesmen whilst I huddled with shopkeepers and professionals.

Even so, it was obvious that Lucas was missing. His rasping voice, which I was told he acquired when a boot, studs and all, crunched into his neck during a rugby match, was gone. Word was that the man had locked himself up in his ramshackle cottage that ever threatens to collapse into the graveyard. Perhaps he wanted time alone.

I was surprised to stumble upon Lucas that Saturday. I had read the morning's papers with its usual depressing fill of car bombs, rioting youths, drugs and starvation in Africa. Even though a fog had fallen on the village, cloaking it in an eerie veil, I went out for a walk, my padded leather jacket keeping me warm. There is nothing like a park filled with luscious foliage to invigorate one's senses, to bring one's thoughts back to earth.

I beheld tall oaks shrouded in mist, their limbs stripped bare and shivering in the breeze. The lawns were covered in the browns and reds of autumn. But before I could go further, I found Lucas slouched upon a stone bench.

The old gravedigger had a stiff hat pulled tightly over his head. His dirty grey stubble threatened to swamp his haggard pinched face. His small shoulders were slumped within a tattered green coat covered in stains. It seemed too big for him. His boots were muddy, which was no surprise for a man of his profession.

'Hello there, Lucas,' I said as jovially as I could.

His eyes darted in my direction whilst his body remained stooped in its sorry state as if frozen by the chill. He grunted and his eyes slid back to the cold hard ground. 'I haven't seen you in a while. You been busy, Lucas?'

I stood in front of him, waiting for an answer. His ragged breath hung in the cold air. His eyes were glazed.

'What have you been doing with yourself?' I said. 'You been ill?'

Lucas slowly took his gloved hands off his knees and clasped them tightly, his body shuddering forward as he did so. He coughed once. Twice. Still he said nothing. I was concerned by his behaviour. This was very unlike the man.

I ran a small art supply shop in the village, selling mainly canvases, paints and brushes. I sometimes organised art courses, usually with a visiting artist from one of the other villages or a town nearby, the nearest being a good forty minutes away. Occasionally we would set up our easels in the grounds of the church for the old sandstone building on a sunny day was particularly striking.

Lucas would inevitably be there, raking leaves, pruning roses, fixing the gate and all the other half-dozen things that needed his attention. He was gardener and church handyman but we all called him the gravedigger. That was his most important, though infrequent, part of his duties. Not being a particularly good artist myself, I would chat with Lucas on these occasions. Small talk of no consequence really although he did ask many questions about brush sizes and cartridge paper. He was an animated man with much to say.

'Lucas, aren't you going to answer me?' I asked.

The gravedigger cleared his throat and slowly looked up. How haggard he was! The man looked like he had not slept for days. His eyes were bloodshot and the creases on his face were more pronounced than ever. It seemed as though his face was cracking.

'I will answer you, Mr Wood,' he said in a quiet voice, his rasp though was unmistakable. 'But it's better you leave me alone.'

'Why Lucas, what's wrong?'

'What's wrong?' he snorted. He pulled off his hat revealing a bald liver-spotted head surrounded by a messy tufts of grey hair. 'You don't want to know. It'll only bring trouble, bad trouble.'

'Oh, come off it, Lucas. Tell me what's this all about.'

The gravedigger got up and pulled the hat back over his head. Mumbling, he brushed past me and hurried up the footpath, up the stone steps and into the gloomy street.

Perturbed by Lucas's strange behaviour, I thought I should let him be. The man obviously had problems he didn't care to share. It was none of my business. So I ambled down the footpath into the park. The leaves rustled. I could smell the damp earth, the fallen leaves. In the distance I could see the lake and the forest beyond.

I stopped. I realised I had regressed into that big-city mentality. Anonymity. Non-involvement. Keep your distance. Those were its hallmarks. I moved here nine years ago to escape its rush, its numbing indifference, its unquestioning embrace of modern technology before all else. There drugs, crime and violence hid beneath advertising billboards and glittering shopping malls. And here I was harbouring that same attitude as if I had never left that wretched place.

I leapt up the pathway, rushing up the short flight of steps to see Lucas's hunched figure a good fifty metres ahead, already veiled by fog. I darted past the old stone cottages, their small front gardens, the low wooden fences and mailboxes. Some had their lights on. I smelt chimney smoke and the stale dampness brought by the fog.

Lucas had slunk past the shops and taken a right turn at the post office. He was in a hurry going at a quick pace for an old man. Some thought he was already into his seventies. He had been in the village for as long as anyone could remember.

I followed him. At the butcher's. I was surprised to see graffiti splattered on the wall. Big, bold and blue. The tag, its vicious curls and strokes were indecipherable. That big city plague had arrived. Our village was changing. Children, the older ones, had taken to garbing in black and swearing was the norm. There were rumours of drugs. This I found hard to believe.

At the post office I saw Lucas's hunched figure climbing the sloping lane, his long coat flapping in the wind. He had to be going home, back to his shack that bordered the graveyard. I decided to drop by later. I didn't want him to think I was following him.

It was almost two and, not having had lunch, I crossed over to Ma Deidre's tea rooms. I was welcomed by a warm fire, pretty curtains and cheerful paintings. Doris, the owner, had grey hair and wore round glasses. She was at the counter, in a white apron, chatting to Mabel. Mabel was a jolly woman in her forties, perhaps a couple of years younger than me, who always tied her hair in a bun. She ran the florist next door.

'I really can't understand what they get up to,' said Mabel, shaking her heads. 'They hardly say a word during dinner. I don't know where they've been. Josie's become so rude. And the way she dresses . . .'

'Maybe you should bring your girls back here,' quipped Doris. 'Get them to work for me again. My customers liked them.'

'Until Belle spilled tea over poor Mr Bentley,' said Mabel, eyebrows arching. 'He was not amused.'

The two women sniggered.

'And what can I get you today, Mr Wood?' asked Doris.

'How about some soup? It's freezing cold out there.'

'Oh, we've got mushroom soup today,' said Doris. 'It's very creamy.'

'How's everything going in your lovely shop?' I asked Mabel as Doris wandered into the kitchen.

'Oh, very well . . .'

So it was after three when I left Ma Deidre's and started up the lane towards the church. As I passed the magnificent trees beside the road, their gnarled tree trunks, their bare limbs still shrouded in fog, I thought of my wife. I still lived in the flat above the shop with furniture she left behind. I had bills to pay and business was slow.

I entered the church grounds and scurried past the squat building, its stonemasonry dark against the grey sky. I had painted it several times. How gloomy was this fog! The gravel path dragged me around the back to the cemetery, the gravestones in several shapes and sizes stood in rows, a few with dead flowers in vases.

This was not a place for the living. I suddenly knew I didn't belong here. But I couldn't let it bother me though. Lucas lived here and it didn't seem to worry him.

I followed the path and came to a grave, the tilted cross surrounded by dead weeds. It was the oldest one. I could hardly read the weathered inscriptions. Mary Elizabeth Stephenson. Born 4th August 1821. Died 17th January 1839. Aged 18. Beside it were newer resting places. The cemetery was filling up, the graves advancing full circle.

A little girl, Sara Batts, had been buried less than a week ago. The mist sat heavily upon her grave's fresh mound of earth and the sad bouquets left behind. A wind swept up behind me and a chill slipped down my neck. I hurried away.

I was glad to reach Lucas's shack. Green paint peeled off its timber planks. Its roof was rusted. There was a crack in a window. A broken pot lay slumped against a wall. I knocked on the flimsy door.

The gravedigger was surprised to see me. He gruffly let me in. Despite the fire in the wood heater, it was cold in that small room. A wooden table and chair stood next to the tiny kitchen. His living area consisted of an armchair, a small coffee table with large stains on it and two stools. A

door led to the bedroom. His home was damp and smelled
of sour milk.

I sat on a stool which seemed solid enough, but Lucas
remained standing, stooped in his tracksuit bottoms and
thick sweater.

'I'm sorry for rushing off, Mr Wood,' he muttered. 'I just
couldn't . . . talk about it.'

'About what?' I said. 'What is it you can't talk about?'

'It's about—' he glanced out of the window, 'what I've seen
in that graveyard. Ever since, ever since I buried that little girl.'

'Sara Batts?' I asked. 'The girl who drowned in the river?'

'Yes, her,' he whispered. 'I don't even dare say her name.
She's . . . she's . . .'

He stared at me, despair in his eyes. His creased face
looked terribly old.

'What about her?' I asked 'You buried her on Sunday,
didn't you?'

'Yes,' he groaned. 'But I still see the girl out there!'

He pointed with one trembling finger at the window, at
the pale headstones.

'Yes, I've seen her,' he whispered, 'stalking amongst those
graves in the dark as if searching for something. No, don't
look at me like that. Don't look at me as though I'm bloody
mad. That I am not!'

'I don't think you're mad, Lucas. It's just . . .'

'Oh, Mr Wood, I do think I've gone crazy half the time.
Since I first saw her in that white dress. I can't think of
nothing else. It's like she's locked herself right here in my
brain and she won't leave!'

'How do you know it's her, the girl you buried?'

Lucas laughed in a croaking voice.

'Not difficult that one, Mr Wood. She hangs around that freshly turned grave over there beside that old grave with the leaning cross. Usually she comes just as it's getting dark.'

'Every night?'

'For the past three nights,' he whispered. 'About the same time.'

'Well, let's wait for her,' I said. 'It gets dark about four. Only forty minutes or so to go.'

'Are you sure you want to stay, Mr Wood? It's a terrible, accursed thing to see.'

'Why don't you put on a pot of tea, Lucas. I've never seen a ghost. So it could be a first time for me.'

'As you wish. And I thank you gladly, for being here, sir. Yes, I will put the water to boil. Yes, yes, tea. Of course.'

He busied himself in his tiny kitchen, then placed two mugs on the stained coffee table.

I tried making conversation with Lucas, but the poor man grew more anxious as the minutes crept by, his eyes darting like those of an injured animal at the window, at the darkening vista of headstones.

Shadows filled the spaces, growing like an evil miasma over the graves, creeping through the undergrowth, grasping the dried-up bouquets left for the dead. Inside, darkness drifted over the moth-eaten carpet, claimed ownership of the kitchen, the dinner table, the lounge area, crawled upon Lucas's gaunt and agitated face.

'Shall we turn a light on?' I asked.

'Better not, Mr Wood. We can see better then. See . . . outside.'

'All right then, Lucas. Let's just wait.'

Lucas really believed something would appear. I wouldn't say that I didn't believe in ghosts nor had I any evidence that spirits did exist. I would keep an open mind. I was afraid though that poor Lucas's own mind was coming unhinged. Spending his time alone in the graveyard, tending the garden, fixing fences, could not be healthy.

Just as I managed to get Lucas into some sort of conversation about his childhood in Eastern Europe, he abruptly stiffened. Even in the enshrouding gloom I knew his face had gone deadly pale.

His body trembled as it got off the armchair and he pointed.

'There,' he whispered. 'There you can see it.'

I moved to the window and peered outside. At first I saw nothing in the foggy darkness.

Then, as I stared, a shadow emerged. It stood unmoving beside a headstone, as though watching me.

I swallowed. Unbelieving.

It was a small figure. Perhaps a child. Sara Batts.

She had ponytails, a flowing dress. Her arms drifted up, sweeping the darkness in front of her.

'Jesus,' I whispered.

Lucas moaned.

The dark figure drifted past the headstones towards the shack, one hand touching the inscriptions as she came. Her dress caught by the breeze. A sleeve billowed.

And then, dear God, I heard a voice. It was hard to make out at first. Then I realised it was a sort of song.

Gravedigger's kiss
Gravedigger's kiss
Come hold me, come stroke me

The sound of thudding earth I miss.

I turned to Lucas but he had retreated behind the armchair, seeking protection from the approaching horror. The voice grew louder. Closer she came.

Gravedigger's kiss, Gravedigger's kiss
Oh touch me, oh feel me
Open my coffin, enjoy our bliss.

Then I leapt, bursting out the door. I ran towards the figure. She tried to escape but I caught hold of her arm.

'No!' she screamed.

'What the hell are you trying to do?' I shouted. 'Just a joke. Oh, it's just a joke!'

It was Belle, Mabel's daughter.

I was right. I knew that voice. She had served me so often at Ma Deidre's. They could have pulled it off if it wasn't for the singing.

'And you. Yes, I can see you. Come out from behind that gravestone.'

A taller figure emerged. It was her older sister, Josie. Josie was about sixteen and Belle a couple of years younger. But from the way Belle dressed in her white laced frock and hair in ponytails she looked much younger. From far away, especially in the dark, we easily mistook her for the dead eight-year-old.

Josie sauntered towards me, her long hair falling wildly to her shoulders.

'You should be ashamed of yourselves! Frightening poor Lucas. How heartless of you both!'

'We're sorry, Mr Wood,' mumbled Belle. 'It was a joke. Please don't tell mum.'

'Hey, we were just mucking around,' said Josie. 'We're not harming anyone.'

'You better come and apologise,' I said. I tried to keep the anger out of my voice. 'That's the least you can do.'

I led the two girls towards the shack. Lucas had turned the lights on. I could see his stooped figure pacing up and down, muttering to himself.

Belle hesitated at the front door. The light spilled on her face. I could see she was scared.

Josie smelled of cheap perfume. Her hair was dyed black and she had thick kohl around her eyes. Her fingernails were long and dark. Her black dress which was pierced by at least a dozen safety pins, revealed her surprisingly ample cleavage. She sneered at me. She was obviously not in the least sorry for scaring the poor gravedigger.

'Please,' said Belle. 'It was just a joke.'

'Oh shut up, Belle,' snarled Josie. 'You're such a bloody moaner.'

'Go on in,' I said.

Lucas sat in his armchair.

'What's all this?' he rasped. 'What's going on?' 'A couple of ruffians,' I said. 'They've been pulling your leg. Real hard, I'd say. A very unkind thing to do.' I glared at the two girls.

'Sit down.' I pointed to the two stools.

Belle sat down. Josie remained standing, pouting her lips.

'You better sit down, Josie. You're only making it worse for yourself.'

'Screw you,' she said.

This was unlike the Josie I knew. Maybe she was on drugs.

'You're caught trespassing,' I said. 'You better sit. I can call the police, you know?'

Josie tossed her hair to one side and made a big show of sitting down. She gave Lucas a suggestive grin and crossed her legs to reveal her smooth pale thighs.

'Well what do you both have to say for yourselves?'

I was disgusted by their behaviour. Scaring an old man so badly. I was sure Lucas was not far from a nervous breakdown. He sat quivering in his armchair, his trembling liver-spotted head was a testimony to his fright.

'We're sorry,' moaned Belle.

'Bugger off!' said Josie, her arms tightly crossed. 'We've got bloody nothing to say. He's just a shitty old man and you're a . . .'

'What?' I barked. 'What am I?'

'A stupid lonely art pedlar,' Josie spat, 'whose wife left you for someone else.'

I stared at Josie, my anger rising. I clutched my hands behind my back and tried not to let any emotion show.

'Don't you want to touch me then, Mr Wood. Feel my body, my breasts, kiss my lips? You know you want me.'

'No, I don't want to touch you,' I said. 'You're only a child. And my wife, she didn't like it here in the village. She went back to the big city. But that's got nothing to do with you.'

'And our frightening this big loser here has nothing to do with you.' Josie threw her hair back and stuck her tongue out at me. It was pierced by an awful-looking ring.

'Lucas happens to be a friend of mine. Are you going to apologise?'

'I'm sorry,' sighed Belle, tears welling in her eyes. 'It was Josie's idea. We just wanted to scare him. It was just for fun . . . '

'He's a horrible old man.' Josie stared at Lucas. The poor man still trembled in his armchair, lips moving but saying nothing. 'We know what that gravedigger did.'

She pointed a black fingernail at Lucas, her bright red lips sneering.

'What do you mean what he did? What are you talking about?' Again I thought that the older sister might have taken a drug of some kind. 'Josie, tell me what this is about.'

'We saw him by the river. That afternoon when the little girl drowned. We saw in the woods.'

'Oh, we just wanted to frighten him,' moaned Belle. 'We wanted him to leave the village.'

'He's a murderer,' said Josie, her eyes suddenly pleading. 'He was there by the river when the little girl was drowned. We saw him there. We know he killed her.'

'That's rubbish,' I said. 'Lucas has nothing to do with Sara Batts.'

I was trying to remain level-headed in the midst of this stupidity. The girls were making it up, trying to worm their way out of their predicament.

'Lucas, please tell the girls you weren't in the forest that day.'

Lucas was bent over, body quivering. All we could see was his liver-spotted head, the tufts of grey hair trembling. He clutched his knees tightly, fingers gnarled, shoulders swaying.

'Yes, yes, I was,' he croaked. 'I was there, Mr Wood.'

'But you didn't kill her, did you? You didn't drown that little girl.'

Making small trembling movements with his head, the gravedigger shook it from side to side. The man had been frightened so badly and now the sisters were making crazy accusations.

'See girls, he didn't kill her,' I said. 'He had nothing to do with her death. Did you, Lucas?'

Lucas got up. He grunted. He rolled one shoulder, stretching his long neck from one side to the other. He stared at the girls. I realised then, as my breath was caught in my throat, that his previous trembling, his swaying body had nothing to do with the man being afraid.

Fury hid in the shadows of his face. His eyes blazed like flames. Beneath the anger I saw an intelligence I had never perceived. He seemed to be tottering on the edge of some decision. He seemed taller. And stronger, too.

'Stop staring at me like that!' snarled Josie. 'You drowned her, you ugly old man. I know you bloody well did it.'

'I didn't drown her, you fool,' he spat. 'I spied the little girl playing so happily by the stream. She was singing to herself as she wandered along, getting her bare feet wet.'

'See, he admits it!' said Josie. 'He was following Sara.'

Lucas ignored her. 'She strolled by the water, throwing leaves into the ripples, dancing around rocks and fallen branches. How beautiful, so fair she was. So innocent in her white dress. Her blonde hair glowing bright in the shafts of sunlight. Oh, like an angel she was.'

He shook his liver-spotted head. His eyes downcast as if the memory troubled him. Then he glanced at me, ever so slyly I thought, before staring again at the two girls. His tongue slid out and licked his tumescent lips.

'No, no, I didn't drown Sara Batts. Not that lovely thing. Any old fool could do that. What fool would want to fill her small lungs with water? No, her beauty, her radiance was something to be savoured. Oh, I can still taste her in my mouth. No, the poor thing was already dead when she hit the water.'

He glanced at me again. His eyes alive and bright.

'Oh, you don't understand . . .. Well, you see, my friends, I drank her.'

Lucas grinned.

I couldn't believe his words. The girls said nothing but stared, eyes wide opened.

For an instance, silence reigned and it seemed that its electrical charge would go on forever.

Until I cried, 'You what? . . .this . . .this is crazy!'

And then, with great deliberation, like a coffin slowly opening, Lucas's mouth yawed before us.

The girls gasped.

'No,' whispered Belle. 'No, no . . .'

'What are you?' moaned Josie. 'Bloody fuck off!'

The gravedigger's fangs, long and gleaming white, glistened in the black cavern of his mouth.

'Girls, girls, you played a good trick,' he rasped through the bowels of his throat. 'We have a legend. Every few hundred years a victim returns from the dead. Comes back to hunt, to feed upon the hunter. I am that hunter. And I thought my time was up!'

He roared with savage laughter. Its ghastly sound pierced horribly in my ears. Black spittle shot from his mouth. The two girls screamed.

Like a spider, Lucas leapt over the coffee table, his knees shooting up high, and he landed silently between the sisters. He spun, crouching as he did so, grabbed Belle by the waist and flung her over his shoulder. She crashed into the armchair.

Then, eyes blazing, he plunged his mouth into Josie's pale neck. Her wild screaming died instantly.

He turned her body around in a slow circle as if they were waltzing. A romantic interlude to violins and champagne. Then he halted and his eyes were pressed up close against mine. I smelt his hunger and that metallic stench of blood.

The gravedigger's arm, gripped Josie's back to stop her from getting away. I could feel her silent horror, her helpless revulsion.

The gravedigger slurped greedily in a low gurgling noise. His mouth made small biting motions. All this while his eyes stared into mine as though conspiring, as though he were feeding for us both. I stared back transfixed by his eyeballs that seemed to grow bigger.

The years fell like rotten leaves from his face. The lines and crevices gave way to a stark smoothness. Dark hair sprouted long and abundantly from his skull.

Lucas, now a young man, was even handsome.

I stumbled back and struck the edge of the dining table, its corner struck my hip bone but I felt nothing.

Josie's arms, which until now had been feebly trying to push the vampire off, fell uselessly to her sides. Her body slumped forward and would have collapsed if it wasn't for Lucas's arm pinning her body to him.

When he had finished feasting, eyes still on me, he gently laid the girl on the floor. Blood, red and bright, trickled down his chin. A drop fell to her pale breast and stayed there unmolested like a single red rose. He wiped his mouth with a tissue from his pocket.

'That's better,' he said in a clear, strong voice that bore no resemblance to the previous rasping. 'Young blood, it's so sweet, Mr Wood. Almost tangy. Quite delicious. Unlike wine though, it doesn't improve with age.'

He gave a small laugh.

'You, you're a . . .'

'A vampire? Yes, isn't that obvious? I've been one for as long as I could remember. But I've only killed when it's been safe. How was I to know these two sisters were in the forest that day. Silly, silly girls they are.'

'What . . . what are you going to do with me?'

'I'm quite fond of you, my friend. We say hello in the pub, don't we? And I enjoyed our chats in the churchyard. It brought back to me memories of painting nudes in Verona. So long time ago now. What shall I do with you? I think I'll . . .' he suddenly turned. 'Ah, I see our young guest is waking up. Poor, poor beautiful thing.'

Sure enough Belle's arm pushed against the carpet. Her hand felt the armchair as if trying to work out her surrounds. She moaned. We watched her rise to her knees, one hand slowly rubbing her arm. Blood dripped from a wound on her forehead.

'Please . . .' she whimpered. 'Oh, please . . .'

Her one eye stared through her fingers at the gravedigger. Wide and scared it was. She gnawed her pale lips. Her ponytails, like dead creatures, hung off her skull. Her frock was impossibly white.

Lucas turned to me and a grin flickered on his angular face. 'We vampires have other needs too,' he said.

He slid like a ravenous lizard over to the trembling girl. With one foot, he pushed Belle to the carpet. She made no sound in protest.

There followed an ugly ripping—clothes, then flesh. And throughout his intrusion, came screams that clawed my mind to madness. Blood, like graffiti, splattered the walls.

I stood, cold claws upon my heart. My eyes were snared
by his brutality. How could any human being . . . no! He was
not human but a creature of evil.

And the foul smell of it!

I wanted to flee but my legs were frozen. Then, as if
awakening from an imprisoning dream, I realised my head hurt
terribly. I was still striking my head backward repeatedly against
the shattered window pane. Warm liquid slid through my hair.

Something struck my cheek. I pulled it off and had to
stop myself from vomiting. Wiping the gristle on my trousers,
I stepped over Josie's dead body and grabbed the stool.

I raised it above my head. I could see the younger girl
plainly now, her pale arm still shaking. Oh, the butchery!
The blood, the open wound, the whites of bone, the slimy
insides uncoiling upon the floor.

My knees buckled and I fell forward, the stool still over
my head. My cheeks were wet.

'No . . .,' I whispered. 'No, no, no . . .'

The weapon slipped from my hands and crashed onto the
coffee table.

'Ah, Mr Wood,' purred the vampire, glancing back at
me. He left the tortured body, the disfigured face and crawled
to me on all fours, his body naked, smeared in blood.

He stroked me on the cheek.

'It is done. Finished now. No need to cry. It'll be fine.
All so very fine.'

Then, his cold, cold lips . . . Fell on mine.

15

SHRINE

'Those British planters found it. Discovered the grave maybe a hundred years ago—when they were clearing the jungle.'

Yvonne had silky short hair, bright questioning eyes beneath pale blue eye shadow and a gold stud through her nose. A necklace with a silver frog locket with emerald eyes sparkled from her smooth pale neck. She was a journalist at *The Star* and, like me, in her early thirties.

'What about the gravestone?' I asked. 'Must be at least a hundred years old.'

'More than that, Malik. Maybe four or five centuries old. Because of its age the locals turned it into a shire. They thought this was a grave of some holy man or even a shaman . . . oh, here's the turn off.'

'I didn't see a sign.'

'That's 'cause there isn't one. It's the first left turn after the mosque.'

The busy main road became a narrow snaking line of bitumen and the hurtling cars disappeared from view. We were suddenly alone, surrounded by wild grasses, coconut trees and fruit stands propped up by timber that now lay rotting. Squat brick houses scattered themselves before us.

'We call a shrine *keramat*,' I said.

'Yep, that's right,' nodded Yvonne. 'A *keramat*.'

'Even we devout Muslims still visit these shrines. We Malays beg for favours, we make blessings and we leave offerings for the spirit.'

Yvonne crossed her tight jeans that squeezed her fleshy thighs. Even though her oversized blouse refused to hide the weight she had recently put on, her dimpled cheeks, the smooth curve of her neck, still brought out a desolate yearning in me. Once, in the darkness of a nightclub car park, I had kissed those full lips. The next morning her text said it could never work. I replied 'Ok' and neither of us ever mentioned it again.

'We Chinese visit these shrines too.' Yvonne dug noisily into her handbag. 'We light incense and pray there. So race and religion doesn't matter. The supernatural, it transcends all that.'

'Very true,' I said. 'Everyone, no matter of what religion, believes in ghosts.'

Yvonne chuckled. 'You Malays believe in our Chinese ghosts and we, well we believe in yours!'

A goat peered from beneath a banana tree, its bitty horns dull and blunt beneath the afternoon sun. It shook its head up and down as if agreeing with my colleague. Its eyes were bright and sharp and its nostrils flared. As we drove past, I searched for it in my side mirror but it had vanished.

'Why does the paper bother with these follow up stories anyway?' I muttered. 'The police have finished their investigation. The villagers have been interviewed.'

'Our readers, they're hungry for more,' Yvonne said as she lit a cigarette. 'It's not just about two mysterious deaths. They wanna know about the *keramat*.'

'I don't get it though. People are robbed and murdered in KL all the time. Just because two people are found dead at a shrine in some tiny village, suddenly it's big news. Just because there may be some supernatural link.'

'Ah Malik, that's 'cause our readers love the supernatural. Normal crimes are so boring. The supernatural gives added flavour. Like lobster instead of chicken in your pot noodles!'

I laughed and told her she was weird.

Bitumen soon gave way to dirt and the road turned bumpy. The car occasionally brushed against a wayward tree branch or clumps of wild grass. Jungle pressed upon both sides. Tall trees and tumultuous undergrowth surrounded us.

'I don't like this,' I muttered. 'Are you sure we're not lost?'

'Don't worry, city boy,' Yvonne said. 'This is the way. I was here last week. Or have you forgotten my story in page two?'

'It was a good one,' I said, grinning. 'Spooky.'

Moments later, the jungle gave way to a rubber plantation. Trees stood in rows and rows into the distance like dark sentinels on a deserted battlefield. A timber house on wooden stilts suddenly sprang out, followed by another and another.

'Stop at that corner,' said Yvonne. 'We can walk to the shrine from here.'

I stopped the Proton beneath a spindly coconut tree, beside a fallen bicycle. I grabbed my camera bag from the backseat, shut the car door and was jolted by the embracing shrill of insects. Yvonne had lit another cigarette and was already walking ahead in her white track shoes.

* * *

Beneath the humid heat of the afternoon sun, lay a deserted village. As we trudged along the dirt road which had been parched and cracked for the lack of rain, I sought out faces in the houses but saw none. Usually villagers would sit on terraces chatting, their children would play in the dusty compounds. Even the chickens that pecked the earth had vanished. And where were the cats that leapt in and out of the monsoon drains?

'Where are they?' I called out. 'All the *kampung* folk?'

Yvonne turned to me, flicking ash on the track. Her nose-stud glittered. Her frog-locket seemed to squirm beneath the bright sunlight, its green eyes glowing warily.

'When I was here last week,' she said, 'I interviewed an old lady. In her raspy old voice, she told me her family would be leaving the next day. That everyone would be fleeing the *kampung*.'

'Why? Because two people were found dead?'

'No, because evil had come.'

I stared at her open-mouthed. My throat dry.

'It started when those two foolish rubber tappers went and broke the shrine. Split the thing right down the middle. No one knows why they did it. The villagers think this was what killed them. Since then the *kampung* folk had seen strange shadows, weird noises 'round the rubber estate. They stopped going to the *keramat* because they were too afraid.'

'But that's no reason to leave.'

'There's more, Malik. The old woman crept right up to my ear, you know, and whispered that something had come to the shrine. Attracted by its power. By the offerings made by the villagers. She had no doubt this something was evil.'

'What is this something?'

'Something . . . unspeakable. Her voice, you should have heard her, it was rasping away in the folds of her throat. I could hardly understand her. All the while the poor thing was trying to hide her face with her headscarf with one hand. Her other hand was clutching mine so tighly. I can still hear what she whispered. She said it killed those two men. A boy and a girl had also disappeared a few days after. And a baby . . . it was found dead in its cot.'

'Allah! What is this thing, Yvonne?'

She stared back at me and grinned. 'This thing, it's supposed to be . . . a vampire.'

'Yvonne, don't play games. What the hell then are we doing here? The villagers have fled. So should we!'

'Don't worry, Malik. It's just what the old lady said, okay? These poor villagers are so superstitious. They believe all those horror DVDs they watch. We need to drag them into the twenty-first century.'

'Is that why you came back? To follow up with this . . . this vampire story?'

'Yes, it's more interesting to read about than two mysterious deaths. I wanted to find out about how the villagers are coping . . . but it looks like they've all gone.'

'Maybe we should head back.'

'No, Malik. I'm gonna do a story on the deserted village. That'd be so cool. And you've got to take your photos of the shrine. It's not far . . . follow me.'

Yvonne turned, crossed the dirt road and took a trail that led down a slope into the rubber estate.

I hesitated. The villagers had reason to be superstitious. Their beliefs had protected them for thousands of years. But if I didn't follow my colleague she would soon be but a small shadow up the trail, engulfed by trees. Then she would be gone.

'Come on, Malik!'

I trotted into the rubber estate and caught up with her. A dank coolness touched my face, my armpits. The insect voices turned quieter, as if they were slowly dying, and except for the scrape of our shoes, all lay silent. Then I smelt insecticide and I thought I understood. I felt a dry tickle in my throat as if chemicals were already poisoning my cells.

Yvonne walked in silence. The rubber estate continued to draw us into its deepening shadows so that the tip of Yvonne's flittering cigarette glowed. I glanced about searching for possible answers, yet not knowing the questions.

The trees had been planted in ordered rows over the rises and falls of the terrain, their scraggly silhouettes stretching out as far as my eyes could reach. Deep cuts had been made into each trunk. Wooden cups, placed there to collect latex, dangled from them. Most had overflowed with liquid; some had splattered the ground like spilled milk. Why hadn't the workers been doing their jobs? Surely they hadn't fled too?

Yvonne turned onto a narrower trail which wended its way steeply between clumps of wild grasses and several trees which, from their lack of foliage, appeared disease-ridden.

'This way, Malik!'

The path now led downwards, past a dilapidated hut probably used for storage or to shelter the workers during heavy rain. Then it curved around several mounds. The late afternoon sun glinted from behind the upper branches.

Yvonne glanced around as if to get her bearings, then she left the path and scrambled up a hillock. I struggled to catch up with her and, without warning, was buried in shadows. I heard Yvonne breathing hard from her exertions. The mass of foliage, the ancient trees and their entangling vines told me that we had entered all that remained of a vast jungle.

Then, my eyes were drawn to a sullen paleness.

There, on the ground, about three feet in height was . . . *the keramat.*

As I stepped towards it, I caught the faint smell of rotting—of leaves and perhaps . . . the flesh of something dead. I expected to see a decomposing civet cat on the ground but only a plethora of twigs and tangling thorny undergrowth stared back at me.

Yvonne's face was pale and pinched. She clasped her metallic frog-locket in one hand as if to hide it from the shrine.

'Look at it,' said Yvonne, pointing. 'You can see that it's . . .'

' . . .broken,' I whispered.

It was as if someone had taken a mallet and smashed it. The stone was split right down its middle. Bits of rubble were scattered at our feet.

'It's as if the thing has exploded,' said Yvonne. 'Why would those two rubber tappers want to smash it?'

I shook my head and stared at the wounded stone.

It was grey and narrow and seemed too tall for a normal gravestone. It climbed upwards in three sections, each curved like tiger's claws.

I stared about us, searching for the best location to place my tripod. The *keramat* was on level ground. It was likely the highest part of the rubber estate. Such places were supposed to be holy like Mount Meru, the holy mountain of Hinduism. The religion of the Malays before they embraced Islam. This was the sort of place a shaman would be buried. The British colonials, respecting local beliefs, had not interfered with the jungle around the grave.

Yvonne squatted and, as if in contemplation she slowly ran her index finger over her bottom lip, then she delicately touched the grave.

As I stood next to her I could see upon the worn stone that curious leaf-like shapes had been carved into it. Then I blinked and in the dappled light, hiding within the shadows, I swore I could see faces. Not only faces, but faces within faces, small and large and each one staring at me. Were the faces pleading or were they full of wrath?

'Touch the stone,' whispered Yvonne.

'I don't want to.'

'Just touch it, Malik.'

Gingerly, I placed a finger on it.

A numbness ran down my finger and up my arm.

'It's cold,' I gasped.

'Not cold, Malik. It's . . . bloody freezing.'

I yanked my finger away. Yvonne was right. The stone was freezing like a block of ice. I rubbed my arm to warm it up.

'I can't explain it,' said Yvonne as she stood up. Her face was pale. 'And what's that?'

I followed her finger. Upon the apex of the grave, just where the stone had been split, sat a small grotesque shape. It appeared to be two miniature cobras intertwined into a ball. It was as if they were suffocating something or keeping whatever it was tightly bound.

'Not sure,' I said. 'Didn't you see all this when you were last here? Didn't you touch the stone?'

'No, the police had cordoned off the area. No one could get close. The bodies were over there and there.' She pointed to two spots on either side of the grave. 'They were covered with plastic sheets . . . Anyway, you should start taking your photos. It's getting late.'

'What about that grave stone? It shouldn't be so cold.'

Yvonne crushed her cigarette under her shoe and crossed her arms beneath her breasts. 'Just take your photos quickly and we'll get out of here.'

I nodded, put down my bag and set up my tripod. I didn't like the shrine. I couldn't understand its natural coldness—as if all the life, all the energy had been stolen from it. When combined with the old lady's story of the vampire, its eeriness, despite the coolness of the jungle, brought sweat to my brow. As I was swivelling the camera into place, I heard a crack.

I turned but saw nothing. Then a shadow darted behind the trees. Then it was gone. I glanced at Yvonne. She was staring in the same direction.

'It's getting late, Malik. Hurry up.'

Her voice trembled.

'What was that, Yvonne?'

'Nothing. Just take your photos and we'll go!'

I brought out the flash. I took five or six shots. The successive washes of light from the flash were all too brief.

'All done?' asked Yvonne.

I nodded and quickly packed my gear.

When I turned to face her again, I found she was gone.

* * *

Yvonne would have had to walk pass me to head back down the trail to the car. That meant she could only have gone in the opposite direction—away from the village.

Why did she want to do that? My instincts told me to flee too. To get out of this place. To run back to the car and drive away.

But what about Yvonne? I couldn't leave her behind. I swallowed hard.

Not knowing what to do, I hurried after her.

The trail led steeply downwards. I hurried past a clump of bushes, which pricked at my arm, its leaves struck my face, and then I was back out amongst the rubber trees. But this area was more neglected and the terrain undulating like the spine of some gigantic creature. Clumps of bushes and tall grass threatened to swallow the track.

'Yvonne!' I shouted, 'Where are you?'

But there was no reply. Only the faint shrill of insects. As if they were fading into some other world where they would be safe from human-kind.

'Yvonne!' I called again. 'You're gone the wrong way. Come back!'

Where was she? Maybe she could no longer hear me. Or could she have stumbled and hurt herself? Perhaps she was unconscious.

I pulled out my mobile phone to call her. There was no reception. And why would there be out here in this forsaken place?

'Shit . . .' I whispered. Where the hell was she?

I trotted down the path, still calling out. The track inclined steeply and, in my desperation, I sprinted down towards a clearing.

Then my body flipped over. My feet were flying. A daze of sky and the tops of trees flashed by as my mobile phone leapt from my hands. My back slammed hard into the undergrowth.

I gasped in pain. It was as if someone had kneed me hard in the back.

Moaning, I slowly turned onto my front.

And then I saw it . . . the thing that had tripped me over.

At first I thought it was a bundle of clothes. But how could I trip over it? My shoes had struck something solid. But not solid as a rock or a branch. The terrible truth lay in its shape.

It was a body.

From the size of the torso, I knew it was boy. He wore blue shorts and a faded T-shirt. I crept forward and his face emerged to meet mine. His was pale and bloodless, eyes wide open, mouth gaping.

As I tried to get to my knees, I nudged a bulk on my left.

I turned . . . and lost my balance.

'No!' I cried.

It was the body of a young woman. She was thin and wore a simple white headscarf. Her eyes were closed and her skin was smooth. Her mouth was twisted as though trying to contain an unspeakable agony. Her sarong was muddy and one plastic blue slipper dangled off her dark toe.

I staggered away. Grasping the branches for support. It felt as though my legs would collapse under me.

I turned as the branches and leaves grasped for my face and, somewhere buried deep in the undergrowth between jungle and rubber estate, my mobile phone began to ring.

'No,' I gasped. 'No, no, not this . . .'

I couldn't deny the tragic reality that a boy and a woman, maybe his mother, could be found dead in a rubber estate. What I denied was the sight further down the trail in the clearing. I blinked, hoping this was a nightmare I would wake from. But my eyes did not lie. This was too horribly real.

Bodies were scattered beneath the trees, slumped or curled up or splayed wide as if awaiting a butcher's knife. Some were men, some women, many were children. There were more than a dozen bodies. None of them moved upon the dry earth. All dead in the clothes they wore: sarongs, blouses, jeans, head scarves, T-shirts. A little girl who was propped against a tree wore a face splattered with latex. An elderly woman, perhaps the one Yvonne had spoken to, lay sprawled faced down, a clump of her white hair dangled out from her headscarf. Her batik sarong was pulled up to her knees so that I could see the long veins in her thin dark legs.

Holding onto the branches, I hauled my way along the trail. This undeniable trail of death. The bodies were scattered on both sides of me as I drew myself along. Still my mobile phone inexplicably rang. The Bosa Nova ringtone I had recently downloaded belonged to another world and here it only reverberated death and despair.

A cloud drifted over and the shadows turned darker and deeper. It was like dusk, yet I could still clearly see the corpses and the scars on the rubber trees.

I stumbled pass a middle-aged man who was incredibly still wearing his *songkok*, his black velvet Malay cap, even though his head was draped back over a fallen log. His dead eyes stared agonisingly up at the trees. It was as if the killer had attacked from above. Despite the half-light, I could see small wrinkles about his eyes and a birth mark upon his cheek. One hand clutched at his heart, one finger snared in the breast pocket of his polyester shirt.

'What happened here?' I whispered. 'Who killed all these people?'

I whirled around and dark faces—boys, girls, women, men, the elderly—stared back at me from their crumpled clothes as though demanding answers.

'I don't know,' I moaned. 'I don't know who killed you all . . .'

'Don't you?'

I froze.

The voice was hers. But it was not quite right. It was completely wrong.

Slowly, I turned around.

Yvonne stood beside a rubber tree. Her stony face cast in shadows.

I realised my mobile phone, if it had sounded at all, had stopped ringing.

* * *

'Don't you know why these people are dead?'

Her voice was icy.

'Because they . . . they refused to leave the village,' I said as my mind spun trying figure out what was wrong with her. 'After the shrine had gone bad.'

Yvonne laughed. It was impossibly high pitched. I had never heard her laugh that way before.

'Why . . . what's so funny?'

'Because, Malik, the shrine—it was *always* bad.'

'What?'

'The people who made offerings, who came to pray, were casting spells to hurt others. The shrine, it attracts bad people. And their enemies were hurt—illness, car accidents, cancer, unexplained deaths. For those who came to merely pray, to seek blessings, I just ignored them.'

'You—what do you mean *you* ignored them.'

'It may look like one but it is no gravestone. It is a *binding* stone. To imprison me deep within the earth . . .'

'What in Allah's name are you talking about, Yvonne?'

'And I was so imprisoned for three hundred years until the binding stone was discovered. And from everywhere, the malicious ones came and knelt before me. Even though I was trapped in the earth, I still could cast spells for them . . .cast bad spells for bad people who wanted to do bad things . . .'

'Yvonne, please stop this . . .'

'Over the years, more vengeful pilgrims came, each seeking greater evils. This made the binding power of the stone weaker. In recent months, hordes of them knelt before me. Until, eventually, when the two men came seeking revenge on a debt collector. Then I emerged right through the centre of the stone. Cracking it!'

'You killed them?'

'Yes . . . I was hungry. I killed these people too.'

'Yvonne, you're bloody crazy, you need to . . .'

'Every single one of them. They came with their holy books and prayer mats and religion. They wanted to cast me out. So I killed them.

'When that was done. I summoned the rest of the village. I sent out a sweet fragrance from the rubber estate. And when they came in their dream-like state, not able to resist my call, I slaughtered them. I bit their necks and slurped their blood!'

Then, very deliberately at first, her head began to turn as if casting an evil look behind her. But instead of stopping, the head continued to move—oh, a neck-breaking twist it made, but how could it?—until it faced backwards!

Still, Allah believe me, it rotated in this impossible way— slowly spinning all the way around—until her eyes were fixed on me again. But this time deep lines were cracked into her contorted face and she was deliriously grinning. As she did so, there was the delicate sound of ripping and the flesh around her throat bloomed red.

'No!' I gasped.

I stepped back, tripped over a branch and fell. Still I stared up at her. But it was not her, this monstrosity was not Yvonne.

The head now began to jerk upwards as if it was trying to escape its confines. Up and up it violently pulled as it shook, its dark hair lashing to and fro. There was an awful ripping sound as the head suddenly lifted—pulling at, dragging out the pink flesh of the trachea—then out, out flopped the bright red lungs.

'What the hell . . .' I gasped.

I had not even in my most horrific nightmares encountered such a creature.

Then this perversion trembled violently and, without warning, it spun upwards and with a deep ugly squelch—like a baby being born—out tumbled the bulging stomach followed by a long trail of grey intestines. This was no baby but a slimy gruesome serpent.

For a second, Yvonne's body stood quite motionless. Then her frog-locket, as if it could no longer bear the disembowelment of its mistress, slipped down her blouse and landed beside her white track shoes. I felt its emerald eyes peering mournfully up at me. Then, like a butchered goat, the ripped-up body trembled before collapsing in a bloody heap.

Hovering above it, before my unbelieving eyes, like a cast of one in a theatre of lunacy, the grotesque thing floated. The demon's head stared, leering almost proudly. Yvonne's nose stud looked like a nail that had been hammered into her contorted face. A face that seemed to hide faces within faces.

The serpent-like demon swayed in the thick hazy air. It seemed to be doing some sort of despicable dance where the silent music wafted from hell. Blood trickled down the coils of guts and tapped onto the earth. The pungent odour of rotting flesh filled my nostrils.

I didn't realise it, but I was crawling on my back, moaning incomprehensibly as I did so, trying to get away. Trying to retrieve my sanity.

It felt as though a hundred cold corpses were caressing me.

I pushed past the man with his *songkok*, the Malay cap that was amazingly still on his head, the one with the birth mark on his cheek. Instead of fear, his face seemed to be filled with pity. I realised my cheeks were wet with tears.

The unspeakable thing slithered its way towards me. There was the soft sound of squelching. Blood still dripping off its tail, its rectum, as it approached. It smelt of shit and a thousand dead things.

'No!' I screamed. 'No! No! No!'

Then, in this nightmare of nightmares, the red lips on that head parted. And I saw them. Long fangs, white as milk, sharp as a cobra's, sprang out from the blackness of that mouth, glistening and sharp in these sickening shadows.

The demon drifted downwards, so close now that I could touch its blood splattered hair, run a fingernail inside the cracks in its face. As for its body, made of slimy lungs, stomach and raw intestines—it dragged over the ground and its very end, its tail, Allah forbid, curled around my left foot!

The head drew closer, as if it wanted to kiss me. Its long coarse hair draped itself around my neck. The fangs dripped saliva on my shirt. Its eyes were burning as though they held the flames of hell.

'Ah, Malik,' it whispered in a cold, dry voice that no longer pretended to be Yvonne's. 'You only had to try harder and we could have been lovers. But I will now feast.'

Out of the corner of my eye, the man beside me still stared, one hand entangled in his breast pocket. But now I saw that his other hand, the one that dangled to the ground was holding a book—our holy book.

Just as the fangs plunged for my neck, I turned, grabbed the Koran and shoved it into the head.

The thing shrieked. It was an awful piercing cry that shook the leaves and shuddered the sky. The demon shot over me and fell into the undergrowth, writhing and screaming.

I got up. Not believing what I had done.

Then I ran.

Away from the scattered corpses. Away from the screeching demon.

I jumped over the body of the boy, the one who had tripped me over. I dashed up the slope, not even hesitating at the broken gravestone. No, not a gravestone but a binding stone. The one that worked for three hundred years until bad people came in their hordes with their evil desires. That undid the binding.

I ran past my camera bag with all its expensive equipment. The rubber estate could keep it. My mobile phone too. I just had to get out alive.

I sprinted down the slope.

The demon shrieked. I glanced backwards and tripped.

I cursed as I got up. Pain tore through my ankle.

I stared up the ghastly hill that could never symbolise Mount Meru. I half expected the demon to be soaring down after me, its intestines dancing, blood speckling the dry earth.

I tried to ignore the pain and stumbled on. My footfalls were heavy in my ears. I went past the mounds and past the rubber trees. Past the cups that dangled from the trunks to collect latex. Cups that overflowed because all the workers were dead.

My ankle throbbed painfully and my legs had slowed. I couldn't make them move faster. My breath came in heaves. Cold sweat covered my T-shirt.

'I'm coming for you!' it cackled.

The voice didn't echo from the other side of the hill—but from the dilapidated hut that stood beside me. The one used for storage or as a shelter during heavy rain. How could it get there so quickly? Could the perversion manifest itself anywhere it chose?

'No . . .' I gasped. 'It can't!'

I needed my own shelter now. From the fury of hell itself. From the possibility that I was going mad.

Again it cackled. This time on my right.

I stopped and turned, expecting the head to be floating at my throat, with fangs ready to pierce it. But I only saw rubber trees, lining up in obedient rows into the distance.

I wiped the sweat from my eyes and tried to recall a prayer. Any prayer . . . *there is only one god but Allah, there is only one* . . .but my memory had forsaken me!

How could it? When I needed it most?

'I can't stop now . . .' I moaned.

I stumbled down the track. The tree trunks and foliage became a shadowy blur. My breath was tight in my chest. Blood rushed through my head.

There was not far to go now. I was sure of it. I just had to make this turn.

My heart soared. *I was right!*

I could see the dirt road and the village up ahead.

Suddenly, sunlight broke through the trees. The cloud had passed. The track was lit up in sunshine.

Breathing raggedly, I pushed my legs hard, trying to ignore the pain, telling them to keep moving as I struggled up the track. Towards safety. Towards the real world. Away from the nightmare. Away from hell itself.

I could see the car now. It was shining in the sun.

It wasn't far. I could make it!

I hobbled as fast as I could. Hoping, praying that nothing would grab me from behind. With each step I took, I felt my hopes rising.

Then I stumbled out of the rubber estate and was bathed in light. The air tasted wonderfully fresh. It was as though the rubber trees that had kept me prisoner had suddenly set me free. Insect shrills filled the air, as though calling out in celebration.

A bird chirped a beautiful melody.

My car gleamed beside the coconut tree, the fallen bicycle, waiting for me.

'Thank Allah!' I whispered.

I glanced behind me. There was no demon following. No head and intestines dancing up the track. There was nothing but rubber trees. It was even peaceful here. Perhaps it was just a nightmare. Or just my mind gone temporarily mad. It didn't matter. I had survived this.

I fumbled for the remote. For a second I thought I had dropped it. Then I felt its familiar shape. I pressed the button and the side lights blinked.

I heard myself sigh.

I opened the door and jumped in.

'Hello, Malik,' said Yvonne. 'I've been waiting for you'.

Her frog-locket.

It was missing.

16

NO KISS GOODBYE

Nash didn't want to meet. Didn't want to talk it over. Just wanted to send messages. Wouldn't take my calls.

We break up. OK?

He wanted to get married and have kids and I didn't want to become a Muslim.

Best for us. Very sorry la.

Nash's words kept coming back to me as I drove out of town. A town once small and quaint but snarling traffic, rampant development, crime, drugs and corruption, had soiled and sickened it.

I had left the tolls and expressways long ago and was curving up a secondary road when a glance at my phone screen told me that my destination was twenty-two minutes away. I thought I recognised a right turning, as I had been to Ping's house once before, but the trusty navigation app had asked me to turn left.

This back road narrowed, then wended past a quarry that cut a deep wound upon a verdant hillside, its mounds of sands and rocks piled up like pulverised bones. One side of the hill had been quarried away, leaving several rust-coloured mounds of various sizes, barren and dry like rotten teeth.

In the distance on a hill, a row of large excavators stood shining new in the sun. There were more than 20 of them, bright yellow and neatly lined up on the barren, dusty ground, but without a solitary person in sight. Were they for sale, idling whilst waiting for a construction job or had the machines finally taken over and buried its workers in the sandy soil?

I shrugged and took the Myvi across a bridge with broken metal guard rails, rust flaking off like torn skin, over a murky rubbish-strewn stream surrounded by stunted trees and moss-covered rocks like deformed skulls.

At first I thought that the app was taking a route to avoid traffic but when it asked me to turn up a driveway, which I did, I knew the app had screwed up; especially when it said in that oh-so-confident voice, 'You have arrived at your destination.'

No I had not.

This is a graveyard!

A Malay one too. From the crumbling, weathered white headstones sloping up toward the jungle, I knew it to be old.

I brushed a bead of perspiration off my forehead, ran my fingers through my hair and, for some reason, his words came back to me as we lay in bed.

I always remember you, baby ku. You mine first love.

Nash was my only love. Nor did I care if his English wasn't perfect.

We were so good together, Nash and I. Then, without warning, I got his message.

We break up. OK?

There it was. Plain and simple. Quite unmistakable.

All over. Not even a kiss goodbye.

'Why won't you tell your parents, your friends about us?' I once asked him as we lunched at a cafe.

'Can't,' he muttered, glancing up from his phone, his eyebrows squeezed together. 'You must want to become Muslim. My parents, they will ask me. Every day they will ask me. So we have to be secret, okay?'

'Okay, I suppose so, Nash. But I can't convert. I don't want to become a Muslim. You know, no pork, fasting and all that . . .'

'They why you ask?'

From behind his metal spectacles, he stared at his empty glass of iced coffee and I thought I saw something die in his eyes. He then scratched his bristles and gestured at the Bangla waiter for the bill. Perhaps that was the start of the end. Or the beginning of a coldness that seeped into our relationship like a dead hand stroking my hair.

I sat in the car, eyes on the graveyard before me. Even though I was twenty-six, I still heard the warm earth calling me, the cold marbled arms of the gravestones trying to embrace me.

One day, you will join us . . .

I blinked.

It was just a stupid cemetery. Wild jungle behind it and overgrown *lallang* before it. Still, I shuddered, switched the app off, reversed down the driveway and sped back from where I came.

When I told her about Nash last night, Ping said: 'Never mind, dear. Someone better will come along. Why do you like Malay guys anyway? Come over to my house tomorrow. We can bake cookies and watch a movie on my laptop.'

But, when I fled the graveyard, I must have missed the turning again for I was soon twisting past a rubber estate, a bleak factory and rows of spanking-new unoccupied shophouses with their metal shutters down, keeping out the world.

Why were they unoccupied?

Cannot sell? Cannot rent? Or were they haunted by ghostly tenants?

I shivered at the thought. This was all wrong. So, once again, I headed back, looking for the turning. Except I found myself going past the quarry, the ruined hill, over the bridge and back to the old graveyard.

Bloody nuts!

'What happened to the turning?' I gasped at the steering wheel.

I almost expected Nash to give his usual answer.

Chill, baby ku. Chill.

But how could I relax? I flicked at my phone to see where I was, hoping that it could lead me out of here but the network was bloody down.

Chee sin!

Just when I needed it most. For the second time, I drove back the way I came. Once again, I saw no turning and, shaking my head in disbelief, drove past that factory and empty shophouses. I drove on as I was sure this route would eventually lead me back to the main road.

Except it didn't.

It drew me on and on, curving, twisting and straightening, repeatedly. I kept wanting to make a U turn, but that would be having to go all the way back and I kept thinking that the junction to the main road was just around the next bend.

All around jungle and palm oil estates pressed in, their leaves like poison, their branches like slithering snakes, yet still I kept following the road, now shrouded in grasping shadows. Occasionally, a dilapidated *kampung* house would peer out like some hungry beast from between the claw-like trees. I was sure now that I was lost and the sudden realisation that I hadn't seen a car, a motorbike, a single person or even a goat since I turned at the junction made me gasp.

Still I drove on, hoping to see signs of life. I felt like crying as the horrible thought that this awful road may never end began to suffocate me. I imagined myself driving on and on, even as darkness fell, until the car ran out of fuel. Or what if it never did? What if I just kept driving down this deserted highway for the rest of my life?

I pushed the mad thought away.

Rain clouds now smothered the sky and the road led me further into its darkening. The clouds swept like a thick black blanket over the top of the trees. Then, rain exploded, splattering hard against the windshield, pounding on the bonnet and all was black and as deep as night. It was so heavy that I had to pull over to the side of the road. I just couldn't see anything. There was nothing to do but wait for the rain to ease.

And wait I did, alone in this rainswept hammering darkness, as images of Nash circled my brain; we were kissing in bed at my condo, he was stroking my hair and nuzzling my neck but his message . . . it kept coming back to me.

You mine first love.

We break up. OK?

I stared into the black, tears in my eyes.

Even though the rain had now become a drizzle, I still kept staring. It was still dark out there. I couldn't understand it . . .

I reached for my phone. It flashed 7.43. I was sure it was only four-thirty the last time I checked. Where had the hours gone? Did I fall asleep?

I turned the key in the ignition.

Nothing.

'No . . .' I whispered. 'Shit . . .'

Again I tried but the engine stayed as silent as a corpse. Why wouldn't my car start? There was plenty of petrol.

I waited a moment, my heart thumping, trying to control my breath. I looked towards the jungle, expecting long-haired creatures to emerge and scratch the car windows with sharp claws.

I bowed my head. Silently, I prayed and kissed the jade Kwan Yin pendant.

Protect me, please. Give me luck . . .

I turned the key again—*No!*—still the damn thing wouldn't start!

I wanted to scream. What was I going to do?

I grabbed my handbag, which, because of snatch thieves in town, I now habitually kept on the car floor and opened the door.

A murky blackness and insect shrills swamped over me.

What waited for me out there?

I'm stepping into the dark, Nash. Stepping out without you.

I needed him here with me now. He would hold my hand, his strong fingers encircling mine and tell me that he would look after me.

But I was all alone and I had to be brave.

I shut the door and a dank humidity embraced me. Rain dripped from trees and behind the muddy smell was the faint scent of rotting leaves and dead meat.

Then, I heard a noise, a distant kind of wailing through the trees. I was about to run back to my car when I spotted a light that flickered through the dripping foliage.

* * *

I quickly trudged up a track towards the silhouette of a small bungalow. By the time I got there, the eerie wailing had echoed into a death-like silence. I knocked on the door and, after several minutes, it creaked open and an old, hunched-up Malay man stood there, wearing a white T-shirt and sarong. His face was dried up and his dull eyes enquired at my intrusion.

I explained what had happened to my car.

He nodded and strands of white hair drifted about his bald head. The liver spots on his face pulsed beneath the fluorescent outdoor light.

'Sorry to hear that, young lady,' he said in low, tired voice. He cleared his throat. 'I don't have a landline and the network is down. It does that often out here.'

'But what am I going to do, uncle? I need help.'

'Oh, don't worry, it should be up again by the morning. You can come back then and call for help.'

'Oh . . .' This was not the answer I wanted.

His eyes flickered at mine. They seemed kind but vague, perhaps even familiar.

'But you can stay here if you like. I live alone. Or you can sleep in your car. It's up to you. Don't worry, young lady, I have a spare room which you can lock. I'm ninety-two next year . . . nothing to worry about.'

He did look terribly fragile. I'd been to a few kickboxing lessons and my roundhouse punch would surely send him sprawling if he tried anything.

'Are you sure you don't mind me staying here, uncle?'

'No problem. Come in, come in. I'm making dinner. Join me.'

I took off my shoes and he led me into his house. We went down a narrow corridor past rooms jammed with household possessions. The thick walls, which were once white, had greyed in patches like cancerous scars and some of the louvred windows had splintered glass and missing handles.

The old man shuffled his way to a tiny, windowless kitchen. He had just opened a tin of sardines and opened a second one for me whilst I helped him chop up sliced cucumbers, onions and chillies.

'Nice to have a woman here,' he mumbled. 'I'm not so good with a knife. Can't see so well.'

I brought the sandwiches to a small plastic table beside the kitchen whilst his gnarled hands carried two glasses of Sprite.

As I sat on a creaky wooden chair, I wished I had dressed more conservatively. I wore my favourite denim shorts, a new chequered blouse and a dash of makeup.

We ate mostly in silence. The old man slowly chewed, sipping his drink with each bite.

As I waited for him to finish his meal and because I found the quiet too uncomfortable, I related the events of that day, especially about how it suddenly got dark.

'Sometimes we lose track of time,' he wheezed. 'I should know. Only yesterday I was a young man.'

Scratching his face, he chuckled. It sounded more like a cancerous cough. Then without warning, he opened his mouth and yanked out his dentures, his saliva dripped onto the tabletop.

I gasped.

'They need a wash,' he mumbled and got up. 'Food gets stuck in them.'

As he rinsed them under the sink, I heard the noise again. It sounded more like a rabid night bird at first before echoing into a distant moaning.

'What's that, uncle?' I asked.

'Spirits,' he said, turning towards me, one eyebrow rising unnaturally high. 'They won't come here.'

'Spirits?' I shuddered.

'Spirits. Creatures of the night.'

The moaning now sounded like high-pitched laughter. The hairs on my arm stood up. He must have seen the fear in my face.

'We are protected here, young lady. Don't worry.'

As if in agreement, the moaning died and what was left was a dead, eerie silence that even the insects were afraid to fill. The old man pushed the denture back into his mouth and cleared his throat.

'Would you like some *teh tarik*? I make a good one.'

I nodded and tried to smile.

'Go sit in the lounge. There are some magazines there.'

So I sat there, flicking through a tattered Time magazine which momentarily distracted me from thoughts of ghosts and spirits. I was sure the old man knew more than he was saying but when he brought two steaming glass mugs into the lounge, I couldn't think of what to ask him. Instead, I sipped the *teh tarik*. It tasted good and warmed my stomach. When we had finished our drinks, the old man said it was time for bed.

Even though it was just past nine, I retreated into the guest bedroom, which was an annex at the back of the house, and locked the door behind me. The one pillow on the thin mattress was stained and the blanket had a rip in it. Above me, the dust-covered ceiling fan rattled as it spun on number two.

I peeled off my shorts, slipped off my bra and lay down. I tried to get comfortable and switched off the bedside lamp, my mind a jumble of thoughts and images. I went over the day's strange events. Why did it suddenly get dark? What was that wailing noise? Was the old man just trying to frighten me? Was he hiding something?

There was no way I could fall asleep.

But I must have for I was startled out of a dream by the sound of the bedroom door creaking.

But I had locked it!

I lay there frozen, my heart beating loudly in my head as I watched.

By the moonlight streaming in through the curtains, the door slowly opened, its creaking merging with the sound of the rattling fan.

The image of my cousin's coffin at the funeral home last year suddenly struck me, his photo surrounded by incense and offerings. Then his coffin, so glossy was the timber that I could see my terrified reflection in it, began to open, creaking open just like the sound of the bedroom door, and his cancerous body slowly sitting up in his over-sized suit and reaching a bloody hand for me whilst an icy coldness like frozen blood seeped into my guts.

And here, in this bedroom, it was his corpse, thin and naked, that stepped through the opening. But as he slunk through and stood beside the window, I saw from his thin, hunched-up posture that this was not my cousin but the old man and his thinning white hair.

I knew what he wanted.

I tried hard to get up but my arms were frozen. There was nothing I could do but stare helplessly at him in his sarong and T-shirt, looking more like a scraggly pigeon than man. For a while he just stood there by the curtains, his pale wiry neck gleaming, his eye flickering, as if he was relishing the thought of what was to come. His rasping breath sent a cold shiver through me.

Then he moved—step by slow jerking step, he came towards the bed, the sound of his bare feet made a sucking noise against the parquet floor. I could hardly breathe as he now stood motionless and he only needed to reach out with his gnarled and greedy hands to grasp my feet.

Cold sweat dripped down my brow.

Get away from me!

I wanted to jump up, scream and punch him in the face. But still my body wouldn't move, my fingers unable to clench, no matter how hard I tried. Did he put something in the *teh tarik*?

More like a shadow than a man, he edged—no, wavered like a black fog, a miasma of evil—creeping slowly along the length of the bed towards me. Step by sucking step.

I shut my eyes.

Nothing happened. The fan rattled. The insects whined. I thought that he must have left the room. Changed his mind. Chose good over bad.

Then I felt him through my blouse. Fingers stroking my breasts, ever so lightly upon my nipples. His breath grew louder, faster. His icy digits sent a loathsome coldness shuddering through my body.

He yanked the blanket away and then, dear God, the weight of his body was upon me. I wanted to push him off, kick at him but my arms, my legs were frozen.

Then he ripped my panties off, spread my legs apart with his bony knees and then . . .

No, no, no!

I felt a searing below . . .

Hot. Knife-like.

I gasped in pain.

He was inside!

I screamed but my voice was dead in my throat.

As he moved, his breath became a roar against my eardrums. Hot and fetid it was, against my cheeks.

Be done with it, you bastard!

But, no, he kept on pushing in and out . . .

Then, then, his lips were on mine.

Cold evil lips of the dead!

My eyes flew open. I yelled and shoved him away.

I could move!

I drew my fist back. I was going to smash his skull. Then I would strangle him to death.

But as he sat at the end of the bed, his face caught the moonlight filtering in through the curtains and I saw not the old man.

. . .but Nash!

'What the hell . . .'

Then his face began to change. His skin turned saggy and lines crossed his cheeks and forehead. His broad shoulders hunched over and shrank. Then, as Nash aged even more, his features shrivelled and . . . I was looking at the old man again. Now I knew why the old man was so familiar.

He was Nash!

But no, it didn't stop there. Older he became, his flesh decaying until the haggard, rotting flesh fell of his face and I was left staring at a gleaming skull.

Then, as I lay bewildered, the rattling skeleton, smelling of rotting meat, crawled over my naked body, and with its bony knees pressed into my bare thighs, grabbed my flailing hands and kissed my trembling lips.

That was when I screamed.

* * *

My back ached. The bed too hard.

It felt like the floor. The surface rough. I moaned and tried to turn over but my torso was too stiff.

I shivered.

Why was the air con so cold? I touched wetness on my cheeks. No, I had not been crying, my blouse and shorts were damp too. I blinked my eyes open and a multitude of stars eyed me through the swirling clouds.

I was outside!

I fingered the soil and smelt its dankness.

I got up, lost my balance and fell on my front, striking my elbow on the earth and crying out. Wild grass stroked my cheek. The ground—cold like a corpse, alive with crawling insects and smelling of dead things—wanted to claim me. I thought of just laying there but when I saw my shoes and handbag, I slipped them on, picked up my handbag and staggered slowly to my feet.

All around me white sculptures rose, poking from the soil. For a moment, I didn't recognise where I was. Then I shivered.

A graveyard!

How . . . how did I get here?

Legs trembling, I stumbled away from the patch of earth that had been my bed but not before noticing beside it a raised mound of soil scattered with flower petals which told me that it was a recent burial. As I edged away, older graves stared at me, their tombstones like white like teeth surrounding me.

What was I doing here?

Where was the skeleton? Nash? The old man?

They were all one and the same in the dream.

But was it a dream?

I could still feel the burning below, even a trickling of awful stickiness down one thigh. I recalled him moving in me in a kind of death-like yet desperate way and I wanted to scream.

Instead, I spun around expecting the skull-headed old man to emerge from the darkness but no, there was nothing but the gathered headstones and the jungle looming behind it. It was then that I realised that this was the same graveyard as the one the app had led me to.

I stared into the semi-darkness. What had happened to the bungalow? Was this a nightmare?

I wanted to wake up now but the sudden thought that if I did wake up, I would die, made me feel faint, for this felt too real.

The sky was now brightening through the trees. The morning, I hoped, was not far away.

I stumbled down the slope, still expecting the old man or perhaps the skeleton to grab me from behind. I glanced back but only saw gravestones, arrayed down the slope towards the road which, to my relief, I now glimpsed past the clumps of lallang. I wanted to run towards it, but seeing the uneven terrain, the scattered branches, the fallen bits of stone and chipped off marble, decided to proceed carefully.

So, with heart lurching, I trudged on and made it to the road. I then followed it and, there it was.

My car!

The Myvi's windshield was covered in thick dew but, otherwise, it was as I had left it. I checked the back seat before I got in. Just in case.

The car started at the first turn of the key.

Yes!

I pulled on my necklace and gave the jade Kwan Yin a grateful kiss, switched on the headlights, flicked the wipers to get rid of the dew and eased the car down the road. I could feel my tense muscles relaxing.

Safe . . . I was now safe.

As I drove past the cemetery, I glanced up at its slope . . . and slammed the brakes.

The headstones were gone!

In its place was the bungalow perched at the top of the slope.

The lights were on. And the front door open.

As I watched, I saw four men who looked foreign, like construction workers or gardeners, carrying out a body. I didn't need to take a second glance, to know it was my corpse they were hauling out the front door. Even from this distance, I recognised the clothes, my chequered blouse and denim shorts. The same ones I now wore as I sat in the car and as I stared unbelieving, even as the sun, red as it was, began to rise above the trees behind the squat bungalow.

Chee Sin!

Just as I was about to push hard on the accelerator, I heard a voice:

'I bring you here, you know.'

I turned and gasped.

He sat beside me, there on the passenger seat, wearing his favourite faded T-shirt, the morning light reflecting blood-like red off his metal-rimmed glasses.

'Chill, baby ku. Chill.'

His face was pale and his lips hardly moved when he spoke. He had his hands on his lap and he stared at them as if they were writhing worms.

'What the hell?' The words trembled in my throat. 'Nash?'

'I bring you here. You think I leave you? Never!'

Then he looked up and his eyes, dead though they were, met mine.

'I die, baby ku. In car accident. Big lorry hit my bike. Not want to tell you. Never want to leave you.'

'What . . . what are you talking about?'

'I die. I pretend to break up with you. Now I bring you here to me.'

'What . . . what do you mean?'

'To stay with me. Forever. Beside my grave.'

'That's crazy!'

'This our family graveyard.'

'Never!'

'The old man, he is me. So sorry, I rape you. Stay, baby ku. You must . . .'

I was going to scream and and push hard on the accelerator. But I already knew all that was to happen.

As I fled, speeding onto the bridge, out of nowhere the old man—my Nash—would leap screeching in front of the car. I would turn the wheel and the Myvi would crash through the barrier. As I plummeted into the river and rocks below, his skeleton would be waiting for me in the murky water, its arms stretched wide as it welcomed me into its bony embrace.

All this flashed through my mind. I took my foot away from the accelerator and turned to Nash. Except he wasn't there. Just an empty seat.

But on the road, in front of the car leaned the old man. Nash in his nineties. He stood hunched up and motionless and in the sky behind him, beyond the wavering trees, was a half moon, barely bright and clinging tenuously to the morning. Then his head swivelled towards me and gestured.

I opened the car door and I thought I heard it creak. As I walked towards Nash, each step became different, more difficult, my body stiff.

I gasped for breath.

As I took his hand, I saw that my hair had grown to my hips and was as white as flour and my arms and legs were bony and liver spotted, my fingers gnarled.

He gave me a toothless, denture-less grin and I smiled back at him.

Insect voices shivered the night. Yes, night had again fallen. Time was tenuous. Above us, in the swirling sky-darkness, the full moon glowed like a distant friend.

Then came the nightbirds, moaning and grieving. But I was no longer afraid. They were spirits that were always all around us. Except I understood their words now.

Hand in hand, Nash and I slowly strolled up towards the graveyard where the tombstones of his relatives circled us, glowing as if in a blissful welcome.

'We home now, baby ku.'

'Yes, Nash,' I whispered. 'Yes . . .'

I took off my shoes, placed my handbag neatly beside it and eased myself back on the patch of soil reserved for me. The one next to Nash's grave.

I closed my eyes and felt his cold kiss which I knew would last forever.

PART 5

MALAY SHADOWS

17

BIGGEST BADDEST BOMOH

Idris Ishak had this *crazy thing* for Zani Kasim; when she walked past nonchalantly as usual, his heartbeat would stop in its blood-filled tracks; her smile would cause his breath to get caught in his throat like a struggling frog. She extruded a subtle, sensual perfume he found himself longing for whilst he lay blissfully in bed, thinking of her warm dreamy eyes, which was far, far too often.

And that was why he found himself on a Singapore-Kuala Lumpur shuttle flight this Friday evening with the other holiday-makers and *balik kampung* commuters. But Idris was on no holiday. He was on serious business. Business that made his hairs stand every time he thought of it and made him almost quiver in delight as he thought about the bounty that would be offered to him.

It all started with Zani, of course. That was a given thing. The day she joined as the Managing Director's secretary was the day Idris fell head over heels in love and in absolute wanton lust for her. She wore a yellow blouse and cosmetic pearls with matching earrings and she whiffed that special perfume of flowers and musk. He was gone. It was oblivion at first sight. Her skirt fell just above her knees and Idris spent that entire afternoon admiring her slim, well-shaped legs, watching them swish against her knee-length skirt. The next morning found him gazing into those warm dreamy eyes, longing to caress her gleaming shoulder-length hair, yearning to press his lips against her fair, smooth cheeks, not to mention those full, cherry-red lips.

There was nothing else Idris could do but beg for a date. Being a mere clerk in accounts receivables, he did not feel particularly confident on whether she would assent to his request. Idris though was quite simply in love and love did strange things to people, and lust produced even weirder behaviour. Idris plucked up his courage whilst hovering over the humming, chemical-belching photocopier. He tucked his bundle of accounts under his arms as if it contained the secrets of a dark universe and ambled over to her.

She had just taken a message over the phone and was tearing out the ubiquitous WHILE YOU WERE OUT slip when Idris found himself in front of her gleaming white desk. His eyes fell longingly on those fair, smooth cheeks, then strayed across to her warm, dreamy eyes.

'Hi, Zani! I'm Idris,' Idris said in a bright, cheerful voice, which he hoped would radiate confidence and friendliness, and mask that blind desire bubbling just below the surface.

'Nice to meet you Idris,' replied Zani. She quickly looked up, and as quickly looked away.

'I'd like to welcome you to Solid Equipments.' Idris wore a Cheshire-cat grin as he imagined himself lying next to that gleaming long hair, stroking it . . . oh stroking it . . ..

'Thanks,' Zani replied, eyes not leaving the newsletter in her dainty fingers.

'Will you have lunch?'

Zani glared up at him with a puzzled look, the cosmetic pearls and her eyes flashing angrily.

'Lunch, you know,' Idris elaborated. 'Have lunch together, you and I—eating together . . . get to know each other. My treat!'

'No, thank you,' Zani snapped, swivelled her chair to face the computer screen and began typing fastidiously—even arrogantly, if one could do that.

'Next time perhaps,' Idris said, his smile dropping like a shattered rock.

'Maybe, maybe not,' muttered Zani as her dainty fingers ran rings around the keyboard.

Idris was crestfallen. Zani was obviously not interested in him. He crept away towards Finance, hoping that the carpeted floor would swallow him whole.

'That girl not your type.'

Idris turned around to see fat Cindy Lam from Marketing with a half-eaten biscuit and a cup of milky sweet tea.

'What do you mean, not my type?'

'Not your type, very action-one. I heard she got three or four boys chasing after her, but she only likes rich people.'

'How do you know this?' questioned Idris.

'I've been sitting in the cubicle opposite her,' Cindy replied, 'heard all her phone calls. Don't waste time.'

'Okay, I won't waste my time with her,' lied Idris.

He was not going to give up so easily. Just the sight of her warm, dreamy eyes and long gleaming hair would lift his spirits and bring a song to his lips. Every effort he made would be worth it, she was going to be his. He knew it. It was just a question of time and effort.

Not wanting to appear too keen, Idris made a tactical decision not to call her for the rest of the week. On Monday, he called her extension and in a deep and confident voice asked her for lunch. He was turned down, the slammed phone ringing like a bee in his ear. He refrained on Tuesday. Wednesday saw his *roti canai* luncheon request rejected. It was going to take more bloody effort than he thought!

By the time Friday had arrived, Idris was in the darkest of moods. Zani had rejected all lunch dates and ignored him when he came up to her with a bunch of fifty-dollar orchids. She just dismissed him as if he was an office boy and the orchids ended up petals first in the bin. To make matters worse, his workmates giggled, even laughed at his every approach.

Cindy Lam kept repeating 'I told you so' all through lunch, making him sick in the stomach. He offered her his *nasi lemak* which she soon consumed without ceremony. 'Not enough chilli,' she said as she chewed the last mouthful.

'I'm going to get her,' said Idris. 'She's mine.'

'How? She ignores you all the time.'

'Somehow, she will be mine. I'll go to a *bomoh*.'

'A *bomoh*, a shaman, a magic-man?' asked Cindy with eyebrows raised.

'Just joking lah,' said Idris as he stood to get up.

'Wait, wait, you sit down.' Cindy watched Idris reluctantly climb back onto the wooden bench with a fed-up expression. 'If you are serious, I can help. My uncle's driver knows a very good *bomoh*. He call him the biggest baddest *bomoh* in the world!'

'Sounds like a Michael Jackson song,' muttered Idris.

'Don't be stupid,' said Cindy with blazing eyes. 'If you really want this girl, this *bomoh* will get her for you. You know my uncle's cousin dying from cancer last year, you know. Went to the *bomoh*, five days later, cancer gone! Just like that, doctors call it a miracle. I call it magic. Powerful magic! Not called the biggest baddest *bomoh* for nothing!'

And so on a taxi with torn plastic seats leaving Subang airport and onto a rattling bus departing Pudu Raya, Idris' eyes were transfixed on a hazy image of Zani, her gleaming hair billowing in the wind, but just out of reach. He headed south in a speeding bus to Seremban to a hotel, a lodging house with eight rooms off a busy street with a rusty air-conditioner and thin musty towels. Idris slept restlessly, tossing and turning as the air-conditioner stalled, started, changed gears, hummed and clanged. How he wished he was tossing and turning with her, pressing his mouth against her fair, smooth cheek, her cherry-red lips. Soon, soon, Idris whispered, the flashing lights outside falling upon his face in a spectrum of garish colours so he looked like an extraterrestrial guest star from *The X-Files*.

A tired, bleary-eyed Idris found himself in a rusty, battered taxi with its Mercedes star missing on the bonnet and a relic of a Chinese driver in singlet at the wheel with one tooth missing. And then up along the windy tree-filled roads, towards Simpang Pertang. Then a turn off into a lane, a dirt track road, scaring a chicken which jumped over the taxi, squawking hysterically. Squeezing past a stubborn goat which no blaring of the horns would budge. Its big glassy eyes, as they crossed paths, transfixed on his, fluttering its eyelids, letting loose a couple of flies that circled the simmering air.

You here to see the Biggest Baddest Bomoh? He heard it say, swishing its beard from side to side. *Power corrupts, absolute power corrupts absolutely. You better know what you're doing! Absolute fool!*

The goat nodded its head and pointed its bitty horns at Idris. Idris fell back on the plastic-coated seat, he could have sworn it spoke and the damn goat was now chuckling away!

Finally they found the house, which to Idris' disappointment was quite ordinary, one in a row of eight, with nothing different about it. Washing on the line, tricycle at the front, slippers and shoes entangled at the front door. This could surely not be the Biggest Baddest Bomoh's house, cancer-curer, witch-doctor extraordinaire. He called out a greeting anyway, removed his shoes and entered.

On a hard, old sofa, below a rotating fan, in front of a large old television, with children yelling next door, Idris was dismayed. This could not be the powerful shaman Cindy boasted of. He had been taken for a ride, all the way up the bloody peninsula. All this way for nothing! Pak Hitam was about thirty-five, lanky, and wore a thin-lipped smile on his spotty face. He served tea clumsily, spoke with a thick, high-pitched Negri accent and said that only true love would win Zani over. True love! What bullshit!

Idris repeated his story with all the semblance of patience he could muster, telling Pak Hitam what he wanted, what he needed. Zani, of all things, Zani, shapely legs, dreamy eyes and all. Pak Hitam talked of love. Idris wanted potent potions. Idris argued that he had exhausted all love's avenues, all *jalans*, all *lorongs*. Pak Hitam had to help or he would kill himself, added Idris for dramatic effect. Yeh, jump into the Gombak River, people did it all the time! That worked like a little miracle. Pak Hitam agreed, taking Idris quite literally and seriously, the fool. Now for the true test. Did this rambling man have the magic?

At first Pak Hitam lit a black candle, muttered some words, made strange gestures with his hand, inhaled deeply and blew the dancing flame out, saying Zani would now be attracted to Idris. With the black smoke drifting by his lips, Idris stopped a curse in his throat. This was not the deal. Attraction was not enough. It was just allurement and others could just as well entice her. After all there were four other men to contend with. Rich guys too!

Another spell, that was what was needed. What kind of spell? An iron-clad guarantee of her, no matter what. No matter what? Yes, she would be his, without fail. Those are difficult spells, Pak Hitam countered. Nothing was too expensive to have Zani. Idris had come all this way, not for a possibility but *certainty*. And surely the Biggest Baddest Bomoh, cancer-curer, witch-doctor extraordinaire, could do this. So you want her, no matter what? No matter what, replied Idris, licking his tumescent lips.

Pak Hitam, with great care, led him behind the house, and up a verdant hill, towards a sacred site teeming with mosquitoes. They climbed a twisting, narrow track for forty minutes and reached a sudden clearing with six red, half-rotting posts surrounding. With each step of their uphill, and somewhat sweaty journey Pak Hitam seemed to grow taller, frame bulkier, voice deeper and on reaching the clearing, he was a different person, with authority and eyes sparkling with power. Absolute power!

Sitting on the damp ground beside a burner, smouldering charcoal, grey smoke blustering up the branches, acrid fumes filling his nostrils, a teary-eyed Idris heard the chanting. The voice raised and fell in dreamy waves and Pak Hitam's eyes, bloodshot and puffy, closed and opened, closed and opened, like the mouth of a hungry fish. The words were a jumble, some with meaning, others a cacophony of tangled words.

When he was done, Pak Hitam uncrossed his legs, stood up and approached Idris and coldly whispered: 'She is now yours.'

She was. For as soon as Idris was back in modern, flashy Singapore, away from jungle, chickens and talking goats, Zani called.

He had just returned that Sunday evening to his one-bedroom flat, when the telephone rang. Zani did not even ask if he was free, she was going to come over *right now*. Idris just said yes, of course, sure thing, anytime, no problem. He abandoned his half-eaten meal of fried rice in the kitchen and paced up and down, straightening posters, stacking magazines, lining up shoes and slippers, spraying air freshener indiscriminately.

Everything was just right. He put on some light background music, combed his hair, changed out of sarong and T-shirt into casual trousers and tennis shirt, with the grinning Lacoste crocodile. Bed made, cushions arranged, curtains closed, lights dimmed. It was going to be perfect. Absolutely perfect. *Pak Hitam came through!*

The door bell rang and Idris tactically waited a few seconds before opening it. *It was Zani in person!*

Idris could hardly believe it. Here she was—glamorous, gorgeous, voluptuous. Glistening eyes, soft skin, full cherry-red lips longing to be kissed, black gleaming hair. And that was just the top, below that was a most alluring and shapely body Idris had ever seen. The red blouse and black skirt would soon be off and he would . . .

The phone rang. Idris cursed himself for not putting the answering machine on. He reached for it signalling Zani to come in.

It was Cindy Lam.

'Can't talk now, I'm busy.'

'How did it go? Did you meet Pak Hitam?'

'Yes, yes,' said Idris impatiently, 'I've got to go now.'

'Did he agree to help?'

'Yes, yes he did.'

He looked back at Zani and grinned. Just ravishing.

'How much he charged you?'

'Not much, not much,' Idris replied as he motioned Zani to enter. Two hundred Malaysian was peanuts for this.

'You waste your money.'

'Why?' countered Idris.

Zani smiled adoringly as she came in. Idris' heart soared. It was going to be a heavenly night. He would soon be lying next to that gleaming long hair, stroking it . . . oh stroking it . . .

'Waste your money.'

'Cindy, I'm willing to pay ten times that. She's here,' Idris said triumphantly, 'Zani is here in my flat!'

'Oh no, dear God!' hollered Cindy.

'What do you mean?' asked Idris irritably, angry at himself for letting her keep him on the line.

Zani closed the front door with a thud that jolted Idris' heart like a gunshot.

'Zani died in a car crash on Friday after work.'

The phone clanged onto the tiled floor, leaving Cindy's hysterical warnings flying aimlessly like a buzzing insect. Idris' mouth was dry and gaping like a hooked fish, his eyes wide with terror. Sweat dripped down his white face.

Zani smiled, the long gleaming hair creeping down, her incisors, long and sharp flashed in the fluorescent light. Her eyes blinked, reddened and turned crimson; her face, like a rotten egg cracked all over, thick green liquid oozed out, spilling in huge globules down her blouse.

'Oh darling, I'm yours.'

'No, no!!' shrieked Idris, as he backed away.

She floated slowly across the room to him, gleaming hair billowing in an invisible wind, arms reaching for an embrace.

Even as Idris felt the hard concrete wall press against his back, he cursed the *bomoh . . . the bloody awful power . . .*

Zani floated down from the ceiling with a hungry smile, mouth open wide, incisors long and sharp, lunging longingly for his throat.

And all Cindy could hear was screaming.

18

MR PETRONAS

Bobby lived amongst a blur of trees on the outskirts of Kuala Lumpur. His real name was Hazbollah bin Abdul Latiff Omar, new IC number 741336-13-54192, but we all called him Bobby.

'Please come now,' he hollered. 'Why, Bobby?'

'It's important, please come.' 'But . . .'

Before I could continue, he'd hung up and I found myself surrounded by tables of ties and handbags, their proprietors slurping and talking and smiling and frowning, and always eating and eating and eating. Chopsticks, forks and spoons, messy fingers.

I tucked my handphone away and fought the escalator crowd into the spiralling heat. Instinctively, I craned my neck to see the twin-towers soaring into the ebullient sky. Fountains splashed behind me and a playful breeze like lover's fingers caressed my back. The crowds sat mesmerised. A security guard eyed a Malay couple walking hand in hand.

An old *amah*, in danger of a heart attack, chased a child wielding an ice cream around the lake.

Bobby was my best friend. I knew that because he did the opposite of everything I told him. I said he was too young to marry but he went and got hitched to the receptionist where we worked. Although that was four years ago, I still called her Cik Normah. They wanted a baby but Bobby was still shooting blanks.

I joined the lines of cars, following the main roads, then took the winding bitumen until I came to Bobby's. The house was small and cheaply built on mosquito-infested land left to him by his father.

My shoes obligingly joined a row of slippers.

'Eh, Ismail, how are you today?' a shrill voice called out.

'Fine, fine, Cik Normah.'

'What's this Cik business, just call me Normah. Bobby's in the garden, at the back.'

I followed her into a house permeated with the giddy fragrance of pounded chillies. Cik Normah wore a lot less make-up since she'd married Bobby, but she was still known as a great beauty. Her hair of henna and Sunsilk was no match for her Mynah-bird eyes which made any male of the species want to covet and protect her in one embrace.

Bobby was in the back garden, thrusting his arms up and down, turning around, then jumping high. Trails of sweat ran down his thin back, his nose swivelled beneath the glimmering trees.

When he saw me, he karate-kicked the air and pointed his fists. I slapped my thighs, clapped and raised my tiger claws.

Bobby attacked, coming at me like a *kampung* chicken with its head chopped off. I danced away, hit the air and crouched low on the ground *Silat Katak* style. He kicked at my feet, and I jumped at him, both of us fell to the grass, laughing.

'Hish, *macam budak*,' said Cik Normah before going back into the house.

Bobby got up and brushed grass off his Adidas shorts. 'Thanks for coming so fast.'

'No problem,' I said, practising a low punch. 'So what's so urgent, you trying to fix me up with some girl again?'

Bobby laughed. 'Well, I wish it was that.'

'So what is it?'

'It's so unbelievable, I don't even know how to tell you.'

'Just tell me.'

'You won't believe me.'

'Just tell me what happened!'

Bobby sighed. 'Two nights ago, right in the middle of dinner, the phone rang. Normah picked it up. When she came back, her face was pale and her voice was trembling.'

'What did she say?'

'Don't interrupt.'

'She said "Don't interrupt"?' 'No, you fool. She said . . .'

Bobby sat down, his back on the wall of the house. He wiped the sweat off with a towel.

'Well, what did she say?'

'She said that someone on the phone said he was going to get her.'

'What?'

'The person said he was going to get her. He said his name was Mr Petronas.'

'Mr Petronas?'

'Yes, that's what he said.'

'Maybe she misheard him. Maybe it was someone from the oil company, Petronas, calling her.' The image of their headquarters, the twin-towers sparkling in the sun filled my head. 'Maybe he wanted to write her a cheque.'

'Ismail, this isn't a bloody joke. He said he's going to get her.'

'That's what he said.' We both looked up. Cik Normah stood by the doorway, lips trembling, sarong tight around her slim waist. 'He said his name was Mr Petronas and he's going to get me.'

'But why does he want to do that, Cik Normah?' I asked. 'And what the hell does "going to get you" mean?'

She shook her head and sat down by the doorstep. 'I don't know.' Then she looked at her husband. 'Tell him, tell him what happened last night.'

Bobby wrung his towel. 'We were asleep. Then I woke up to a sound, a noise at the window. I got up, drew the curtains and saw it.'

'What did you see?'

'I'm . . . I'm not sure. The first thing I saw were the eyes. Then, I saw the outline of a head and a face that was all black. Suddenly, the thing ran and jumped over the back fence.'

'But Bobby, why do you call it a *thing*?'

Bobby bit his lip. 'It was black and hairless. And the eyes, they were red, blood red, burning like hot needles into the back of my brain. That was no man.'

* * *

I agreed to spend the night with them, just in case the thing returned. I sat in their kitchen drinking coffee and reading the *Malay Mail* whilst Bobby and Cik Normah waited in the bedroom.

Just after one, I heard a rustling in the bushes outside. As I unlocked the door, Bobby appeared at my side. He gestured excitedly with his hands, I nodded, putting a finger to my lips.

I opened the door and we both stepped into the garden. We were met by a hungry darkness.

'Bloody mosquitoes,' I said, slapping my face. 'They're biting me all over.'

'Look, Ismail.' Bobby pointed to the fence. 'It's there!'
'Where?'

'There, can't you see it?'

At first, I saw nothing, then a muscular outline of a tall man standing by a tree emerged. I decided that it, he, she, or whatever, must have been an 'it' for when the figure looked up, eyes like bleeding crimson flames met mine.

I felt my bladder almost let go—until Bobby yelled. 'Get it!'

I stumbled after a sprinting Bobby.

At that very instant, the thing hurtled across the grass towards us.

Just as I thought my friend was going to crash into the figure, it leaped into the air.

We turned but it had disappeared. All we saw was the outline of Bobby's house beneath the night sky. 'Where's the damn thing gone?' Bobby shouted.

'Shit, I don't know!'

Then the clouds moved and a black figure squatting triumphantly on the edge of the roof revealed itself, a sinewy silhouette against the backdrop of a half-moon.

It peered down, red eyes blazing. Slowly, it reached forward as if to pick something and, all of a sudden, an object came soaring through the air.

'Shit,' cried Bobby. 'It's throwing down my roof tiles!'

We retreated to the fence as more tiles rained down on us. One hit the fence post and shattered. Another struck Bobby on the head, he fell moaning on the grass.

There came a crash as the thing leaped through the roof cavity, breaking through the ceiling.

'Normah!' gasped Bobby. 'We have to help her, the thing's jumped into our bedroom!'

I rushed back inside the house, through the kitchen, down a corridor. Bobby followed, holding his injured head. I reached the bedroom and tried the door.

'Locked,' I cried. 'The stupid thing's locked!'

'Move aside!' Bobby stepped back and his leg flew at the wood.

Bobby dragged himself up from the floor.

Door one. Bobby zero. I madly thought.

Then from the bedroom came a high-pitched laughter which turned my blood cold. I thought the bowels of hell had opened and the Syaitan himself had come to share a joke with us.

'Bobby, got a parang?'

Bobby stared wide-eyed at me, then as if he'd come out of a dream, he ran off and came back with a big spade.

'That'll have to do,' I said.

Between the two of us and the digging implement, we managed to crack the door open.

But minutes had passed. Minutes in which anything could have happened to Cik Normah.

I gave the door one last shove and we both fell into the room.

In the ceiling was a gaping hole. A dark cloud partly hid the moon.

Bobby switched the light on.

Upon the bed, a figure hid beneath white sheets. Dark stains like leeches covered the material.

'No . . .,' Bobby whispered. He stepped forward so tentatively that I thought the floor was burning the soles of his feet.

I crept forward, my heart bashing away like a *kompang*. To my relief, there was no sign of the black thing.

Bobby reached the bed and pulled the sheet away.

Cik Normah screamed.

Dark patches covered a face riveted in terror. Beside her was a torn nightie with fingermarks on it. Then I realised she was naked and averted my eyes but not before seeing the same dark stains all over her body.

'I'll call an ambulance,' I gasped. 'You'll need to find some bandages to stop the bleeding.'

'Please don't die, Normah,' whimpered Bobby. 'Please don't leave me.'

'I . . . I'm . . . not hurt,' she said. 'I'm . . . I'm okay.' 'But the blood!'

'It's not blood, Bobby.' I looked up and saw that Cik Normah had pulled the sheets over her body, she raised one hand and a slick of black slime flowed down her fingers. 'It's, it's . . . I don't know what it is!'

Bobby caught some of the liquid with his hand. 'What is it, Ismail?'

He passed me a couple of drops. I rubbed the greasy substance with my fingers, then put it to my nose.

'Oil! It's black oil!'

'What happened here?' Bobby said to his wife. Normah shook her head.

'What happened?'

'I was looking out of the window at you both when it jumped through the ceiling. I tried to run but it grabbed me. It was strong and all greasy, and . . ..' She burst into tears.

'And?'

She shook her head.

'What happened Normah?'

She continued sobbing.

Bobby looked up at me. 'Maybe you should leave us alone for a while.'

I nodded and left the room.

* * *

Bobby didn't make a police report. He didn't think they'd believe him. How could they help anyhow? How were they going to arrest a mythical creature that covered itself with black oil so no one could grab hold of it? Or perhaps oil oozed naturally from its skin like it did from the earth?

After all, if man was fashioned from mud, then oil seeping from man could be conceivable. Yet could this not be some kind of awful joke?

Mr Petronas, indeed.

But no one was kidding. Cik Normah had been attacked and, although Bobby had not said it, I knew much more had happened.

This creature had raped her.

The unkindest of wounds came a few weeks later when we found out Cik Normah was pregnant.

As the months past, her stomach grew bigger and, although Bobby tried to dismiss it as his imagination, he did say that she'd begun to smell somewhat oily.

Bobby was becoming even thinner. His hair was falling out. He said staying at home with Cik Normah was like living in an oil refinery. He'd stopped smoking too. He didn't want to burn the house down, he jokingly said but neither of us could manage a smile.

And his trembling hands weren't due to nicotine withdrawal. He was shit scared.

We discussed abortion but Cik Normah refused to hear it.

'Maybe it's your child, Bobby,' she said, eyes flashing. 'How do you know it's not. You'd be killing our own flesh and blood.'

She was right. We didn't know for sure.

* * *

It was during the sixth month of her pregnancy, when I was sending them home from work when Cik Normah screamed: 'It's coming, it's coming!'

'What, right now?' Bobby yelled.

We were in a huge traffic jam in Jalan Ampang and I knew we wouldn't make it to the General Hospital on time, not from the way Cik Normah was wailing.

'Bobby, she's going to need help now!'

I turned towards the nearest building. Drove down the side, stopped the car and we both helped her out.

The irony of it still fills me with anger and, dare I say it, a twisted kind of sick hilarity. Cik Normah lay there in Bobby's arms, next to the lake, her maternity dress from Metrojaya soaked in blood.

The fountains danced in the air whilst she kept on screaming.

I wanted to run for help but I knew our time was up. So I went on my knees to help bring the baby out.

A warm spray hit my face. Viscous liquid trailed down my cheeks. I rubbed it off and realised what it was. For no rhyme or reason, a ferociously stupid thought came to me . . .

We've struck oil.

Then this tiny hand slipped out of Cik Normah and waved. That's right it moved to and fro, so gracefully as if saying hello at a wedding at The Ritz-Carlton. Then the rest of the greasy thing spilt out, it's body all black as it slid on the pavement on its protruding stomach.

A crowd had gathered by then, but they stepped back when the baby crawled across the pavement, a couple of times slipping on itself and falling face first. Then it got the hang of it and, like a monkey, sprinted past the bewildered faces, before leaping up a pillar.

It glanced at us with mischievous human eyes. That's right, human eyes no different from yours and mine. Pitiful, intelligent eyes, it had.

And I only realised it had a mouth, when I saw its thick black lips stretch up its cheeks into a grotesque smile, a red tongue flickering inside.

Then, as if satisfied with what it'd seen, it reached out with one pudgy hand and started to climb. The umbilical cord trailing behind it.

I craned my neck as the *bayi minyak* ascended higher and higher, leaving oil stains on the polished metal wall, now red with the setting sun.

As it went past the skybridge, it became nothing but a black dot. It climbed on and on, whilst the crowd below silently stared, mouths open. The baby scaled all 88 stories, occasionally stopping as if to rest, and then continuing until it got right to the very top.

For a few seconds it balanced itself like a tightrope walker on the sharp tip of the spire. From there it could see beyond the city, beyond the scattered trees and hills, perhaps even the oil tankers plying the Straits of Malacca. Perhaps it could even see into our hearts.

Because then it jumped. High in the air, high above the tallest building in the world.

Before falling.

Before impaling itself on the metal rod. I thought I heard it crying, a soft whimpering like a breeze through tired trees.

On the spire it melted. Whatever lubricant its little body held dripped down the metal cladding. The authorities sent a helicopter up but they only found stubborn oil stains.

Cik Normah died from internal bleeding. Bobby floated her in the lake and disappeared into the shimmering night. It took several days to get the redness and oily residue out of the water. No one ever heard from Bobby again.

As for me, I still can't visit a petrol pump alone.

19

IN THE VILLAGE OF SETANG

I was nineteen when my mother died of a fever which she contracted after her labours in the soggy paddy fields. Soon after her white shroud was swallowed by the crumbling earth, I received word that Mak Ina, my aunt, wanted me to move to Setang, the village where our territorial chief resided. Mak Ina worked as his head cook in what she called his 'palace' and, as she was already seventy, she needed help in her daily duties.

Setang was half-a-day's walk from the village of my birth, but because of my club foot, it took all day to get there as I hobbled down the track between jungle, gambier plantations and tin mines dotted about the sacred limestone hills. I arrived with my body aching, staggering with my bundle of clothes just as the insect voices mounted a shrilling octave. Then the Maghrib prayer-call came echoing like a wind and descended upon the valley.

At the village check point, two Japanese soldiers leaning lazily against a coconut tree, with their khaki leggings half undone, asked me what I was doing here. I told them my business and the one that looked sulkiest and half-sick spat on the ground before waving me through. I hobbled past wooden houses on stilts, perched above their small dirt compounds of weary fruit trees and empty chicken coops. An old man, smoking a cigarette, fiddled with a wreck of a bicycle. Beside him a scrawny monkey sat, tied to a wooden post, tearing up a rotten papaya whilst its mournful eyes stared at me.

About fifty families lived in Setang, the most important of which was Dato Nan's. The territorial chief's house, I had heard, was five or six times the size of a normal one. Even as I followed the track alongside several geta perca trees, I could see its timber, the colour of burnt umber, spanning across the hillside like a monstrous crow nestled on a verdant landscape.

I had never seen such a huge house and my mouth widened as I drew closer. Its sturdy dark planks, its looming walls seemed to hold up the purple sky. Sloping up steeply was a thatched roof and, above it, the evening star was winking. Was it warning me or welcoming me? I didn't know. After my mother died, I felt I had nothing to live for, but here, no matter how unpromising, a new life was beginning.

I hobbled around to the back and found Mak Ina chopping pungent-smelling onions in the small building that housed the kitchen. She was a small and round grey-haired woman, who moved with great deliberation. After warmly greeting me, she passed me a drink of water mixed with lime juice and sat me down on a *mengkuang* mat, which is a mat made from pandanus leaves.

'Any trouble with the Japanese?' Mak Ina asked, speaking slowly in a sing song voice. 'You shouldn't have come alone, you know.'

As she spoke, my aunt's lips and tongue were dancing flames of orangey red for they were stained from a lifetime of chewing betel leaf filled with areca nut. She once told me that it gave her not only the energy but the inspiration to cook delicious food. But that was a long time ago.

'There were some along the way,' I replied. 'But they left me alone.'

'That's good,' she sighed. 'Well, Yan, you're lucky to be working here, you know.'

'I know that, aunty.'

'I didn't really need extra help in the kitchen. I can get help from the other servants. But you needed looking after. Luckily, Dato Nan agreed.'

'I know. Thank you.' I rubbed the sweat off my forehead and retied my long hair.

'After your mother died, I knew there was no one to look after you. You and I know that marriage is out of the question . . .'

Mak Ina didn't elaborate and so I simply nodded, indicating that I understood what she meant.

She was, of course, referring to my club foot—and to the black birthmark, the size of a guava on my cheek. No boys from my village had ever shown an interest in me. Perhaps that is also why the Japanese soldiers left me alone. There was once a boy though, but he married someone else. That too was long ago.

Mak Ina continued with a cursory description of the household duties that were expected of me.

'Another thing,' she said, turning to me in almost a whisper. 'Don't venture out of the servants' quarters after we've turned in for the night. Even if you can't sleep.'

'Why's that, aunty? Is it the Japanese?'

She shook her head.

'Then why?'

'Just don't, Yan.' She shrugged her small shoulders. 'All we have tonight is tapioca. Now let's see you slice that one up. I want to make a boiled salad of it.'

A few days later, well after Mak Ina had extinguished the kerosene lamp and we five servants were all lying on our mats, I realised my necklace was missing. I had carelessly left it hanging on a delicate branch of the Frangipani tree beside the old well.

Though not expensive, it was my mother's and she gave it to me a few months before she succumbed to her fever. Other than the bundle of clothes I had brought with me from my village, it was all I had.

Two of the other servants were already breathing heavily. Carefully, I got on my feet. Moonlight crept in through the gaps beneath the wooden shutters and this was sufficient for me to pad my way to the main door.

'Don't go out, child,' a voice said.

It was Mak Ina.

'I forgot my necklace,' I whispered. 'I'll be very quick. It's just by the well.'

'Get it tomorrow,' she insisted.

'It might be gone by then, aunty. I'm so worried . . .'

I heard her sigh.

'You're a careless one, Yan,' she whispered back. 'Off you go then. Get it and come straight back.'

The door creaked opened and insect shrills suddenly filled the air. The dirt compound outside was bathed in eerie moonlight. A breeze swept through my hair and rustled the leaves of the trees.

The stone well was perhaps a hundred feet away and beside it stood the silhouettes of two Frangipani trees. To my left loomed the long main building. Its curving shadows reminded me of a *parang*, the long knife used for many things, including slaughtering animals.

I crept down the wooden steps and hurried across to the well. The wooden bucket attached to a rope was cast carelessly to one side. A pool of dark water like freshly drawn blood floated beside it. I quickly searched the two trees, my fingers running along the small branches, feeling the rough knobbly bark.

But the necklace was gone.

Perhaps I was mistaken. Where else could I have put it? I was sure I had left it hanging on a branch, its silver chain glinting in the blazing sun.

Just as I was about to hurry back to the servants' quarters, I heard a sound. It was the snap of a twig. It was almost masked by the gushing noise of the stream behind the orchard but I had definitely heard it. I stared hard between the tree trunks and branches of the fruit trees but saw only shadows.

Then came another sound.

Something scratching the ground. I should have fled then. Instead I foolishly crept forward. Perhaps I thought it might be someone who had found my necklace. Or perhaps I was just curious. The sound of my heart pounded in my ears as I moved cautiously from tree to tree.

Beyond the orchard, the stream shimmered. It made a loud cascading sound as water flowed over small rocks which appeared remarkably white in the moonlight and resembled large eggs, some of which were broken. Then I saw it, crouched on the bank, an unmistakable muscular shape.

A tiger!

Perhaps the stream had masked the sound of my footsteps and the beast did not hear my approach. But now I was afraid to turn back, afraid that it would chase me as I retreated to the servants' quarters. So I hid behind the trunk of a rambutan tree and watched.

I saw the rhythmic movement of its body as it breathed the night air. Its ears twitched as if it was bothered by insects or perhaps, more worryingly, listening for prey. Occasionally, it would stare up at the jungle across the stream. Then, I must have glanced away for a second, for when I looked up, the tiger was gone.

I swallowed hard.

What if the beast had seen me? Smelt me? Perhaps right now it was circling behind me, stalking within the shadows of the fruit trees, getting ready to pounce?

Barely able to breathe, I stared at their misshapen silhouettes, listening hard, ready for the animal to charge. What I would do, I didn't know. I picked up a large stone from the ground as a weapon and held it close to me, between my small breasts. As I waited, the moon peeped between the branches, the stars glittered in the foliage. When I was sure the tiger was no longer waiting for me, I crept in the direction of the well.

Just as I reached it, I heard a sound. It seemed to come from beneath the steps that led up to the kitchen building.

I knelt behind the stone work and then, suddenly, a figure stepped from the shadows. He was tall, muscular but slightly hunched. As he turned to climb up the steps, moonlight gleamed upon his long white hair that fell upon his broad shoulders. Even at this distance, I could make out his dark and angular features.

It was Dato Nan!

He was the reason we were all here. He was the chief of this district. This was his 'palace' and he was perhaps the most powerful man in the state, second only to the sultan.

Dato Nan was wearing his bed clothes—a sarong and a light blue pyjama top. At the top of the stairs, about six feet from the ground, he pushed open the kitchen door and disappeared inside. Pulling up my sarong, I raced around the side of the building soundlessly in my bare feet just in time to see him leave the kitchen building and stride along the timber bridge that led to the main house.

It could only be him!

His white beard caught the light of the kerosene lamp inside the entry hall as he entered. But that was not before he hesitated and glanced behind him. He stood there for a long moment. Then he turned away and firmly shut the door.

* * *

The next morning, when I was hanging out the clothes behind the servants' quarters, Mak Ina pulled me aside to ask me why I had taken so long to get my necklace the night before. She said she must have fallen asleep as soon as I had left and when she awoke I had not returned.

'I was about to go out looking for you, Yan,' she chided in a slow sing song voice. 'Then the door opened and you came in. Thank Allah you're safe!'

'I saw something strange,' I said. 'I didn't want to tell you last night. I didn't find my necklace but I saw something else . . .'

I then quickly told her what I had seen.

Mak Ina shifted her small round body beneath the scorching sun. She pursed her lips and scratched her grey hair as she listened.

'You mustn't tell anyone else about this,' she whispered. Her face was grave and beads of sweat peppered her brow. 'You shouldn't have seen what you saw.'

'But why?'

'It's a secret. A dark secret.'

'Tell me about it, aunty. Please!'

She glanced behind her towards the house whose timber shutters stared ominously back at us.

'Long ago, child,' she whispered. 'There was a dispute between Dato Nan's great grandfather and a cousin-in-law of his. It was over who would become the next territorial chief. As you know, it's hereditary but governed by customary law.'

I nodded, encouraging her to continue.

'Anyway, one day when this cousin was bathing in a hut made of palm leaves beside the river, a tiger leapt in and killed him. The villagers found his torso floating down the river. The palm leaves were smeared with blood. A village boy saw the tiger wading across the river.'

'Where's this river?'

'I haven't taken you there yet, child. You'll need to follow the stream until it flows into the river. It's called the River Setang. It'll take a bit longer than the chewing of a betel nut to get there.'

'It's quite normal for chickens, goats, even cows to be killed around here,' she continued. 'If traps or hunting parties are organised by those who are ignorant they are quickly ordered to leave the tiger alone. Many think it's some sort of a sacred creature that cannot be touched. But those closer to Dato Nan's family know better. The tiger legends have always been with us.'

Her orangey red lips and tongue were fiery in the bright sunlight, then her eyes stared right into mine. 'You know, this has nothing to do with your father. That was a terrible thing. But there is no connection between Dato Nan and your father's death. You must know that.'

I slowly nodded. I did not want to speak about my father. Not now, anyway. He used to kiss me on the forehead, then gently touch my cheek. It made my heart soar.

He would tend to our small orchard, his dark back gleaming in the hot sun. His thin moustached face, the drooping narrow eyebrows spoke of his hard labours to feed and sustain our family. But he always made time for me, showing me games with polished stones on a wooden board he had crafted.

'You must know, Yan, that his death has nothing to do with our legends. That was seven years ago. It's all history now. We learn to forgive and forget. For instance, the British were our enemies seventy years ago but today we want them to save us from the Japanese.

'Yes, I was only a child when the British soldiers marched up the hill into our district. They looked so fine in their hats and red uniforms. After they had left the paddy fields and marched into the jungle, our men ambushed them. We attacked them with spears and parangs, krisses and guns. Oh, what a shameful day that was for the mighty British and their empire! The thing is, some of their soldiers were also killed by tigers. There were two of them!

'This was all when Dato Nan's grandfather was still alive. But these British returned, this time with artillery and ten times more soldiers. They came on two sides and we were defeated. Many of us Malays died. That's how we came to be under British rule. Then, of course, the Japanese came with their planes and tanks. We thought they were liberating us— but they're far, far worse.

'As for those British, they did conduct a tiger hunt but never found their man-eating tiger. So you see, our village has a reputation for tiger attacks. Always has. But no one has ever killed or captured a tiger. Except for that one time . . .'

'When was that, aunty? What happened?'

By this time, Mak Ina and I were sitting beneath a banana tree that held on tenuously to its dead brown fronds. A black and white moth flitted over the wild grass, then disappeared as though it was never there.

'Ah, you see, child,' she said. 'There was this one time when a man moved in from another district. He had never heard of the legends. So one early morning, when he came across a tiger eating the carcass of his goat, he raised his spear and flung it at the beast.'

'What happened then?'

'Well, the next day, Dato Nan's father, returned back to the house with a deep cut in his thigh. Nobody knows how he got it. But everyone was whispering the same thing!'

'Are you saying, aunty, that Dato Nan's father was a were-tiger?'

'Yes, a shape-shifter!'

'That can't be!'

'And Dato Nan is one too,' she whispered, her eyes blazing. 'It passes from father to eldest son. That's the story anyway.'

'But it's just a story right?'

'Yes, yes, child, just a story. But Dato Nan has five daughters. No sons. So when he dies, his position as territorial chief will go to his younger brother. Then we won't have any more problems with tigers around here.'

* * *

The next day, as I helped prepare the evening meal, I received word that Dato Nan wanted to see me. So, from the kitchen, with my heart thumping, I followed the narrow covered bridge which connected it with the main house.

We servants used it several times a day to bring food from the kitchen. It was mostly curried or fried tapioca, sometimes with other vegetables, rarely with meat. The Japanese helped themselves to all our supplies. The reason the kitchen was kept separate from the main house was in case of fire. The kitchen had been ablaze twice in the palace's hundred year history and the separation of the two buildings was what saved it. Of course, we servants only whispered the word 'palace', for only the sultan was allowed to call his home that.

I pushed open the back door and entered the main building. I stood in a narrow dark hall. Mak Ina had told me that its walls used to be decorated with family heirlooms which included Chinese porcelain, pewter plates and silvery cutlery. Under the Japanese occupation, all of these had been hidden and only a painting of Dato Nan's father hung here.

From the hall, the building divided into two. To the left was the reception room where Dato Nan would receive visitors. Beyond the reception room was Dato Nan's bed chamber.

The other half of the building was to the right of the hall and it was reserved for family members. The first room was a dining area where mengkuang mats were spread out for meals. This was followed by two family chambers shared by Dato Nan's two spouses and children.

Instead of turning either way, I continued through the hall and out to the balcony at the front. The balcony was expansive and stretched out on both sides, like wings. This space was used for family activities and it often caught a cooling breeze from the jungle. From here, a set of stairs led to the main entrance at ground level.

At the far end of the balcony, three of Dato Nan's granddaughters played a dextrous game of hand clapping. Dato Nan was lying casually on a mat at the other end, just outside his bed chamber. His gaunt-faced grey-haired massage lady, in sarong and white blouse, was rubbing his feet. She nodded when she saw me. As I approached, stooping my body to show respect, I smelt a mix of coconut oil and herbs.

Dato Nan wore a loose sarong. He was bare-chested and his nipples black. His long white hair was like sand over a small pillow whilst his white beard and thick eyebrows floated like clouds above the umber timber floors. Deep lines ran through his dark angular face.

'Ah, it's you, Yan,' he said when he saw me approach. 'Come, come closer. No need to be afraid.'

Although Dato Nan was in his sixties, the muscles on his biceps and chest were firm upon his dark leathery skin.

'I want you to learn to massage,' he said in a voice that echoed deep inside his chest. 'No use spending all your time in the kitchen. I'm getting old and my body needs more and more attention.'

Then he laughed. It reverberated up in the dusky timber rafters sending a sparrow fleeing from the balcony rails.

Without warning, his hand flashed up and grabbed the air. He was so fast, I hardly saw its blurring movement.

'Mosquito,' he said. 'They spread disease and must be killed.'

He showed me the striped body of the insect before rubbing the blood off on his sarong. For the first time, I noticed his long, sharp fingernails.

'Now, come here, Yan. You can start by rubbing my neck and shoulders. I've had too many discussions with those troublesome village chiefs today.'

I used to massage my father before he died, so I knew the various pressure points. Dato Nan, smelling faintly of vinegar and strongly of clove cigarettes, was a lot older but a lot more muscular than my father. His skin was tough and strangely warm beneath my fingers. He sighed as I pushed my thumbs into the tissues around his neck. I could feel the tension in the knots in his sinews.

As I massaged Dato Nan, I wondered if he was a were-tiger. But mostly I thought about my father, how he died and how unfair it was.

A crow cawed incessantly close by, its lonesome voice shuddering an awful darkness in my head. It sounded like a warning.

* * *

One night, not long after I began massaging Dato Nan, I heard a deliberate scratching in the dirt beneath the timber floor of the servants' quarters. I opened my eyes and listened. There was hardly a sound. Even the insects had gone quiet.

There it was again. Something dragging its sharp claws against the earth.

I could hardly breathe.

Then I heard it. A low growl of a large beast.

The thought of the thing stalking just beneath me sent my heart beating like a *kompang*, a Malay hand-held drum used at important events. But what events were unfolding this awful night?

I heard footsteps now—very slowly—climbing up the wooden steps. The timber creaked. It groaned as if in fear. There was a loud scratching, right against the door.

Then suddenly, silence . . .

All was quiet, moment by terrible moment.

This soundlessness went on for so long, I felt like screaming. I dared take a step forward, my club foot rolling on the floorboard. Suddenly, there was a great crash as something heavy slammed against the door. It roared like thunder.

But the door held!

Then it struck again. This time, the door crashed to the ground.

A flash of white leapt in. It stood facing me, its sinewy body occupying almost half of the space in the servants' quarters. I edged away towards the far wall. I wanted to scream but nothing came from my mouth. There should be four other women sleeping here, including Mak Ina.

But I was alone.

An incandescent glow spilled in through the broken door. The tiger's fur gleamed. It was almost white in the moonlight and shimmered like some divine being. The animal's eyes shone as it padded forward. One paw delicately touching the timber floor, followed by the other. It seemed to know exactly what it wanted.

Sweat dripped off my forehead.

'What do you want?' I whispered.

Now I could see its orange fur. Its black stripes. The white long whiskers. Its eyeballs, small and black, peering deep into mine.

'Leave me alone, please!'

Then it leapt.

It pushed me backward and toppled my body to the ground. It pawed my bare legs. I tried to crawl away on my back, using my elbows. But it clambered on me. It was heavy and smelt of blood and raw meat. Its teeth were large, sharp and dripping. I thought it was going to tear out my throat.

It growled and with the swipe of his front paws, flipped me around. With several jerking tugs, it tore off my sarong.

I do not want to describe what the tiger then did to me.

But, after several nights of the same nightmare, I had to tell Mak Ina about it.

'You should not have such dreams,' she said.

But I did. And the same dream continued.

I began to enjoy the animal's visitations. I looked forward to it. There was always fear. But fear was followed by pleasure. Pleasure I had never known.

Little did I know that these dreams were a prelude to something more for one night, just before we turned in to bed, there was a knock on the door. It was one of the servants that slept with Dato Nan's grandchildren in the main building.

'Dato Nan wants you,' she said. 'He has back pain and needs a massage.'

I yawned and rubbed my eyes.

'Come quickly,' she said.

I pulled off the sarong that I used as a blanket and followed her. We went up into the kitchen, then across the bridge and entered the house.

'He's in his bed chamber,' she said as we entered the hall which was lit by a single kerosene lamp. Then she disappeared.

I opened the door on my left and entered the reception room.

This was where Dato Nan would sit on a large mat for his meetings with village officials. I knew that hanging on the walls, were a collection of krisses and spears, but these were now just shadows. Beyond this reception room was Dato Nan's bed chamber.

I knocked on the door.

'Come in,' he answered.

I entered, putting my right hand forward and stooping low.

'Ah, it's you, Yan,' he said in a deep voice. 'Come over here. My back is sore.'

'Yes, Dato Nan,' I said.

He was lying on a bed. It was the only bed in the house and was a gift from the British many years ago. He turned onto his stomach as I approached. I knelt on the floor and began to massage his back.

'That's good,' he said. He gestured towards the kerosene lamp beside the wooden shutters. 'Blow it out. It's too bright.'

I did as asked and returned to kneading his back.

Then, he turned over and took my hands in his. His were large and very warm.

'You're mine, Yan,' he said. 'All mine.'

He stared into my eyes, before drawing me to him.

His hands slide beneath my blouse and he caressed my small breasts. Then he undid my sarong and pulled me on the bed.

That night, I knew that Dato Nan and the tiger were one and the same. It was not so different from my dreams.

Fear and pleasure merged and mingled as he changed his form over and over in the deepening shadows.

* * *

There was endless cooking in preparation for our wedding. Such events were usually held in the compound outside where mats would be spread for guests attending the dinner.

There were no chickens to slaughter as the Japanese had taken them long ago. Instead, the kitchen staff chopped coriander and galangal, they pounded tamarind, turmeric, garlic and ginger, all for a tapioca curry. The smell of cooking scented the air. As the bride-to-be, I was not amongst them, even though I had offered several times to help.

That night, to the sound of *kompang* drums, about a hundred or so villagers, mostly relatives, sat in groups of six around the meagre dishes we offered. It was a small affair because the Japanese occupation turned everyone frugal. For the same reason, there was no traditional cock-fighting contest that day.

As I sat on a timber dais next to Dato Nan, I could not fathom why such a wealthy and powerful person could be bothered with this club-footed, birth-marked face girl. He could have anyone he wanted in the village. I wondered how many of them knew that he was a were-tiger.

There were rumours about the family, but who knew for sure? Was it only me, or did his other wives know his secret?

Dato Nan's ex-wife resided in the village with her grownup daughter. As for his two current wives, they and their girls would continue to live in the two sleeping chambers at the other wing of the house.

Dato Nan insisted that I share his bed chamber.

'Now I can be at peace,' he whispered to me one night after the wedding. 'Now that I have a son, at last, growing in your belly.'

I spun around to face him in bed.

'What?' I whispered, staring wide-mouthed.

'I know these things,' he chuckled, stroking his beard. His white hair was draped flamboyantly over the pillow. 'It's one of the instincts we were-tigers have. The other instinct I had was that you were the right one for me. Ah, to have found you so late in life.'

He stroked my long hair and smelt it. 'You know, you're the only one I've appeared to in my true form. I was born a were-tiger. It's something that is passed from eldest son to eldest son. You've been very brave. I knew it that first night when you saw me by the river. You didn't run away. You stayed and watched.'

His dark face, etched with deep lines held a knowing smile. In his stern eyes, I saw a kindness I had not seen before. Then he reached under his pillow and pulled something out.

It was my necklace!

'Thank you!' I said.

'I found it hanging on a tree beside the well,' he said. 'I didn't know who it belonged to. But when you came out looking for it, I knew it was yours. I had already changed form and I was watching you from behind the trees.'

'I didn't know that,' I whispered. 'I've always heard stories of were-tigers. But my mother, she told me they weren't true.'

'Well, now you know that we're real, don't you, Yan?'

He scratched his beard and stared up at the beams beneath the roof, as though mesmerised by its structure. 'This magic is passed down through the generations. My great great grandfather came here from a village in Sumatra. He came on a boat, across the sea, then up the River Setang. He was a were-tiger. But he was not alone, there were many.

'There was a village deep in the jungle where all were-tigers lived together in human form. But when they stepped out of the village, they would turn into tigers. But my ancestor, for some reason I know nothing of, was forced to flee the village. And so he fled across the water to this land. It was a good thing too. For years later, all those were-tigers were hunted and killed. The jungle was burnt and, with it, our tiger village.

'My great great grandfather could take on human form whenever he wanted. But because he could only mate with humans, this gift, his magic, is only passed from eldest son to eldest son. With no sons of my own, I thought it would end with me and for many years I was happy. This gift is in so many ways a curse. I've tried so many nights to not succumb to the instinct deep within me, but the desire to stalk and kill is so strong. I cannot resist it!

'So for many years, I was content, knowing that this curse would not be passed. But then, as time went by, as my body grew old, I realised that what a loss it would be to not have were-tigers in this world. And that is why I asked Mak Ina to get you.'

'What?' I blurted. 'Me? You mean Mak Ina knew all along?'

'Yes, she did. She told me about your family. She told me about you. You know, my father had a club foot too. So I just knew that you would give me a boy.'

'How? How could you know that?'

'I just knew, but it's so much more than that, Yan. Your family is from the same tiger village my great great grandfather came from in Sumatra. The magic is strong between us. Your family was descended from were-tigers too but the magic never passed on because your grandfather didn't have sons. Now, finally, we can start our tiger village again!'

Somewhere in the building a gecko called out.

'Ah there,' he said. 'The *cicak* agrees.'

He then turned over, rocking the bed and was soon snoring.

A night bird wailed from far away but, for me, sleep would not come.

* * *

Three months after our wedding, I heard shouting and loud commotion outside. I leapt from the mat in the dining area and rushed out to the balcony.

Three villagers were carrying Dato Nan towards the house.

'Open the door!' I shouted.

A servant rushed down the steps and pushed open the front door at ground level. The villagers hauled my husband up the steps and onto the balcony.

Blood dripped from his body.

'Put him over there,' I ordered. 'Be gentle!'

I ordered the servants to bring water and towels. By this time the rest of the family, including his other two wives, had congregated around Dato Nan.

His body was splayed outside our bed chamber, at almost the same place where I had first massaged him. There was a gaping wound in his chest. His wives, including myself, tried to give him comfort, fanning him and wiping his forehead.

He drank water then coughed it out. His breathing was ragged, his beard shuddering as his body shook.

I held his hand and it trembled in mine. I knew then that I truly loved this man even though I had been manipulated, even though he was older than my father. For doesn't love transcend all things?

I looked into my husband's eyes. They blinked and were filled with despair. We bandaged his wounds but could not stop the blood. It spilled on the floorboards and trickled down a gap between them, falling far down to the earth below.

'Take care of our son,' he whispered to me. His eyes were watery and pleading.

'Yes, of course,' I said and caressed his limp hand.

I stared up at the rafters, feeling terribly helpless.

Then my husband closed his eyes and I thought I heard a quiet growl.

Not long afterwards, he was dead.

He had been out hunting the night before and had stumbled upon a camp of Japanese soldiers. They had heard the stories about tigers in the area and had come in search of trophies. One of the guards had fired his machine gun in the dark. Two bullets struck my husband in the chest. He had spent the rest of the night trying to get back home.

The day after his funeral, I stood in the kitchen and stared at the dirt compound. The well, Frangipani trees, the orchard beyond were covered in an early morning mist.

'How are you, child?' said Mak Ina as she boiled some water in a dented old pot.

'I'm fine,' I said. 'It's Allah's will.'

'Yes, it is, Yan. They'll find you a house in the village for the whole family. Dato Nan's brother will move in here.'

'I know,' I said. 'That's how these things work.'

'They say the Japanese will surrender soon. A huge bomb exploded in their homeland.'

'I hope so. We need peace. All of us. I think I'll go for a walk now. Down to the river.'

'Why there?'

'I like to see the water flow. Always moving. To some other place. To some other time.'

Mak Ina stared curiously at me and then sighed.

I brushed against the gnarled branches of the Frangipani trees as I drifted past the well. I glanced back at the long, umber-coloured house. The wooden shutters seemed to shy away from my gaze.

Then I followed the track behind the orchard. It wended its way beneath the jungle trees, beside the gushing stream. It may have been saying a thousand things, but I heard none of it. The rocks that looked like large eggs in the moonlight, now resembled blood-covered fists or perhaps even giant bullets.

Insect-calls led me on even as the sun glinted from behind the tumultuous foliage. There was a rustling in the branches. Monkeys perhaps. But I did not stay to look at them. Eventually, I found myself where the stream spilled into the wide River Setang. It was wreathed in thick drifting mist.

It was here that my husband's ancestor had killed his cousin-in-law over the succession of territorial chief. The bathing hut made of palm leaves was long gone but I guessed it was located somewhere along the shore I was now passing which was filled with wild grasses and several hovering dragon flies. A small boat was pulled up on the bank but there was no one around.

I sat on a rickety timber jetty, my feet dangling over the muddy-coloured waters. The timber was cool and coarse beneath my soft sarong.

I placed a hand firmly on my belly. It had grown but was not huge yet. I felt the stirrings of my son in the amniotic fluid. Felt what must have been his elbows pushing slowly, rhythmically against my stomach.

My son, who would one day be a were-tiger.

As I too was descended from them, all my son's offspring would be were-tigers. This was my husband's wishes. He wanted a tiger-village again, perhaps somewhere hidden deep in the jungle.

What did he say?

What a loss it would be to not have were-tigers in this world.

I wiped away my perspiration with my sleeve, drew back my long hair and stared at the insects darting above the fast flowing waters. A kingfisher swooped through the air and picked up a small fish. Then it was gone. Perhaps I had only imagined it. Like the trees, the river, the wild grasses before me that were so misty-veiled. Perhaps life itself.

What were were-tigers? Humans who turned into tigers? Or tigers who turned into humans? I didn't know. I didn't care. All I knew was that tigers ate animals and often humans too.

That was how my father died.

I was twelve and sick with a fever and he had ventured out to the jungle that evening to gather camphor needed for medicine. He had collected some but needed more. He had almost reached the waterfall when the tiger attacked. They only found his severed head. It was nestled above, stuck in the aerial roots of a Ficus tree.

Did the man-eating beast play with my father's head as though it were some kind of ball?

In my child's mind, I had vowed I would find the tiger and kill it, this animal that had stolen my father from me. It was a vow I had never forgotten.

What a loss it would be to not have were-tigers in this world.

Would it be such a loss?

Disfigured shadows now hid in the mist. Were these the ghosts of were-tigers emerging? My lips trembled. I watched my bare feet swaying beneath me.

Forward. Backward.

Was that a drop of rain or a teardrop?

Forward. Backward.

They had no right to exist.

Not now. Not ever . . .

My feet seem too tiny.

They are falling into water.

There is a splash and coldness grips my body.

Bubbles shoot to the surface. Except for my sarong drifting like a net, all is cloudy before my eyes.

But my mind is clear.

There will be no more were-tigers in this world.

Not a single one.

I open my mouth and drink the river.

Drink life from my body.

My husband's ancestor had sailed up this river. Together with my unborn son, we now float down it.

Away forever.

20

MIDNIGHT RAIN

'Stupid assignment,' Fidrus muttered.

Fidrus was 20 and lived with his parents and, as an only child, was used to having things his way. Except for the glow from his laptop, darkness like an ill-worn cloak shrouded his bedroom.

Struggling in his third year at college, he was desperate as he had to submit his assignment the next day or he would fail the unit. So he sat, well after midnight, hunched over a course book on his tablet, typing into his laptop and occasionally distracting himself by checking his phone for messages or flicking through a babe-hunting app.

He liked video games, clubbing and girls, yes, especially girls, and, because he had spent so much time on these 'hobbies,' *trouble* was now his best friend. He could hardly concentrate as the text crawled spider-like before his eyes.

He sauntered to the bathroom to comb his hair which was cropped on the sides, and left long and dyed a dirty blonde on top which he knew the babes swooned over. He applied moisturiser to his cheeks and forehead, admired his looks and grinned.

But his lips drooped as he dragged himself back to his desk and tapped away at the keyboard, hoping that his answers were correct or at least close to it. Usually his friend, Zudin, would send him stuff to copy but he was recovering in hospital after a bout of dengue.

Just as he started to type a semblance of an answer, he felt an oddest need to look out of the window. He tried to ignore the feeling, but he could no longer concentrate.

Got to see what's there.

This thought came to him several times like a buzzing fly that refused to go away. He shut the lid of his laptop and, craning his neck, his one eye peeked through the curtains.

At first, it only saw the city skyline in the distance. The Petronas twin towers flashed amongst a plethora of other scintillating skyscrapers. Pushing aside the drapes, he spied Genting's far-off glitterings. His eyes slid past the expressways, the neighbouring apartment blocks, across the shophouses and down to the condo swimming pool with its inviting turquoise waters brilliantly lit up, even at this late hour.

Movement!

There beside the shadowed garden bed. He screwed up his eyes and saw a figure in a black gown standing in front of a stand of tall bamboos as if trying to merge with their narrow fronds.

A woman.

From several stories above, he didn't know how he knew. He just did. Perhaps, he mused, it was because he had an affinity for females. He found this notion not the slightest bit amusing as he stared at her. From her slim figure, he guessed she was young.

She stood there quite still. She could have been a statue but Fidrus could feel her presence, perhaps even her quickening heartbeat, several storeys above in his bedroom. He felt a chill, not one that blew from the Daikin air con, but rather a coldness rising in his chest that brought a foreboding, as if he knew of ghastly things to come.

He wanted to turn away. To let the curtain drop and rush into bed and hide beneath the warm blanket. But Fidrus wanted to see what this young woman was doing.

The figure stood unmoving as if she was mesmerised by the shimmering waters. Then, slowly, in a dream-like way, she glided forward, her loose gown rippling.

She suddenly looked up.

Right at him, he was sure, and that was when he saw that her face was hidden by the black cloth of a niqab.

It brought a tightness in his stomach.

'A ninja . . .' he whispered.

That's what Zudin called them.

'Hey, she's got a nunchak,' he would say, elbowing him. 'She's gonna jump out and smash your head in!'

Fidrus would laugh and punch him playfully in the stomach and Zudin would pretend to block it and dance out of the way.

But now Fidrus wondered what a ninja was doing at the pool area so late at night. Other than being dressed in a niqab, which he found disturbing enough whenever he encountered such people, he felt something was very wrong with this woman.

Terribly wrong.

For awhile, she stood at the pool's edge.

He heard the faint drone of a motorcycle and perhaps even a mournful voice singing from far away.

Then, without warning, the figure leapt, her body hanging in the air for a split second like a soaring crow.

There was hardly a splash as she fell in.

Her body sunk like a black concrete block right to the bottom . . . falling deep, so deep . . . without moving once.

Fidrus jumped to his feet.

His first thought was to shout out to his parents for help. But then he realised that they were out Latin dancing. He needed to act quickly. But should he even help her?

Before he knew it, he was already out of the apartment. He pressed the lift button. He paced up and down waiting for it to arrive. When the doors finally opened, he thought the woman would have surely drowned.

He got off on the recreational level, dashed past the sauna, almost bumped into a startled security guard slouching beside the small library with its shelves of yellowing books and sprinted to the swimming pool. He stood panting at its edge lined with pavers, eyes searching.

There!

The figure lay unmoving, a black mannequin at the bottom of the pool.

Without thinking, he threw off his slippers and dived in.

The cold water sent tremors through his body. But it heightened all his senses. He could feel his breath, every movement of his taut muscles.

He grabbed the woman, expecting to feel her arms, solid beneath the gown but . . . there was nothing.

Just cloth!

Where is she?

He couldn't understand it.

He grabbed the gown and pulled at it, expecting to see a body beneath it, prostrated at the bottom of the pool. But no, there was nothing there but bright blue tiles staring back. Desperate for air, he poked his head out of the water, dragging the gown with him.

By then, three security guards were at the pool's edge, talking excitedly to themselves in Nepalese.

They helped him pull the gown out. Water trickled from it as they yanked it. A security guard, the oldest looking one, was left holding the garment. Making a distasteful face, as if it was a dead creature, he dropped it, the black material flopped to the tiles, making a slapping sound.

Fidrus eyed the rippling waters, hoping to see the young woman somewhere in the pool. But there was nothing but bright tiles. Except that in one corner beside the metal steps, lay her black shoes, one sitting neatly on top of the other. He wondered if he should retrieve them but he suddenly felt drained, as if the act of dragging the gown from the water had sapped all his energy.

Above him stood the two apartment blocks, framed by tall bamboo plants and beyond it were the silhouettes of palm trees and a timber pergola behind a line of plastic deck chairs.

There was no sign of the woman.

Where the heck did she disappear to?

'Come, come,' the security guard said. 'Out, out. Pool close nine. Tomorrow swim.'

'Okay,' Fidrus muttered. 'I didn't come swimming, I was trying to save . . .'

'You get, okay?' The security guard pointed at the pair of submerged shoes.

Fidrus sighed.

'Sure . . . sure. No problem.'

He turned but just as he was to gulp the air and dive in, a pair of hands flew out of the water and grabbed his hair.

They yanked his head under water. A storm of bubbles shot up before his face. He struggled for air. His chest tight and close to bursting. Before him, a face, young and wide-eyed, stared back. Even as he fought to get back to the surface, he could see her black hair flowing down to her shoulders and exposed breasts. Her face was oval and so smooth and he knew that if he touched it, he would be lost forever. Her eyes were bright like sunshine even at this midnight hour.

Then she let go and he burst to the surface, spluttering and coughing.

She laughed as she rose up with him. She tossed her head and beads of water flew off her long hair like dripping stars.

The security guards chortled from the edge of the pool.

Suddenly, clouds burst open and rain came hurtling down, sending thousands of mini-explosions onto the surface of the pool. He stared skyward and the moon shone into his eyes.

It seemed to be laughing too.

* * *

Fidrus woke up and found his head on his desk, his arms bent beside the laptop and tablet.

He sighed and shook his head.

The dream. That damn dream again!

He massaged his neck.

The same one three nights in a row.

He got into bed and shivered. It took him a long while before sleep's warm-fingers claimed him.

In the morning, Fidrus managed to upload his assignment on time. He had answered every question, not very well, he knew, but at least he had made an effort.

'Try your best,' his father had said just the other day. 'That's all I ask.'

His father had intense eyes, a grey-flecked beard and round glasses and people were always saying that he looked liked Yusof Islam although Fidrus didn't know who Yusof Islam was. Perhaps he was an ustaz of some sort.

'But I worked so hard, Abah,' Fidrus lied. 'I really did my best this time.'

'I don't think so. You party too much. All those late nights with your buddies. And all those girlfriends of yours. Doing your best means putting in both time and effort. You do neither.'

His father shook his head.

'But, Abah, . . .'

Fidrus spewed a raft of excuses and tried to keep a straight face because he knew they were obvious lies.

Luckily for him, his father was a liberal man who had once played in a punk band in pubs whilst studying in London. He was pretty sure his father had smoked ganja too.

'You're lucky I'm not of my parents' generation,' his father added. 'They went through the war. They did it tough. So they wanted us, their kids, to be tough too. That's why they were hard on us. You, Fidrus, you're spoilt. We've given you everything. You've had too cushy a life.'

Fidrus nodded and tried not to yawn.

It was the same old story. Of course, he enjoyed all the comforts in life. But was that his fault? He found it hard to study too. He just had to glance at his phone to know that life had too many distractions.

That afternoon, the mother of all distractions bumped into him. He had returned from college as the sun blazed its infernal heat outside. He hummed a Chainsmokers tune whilst waiting for the lift in the air-conditioned lobby when he heard soft shuffling footsteps. A whiff of perfume touched the hairs of his nostrils, making him turn to the thin, all-black, niqab-clad figure behind him.

Ninja!

This one had a black veil that covered her entire body. There were a few who lived at the condo. He'd seen some in shopping malls. Even on billboards. He couldn't help staring at these creatures as they looked so alien.

Even scary.

She wore a small, fashionable orange backpack though it looked odd against her extreme raiment.

What was in it? The Quran and prayer books? Or did she lead a normal life and went to college like everyone else?

Whatever she did, she was not of his world.

In his world, he would wander with the guys to their favourite clubs. The bouncer sold them dusky red pills which would send them dancing like broken puppets until the morning light slithered over the shophouse roofs. He often told his parents that he was bunking with Zudin . . . so he could do whatever he liked.

Sometimes, when they had extra money, they would slink into massage parlours for sex.

This ninja girl though was most likely obsessed with her daily *salat*, extra prayers and attended sermons all day long. He crazily thought that she would burn down *tahfiz* schools too, just to send the dead kids to heaven.

He glanced at her again and a notion shifted in his head.

Her mascara-painted eyelashes whispered something else, of seductive promises, whilst her bright, sparkling, dark brown eyes posed a hundred questions that tugged at his heart.

They seemed so familiar . . .

It's that girl from my dreams!

He was sure of it.

He hadn't seen her wandering around the condo before. He would have noticed her and her flowing gown that seemed to absorb all colours in the lobby so that the marble floor, its rows of metal letterboxes and leather lounge sets seemed bland. The brightest thing was her backpack which blazed like sunshine in a cave. The shoes, barely peeking from beneath the gown, had to be the same soft ones he had seen at the bottom of the pool.

'Hello,' he said.

He was surprised that he opened his mouth to this ninja. Why the hell would he be interested in someone in a niqab?

The dream. The damn dream. That's why.

She nodded and perhaps she even said hello. But he wasn't sure. If she did, it would have surely been in a soft girlish voice which got lost in the folds of her face covering.

He recalled her slim seductive body, smooth and naked in the bright blue swimming pool. It too was now engulfed in the folds of that tent-like gown without so much as a hint of the delightful curves he had beheld in his dream; no shoulders, no breasts, no stomach, no hips, no thighs, no knees.

Yet this had to be the girl that dunked his head in the water and laughed at him three nights in a row. He could still hear her chiming, teasing laughter. He could still see her long black hair drifting in the water, the slope of her neck, the curve of her shoulders, her perky breasts and the black mound below. He had seen these shimmering promises in a single glance as he fought for breath amongst the burst of bubbles.

The lift doors slid open.

With a gloved hand, she swiped the key card and pressed her floor button.

He imagined her flinging away her brown gloves and with a soft delicate hand stroking his cheek and reaching beneath his pants.

He hung at the back mirrored wall whilst she stood beside the buttons as the lift ascended. Within these confines, her perfume grew stronger, but there was something else, another scent, oddly familiar, somewhat unpleasant.

Was it a scent extreme Muslims wore nowadays? It couldn't be, for surely perfume was *haram* to them. Or only if it contained alcohol? Fidrus had to admit he had no idea.

The doors slid open and, in a slow gait, the girl drifted out like a gentle black breeze in a war-torn desert.

'See you,' he called out. 'My name's Fidrus!'

She turned around and, in that movement, he glimpsed a curve of her buttock pressing against her gown. Her recalled her naked body and swallowed.

She nodded as if she knew. Her eyes of a thousand promises sent a warm stirring into his loins. And if he could touch her smooth, smooth cheek, breathe in the scent of her hair, he would be lost forever.

The doors slid shut.

He felt an almighty erection poking hard against his track suit bottoms. Getting off on his floor, he fumbled with the keys to the condo and scurried to the toilet.

Breathing hard, heart thumping, he yanked his pants down and closed his eyes. After a moment of pleasuring himself, from his open mouth came a hound-like gasp for his stroking hand had incredibly melded into her lips!

How soft, how luscious they were!

Her eyes, bright and lusty, glanced up at him just once, then fell back to his groin . . . her lips still hidden behind her face covering. Her hair, which should have been flowing over his naked thighs, was still shrouded by her headscarf. But when he saw that she was otherwise naked, when he beheld her fair, smooth naked body, writhing on the tiles, he collapsed off the toilet seat.

He lay on the floor, panting, eyes on the ceiling light, the cornices, the small stain above the shower, wondering what in heaven's name had just happened.

Am I mistaking heaven for hell?

The vision of the naked girl had, of course, disappeared. He cleaned up the mess with a wad of tissues, wandered into his bedroom and snuggled against his pillow, his mind only on her.

He saw the ninja again the next day at the lift lobby. He swallowed hard. He could barely mumble a hello as he stood beside her, breathing in hints of fragrant perfume and the curious smell behind it.

'Hello, Fidrus.' she said. Her voice was girlish and shy. 'How are you today?'

'Oh . . . eh. I'm fine.'

'My name's Afeza.'

He hardly dared stare into Afeza's gorgeous green eyes, eyes that seemed all too aware of his misdeeds.

Green eyes?

Weren't they dark brown?

Perhaps she was wearing contact lenses. But why would a ninja wear coloured contact lenses, use perfume and wear makeup? Perhaps, she wasn't really a ninja at heart. It was just peer pressure. That was it. She was just a pretty girl dressed up piously.

His hopes soared as they ascended in that confined lift space, her odd fragrance making him giddy, and as she glided out, she glanced back.

'Come tomorrow, Fidrus. For tea.'

Afeza's voice had a hint of an English accent.

'Really?'

'Three-thirty. Unit 6-04'

'Yes, I'll . . .'

But the lift doors had slid shut.

He could hardly believe the invitation.

It was just awesome!

* * *

The next day, Fidrus got home early, skipping his usual computer gaming sessions with his college buddies. He showered and changed into his new Hurly T-shirt and Rip Curl track suit bottoms. He combed his hair to get it perfect for Afeza.

His hands were sweaty even though it was only just after three. Twice he had to wash his face which was hot with excitement. As he lay on his bed trying to control his heartbeat and a shivering excitement in his cold chest, he glimpsed a fly trapped in a spider's web outside the window. He was fascinated by its struggle to escape but he didn't know why.

Perhaps I shouldn't go . . .

And what would his father think of him going with a girl in a niqab? Of course the liberal man, the moderate Muslim, wouldn't approve.

Just last year, whilst he was messaging several girls on his new iPhone, his mother emerged wearing a light purple *tudung*, the loose folds covering her hair, neck and breast.

'Don't be angry, okay?' she said to his father who glared as if an alien had just stepped into the lounge. 'This is what good Muslim women do.'

'That's ridiculous,' he growled, removing his glasses and dropping them nosily on the dining table. 'The Quran doesn't say a woman should cover her face. Nothing about covering the hair either. So if you want to wear a *tudung*, why don't you go all the way and cover your face as well?'

His father snorted and returned to his tablet.

'I'm just doing what everybody does,' his mother sighed. 'Anyway, this is a silk chiffon, it's branded, you know. Sugarscarf. Very fashionable.'

'I don't care about fashion. Malay women didn't wear the *tudung* before. Just look at all the old photos. Now we think we're Arabs. We're pretending to be so very pious. Even young girls, toddlers, are covering up. Which man is going to look at a girl that age? You tell me.'

'You're never heard of pedophiles? Anyway, their parents just want them to get used to it. Just because you're not religious doesn't mean you can go and criticise everyone.'

'Wearing a *tudung* doesn't mean you're religious. There are many people who pray five times a day but they're gossiping and back-stabbing. They're taking bribes and committing adultery. I'm more religious than all of them!'

His father got up and stormed into the bedroom.

For days, his father refused to go out with his new hair-covered wife despite all the designer and highly-fashionable scarves she wore. But eventually he relented. After all, what choice did the man have?

Fidrus didn't care one way or the other. He got up from his bed, caught his reflection in the mirror and winked. Women could wear whatever they wanted as long as they were willing to go naked on demand.

He thumbed a message to Zudin.

I've got a date, bro. With a ninja!!!!

Talk shit as usual. Came the immediate reply.

Zudin was probably on his mobile, watching porn or gambling, even though he was still recovering in hospital.

It's for real, man.
Don't gimme shit bro.
I'll send you photos. It's damn real!
Ok. She's gonna nunchak you
Not if I nunchak her first. Lol
Where you find her?
Tell you later. Gotta go bro.

Fidrus pocketed his phone. He checked his hair one more time before slinking out of the condo.

Knowing that his lift key card wouldn't give him access to the 6th floor, he scurried down the grey-tiled stairs; quietly he went as he tried to soften the echo of his footsteps which announced the imminent rendezvous. At each landing there was an open-air view of the limestone hills beyond and, each time he beheld them, they appeared more and more like teeth.

Am I being stupid?
She's a complete stranger.
But she was a girl.
A girl he wanted to screw.
Maybe she's got a nunchak, but I do wanna fuck!
He sniggered at the thought.

He wondered if Afeza would be wearing normal clothes at home with her face and hair coverings removed. Then maybe he could put his hands up her blouse and then he would unfasten her bra. The thought of seducing her brought a warm stirring below.

Hardly able to breathe, he rang the doorbell.

The door opened, revealing Afeza in her usual black gown with her face covered.

Shit! Shit! Shit!

His stirrings coldly withered as he took off his Nikes and left them at the front door. He stepped inside as air-conditioned air slid its cool fingers around his neck and cheeks.

A poster of multi-coloured faces hung above a plush blue sofa whilst a wooden antique clock winked from a side table. Upon an antique-like coffee table, a crystal bowl depicting several circling nude women shimmered beneath a chandelier.

Afeza had to have rich parents. But if she was so religious, why did she have a bowl depicting nude women?

'Like my place?' Afeza's soft voice asked from beneath her face covering.

'Oh . . . it's great. Really cool.'

'Thanks. Please sit.'

She brought out a tray laden with chocolate biscuits, mini-eclairs and a glass of orange cordial.

'I'm glad you're here.'

'Me too. Very happy . . .'

From the sofa, Fidrus stared into her lovely eyes and her mascara-thick eyelashes. He wanted to rip off her face covering and kiss her soft lips right there. Lips he remembered from his dream and when he pleasured himself so deliriously in the toilet. Perhaps she would remove it herself . . . later.

There's lots of time.

The rest of the afternoon and perhaps even into the night.

She lowered herself onto the rug and sat down, placing one gloved hand on the coffee table. He glimpsed her sock-covered foot on the carpet, protruding from her gown, and wondered if she felt hot beneath all those black layers.

'So how old are you, Fidrus?'

'I'm 20. What about you?'

'I'm 19.' Afeza's eyes twinkled.

'Oh, only 19? That's a good age.'

An innocent age.

Definitely a virgin.

'Your condo . . . it's so nice, Afeza. Like a 5 star hotel.'

You have a 5 star body too.

He had seen its promised delights in his head. He had imagined his hands roving over her smooth skin.

'Thanks, Fidrus. I designed it myself.'

'I'd like to own a place like this . . . one day.'

Even though her mouth was hidden by black cloth, he thought Afeza smiled at his notion. Her eyebrows did a little dance and her eyes, he was sure they were laughing. He wanted to say something but instead helped himself to a biscuit. He sipped the orange cordial and grinned stupidly at her.

For a while they said nothing whilst Afeza's fingers, beneath her gloves, softly drummed against the coffee table.

Fidrus jerked when he heard the door bell ring. Afeza got up, a black fog that glided quickly to open the front door.

He heard a woman's hushed voice.

'Meet . . . my friends,' Afeza called when she returned.

Fidrus stood up. His mother would be proud, for he wasn't he being so polite? Doing what she'd taught him?

He wondered what his father would think though. He pictured the man staring through his glasses and stroking his beard disapprovingly.

You shouldn't be here, son, he would mutter. *You're spoilt rotten and you only think of having fun. Do you think you'll never get old? Be wise, son, be wise. What are you doing wasting your time in this girl's condo? And look what these awful people are wearing . . .*

Two women in sombre gowns with veils falling over their bodies clouded behind Afeza; together they were a mass of black. One ninja was taller than the host whilst the other was shorter, fatter and wore dark glasses, with the frame's plastic arms pressed over her *tudung* like a goggle.

They could dress as they wanted. It was a free world. As long as they didn't bother others, he was fine with it. He wasn't going to tell them what they should or shouldn't wear.

But they'll force others to wear such clothes, his father whispered, whose warm breath he could almost feel against his ear. *These people are holier than thou. Don't you know that, son? These extremists only make misery.*

The two ninjas nodded and sat down on the sofa, on either side of him. He could smell perfume, but beneath that some whiff of something else.

Something unpleasant.

'So you are Fidrus,' said the shorter woman with the dark glasses like goggles, once she had arranged the cushions behind her back. From her voice he guessed she was in her thirties or forties.

'Yes, I am.'

'I'm Mafuzah and my friend here is Naleen. You can call me Maffy.'

Naleen nodded at him, her eyes blinking rapidly. She reached with one gloved hand and scratched her socked foot.

From their voices, body-shapes and whatever that narrow postbox slot revealed of their faces, he guessed Naleen was about the same age as Maffy.

'Have some eclairs,' Afeza said, who had resumed her position on the floor.

'Yes, have some.' Maffy placed two pieces on a plate and passed it to him with her gloved hand. 'Looks sooooo delicious.'

Her face drew close to his and he saw his worried reflection in her sunglasses.

But what's there to be worried about?

Perhaps he didn't like being sandwiched between these two older women dressed in black with faces covered.

'Would you like an eclair, Naleen?' Maffy asked. 'Or a biscuit?'

Naleen shook her head.

'Oh yes, I forgot to say that Naleen doesn't speak.'

'A vow of silence or is she . . .'

'No, Fidrus, Naleen just doesn't speak.'

'Ah, ok . . .'

Naleen pulled out a tissue from her gown pocket, pushed it beneath her face covering, glanced at him worriedly, then sneezed. Then she snorted and blew softly into the tissue.

She withdrew the crumpled tissue and was sliding it back into her pocket when Fidrus noticed dark stains on it.

'What are those . . .'

'Have your eclairs,' Afeza said in a firm voice.

Her once-sweet eyes stared back intensely.

Could Naleen have been coughing blood? He doubted it for the marks were black not red.

'You'll like them, Fidrus. The eclairs are really delicious. They'll sweeten you up.'

'Ah . . . okay, sure, I'll try them.'

The mini-eclairs were indeed sweet and filled with chocolate cream. When he had finished them, he took a gulp of the orange cordial. He was still thinking about the black marks when Afeza asked him to stand up.

'We just need to cover up the sofa, Fidrus.'

Fidrus got up uncertainly as Maffy took a thick transparent plastic sheet from beneath the coffee table. The two women unfolded it and draped it over the sofa.

'What's this for?' Fidrus asked as he helped them tuck it over the back of the sofa and against the wall.

Maffy laughed. 'You'll see . . . don't look so worried.'

When the sheet was in place, the two women sat down, the plastic making a distinctive rustling sound against their bottoms.

'Sit down, Fidrus,' Maffy said.

Fidrus joined the two women on the sofa now covered up by the plastic sheet.

'Please eat more,' Afeza said. 'Don't be shy . . .'

He sipped his orange cordial and helped himself to a biscuit, except he couldn't taste either. Something strange was going on.

And why aren't the women eating?

He wondered if he should make his excuses and leave.

Yes, his father whispered. *You should never have come here, son. Make your excuses and leave . . .*

From the corner of his eye, he glimpsed Naleen staring at him as if he was a piece of supermarket meat wrapped in cellophane. He turned to Maffy who had taken off her goggle-like glasses.

There were pink streaks in her narrow eyes and the skin around them appeared to be peeling. But there was something else, there was a keenness, a hunger, in her shifting eyeballs.

Before he could say anything, Maffy placed a hand on his shoulder and pulled him towards her. In a single motion, she yanked his T-shirt over his head and flung it across the room. Before he knew what was happening, she was kissing his nipples beneath her face covering.

He gasped.

Afeza rose from the carpet, slipped over to him and yanked down his track pants and boxer shorts.

This . . . he couldn't believe, it was beyond his most erotic dreams.

So that was the reason for the plastic sheet. They didn't want to mess up the expensive sofa!

Meanwhile, Naleen was kissing him behind his neck and, even though she couldn't speak, she was making moaning sounds.

As for Afeza, she was licking him below!

His body quivered as the three women licked, sucked and kissed his entire body. The plastic covering made urgent rustling noises beneath him.

He closed his eyes and groaned.

This was heaven on earth!

He couldn't wait to tell Zudin about this. His clubbing buddies would reckon he was hallucinating on some new party drug.

Naleen made sucking sounds on his neck whilst Maffy slurped at his nipples and Afeza made him delirious as she licked his hardness below.

He suddenly opened his eyes.

This is crazy shit . . . they've still got their headscarfs and face coverings!

'Take them off!' he cried. 'I want to see your faces!'

'Yes!' Maffy shrieked.

'Of course!' Afeza chimed.

Naleen made a squealing noise, like an animal that had been caged for too long.

Afeza stared up at him and in her lovely eyes he saw not only lust but the same hunger.

Then he glanced at his groin.

'What the hell . . . is that ink? What have you done?'

'Don't you want to see my face?' Afeza clutched at his thighs. 'Like in your dream!'

'My dream? How did you . . .'

Before he could finish the question, Afeza had pulled off her gloves and flung them to one side.

'Your hands?' he gasped.

'Surprised?'

'They're . . . they're all black!'

They were more than that. They were *oozing*.

'You're not racist are you, Fidrus?' she laughed, as she slipped off her socks to reveal slimy ebony feet.

Then she pulled off her headscarf and ripped off her face covering.

'No!' cried Fidrus. 'No! No! NOOO!'

He had a good reason to object so vehemently.

For Afeza had revealed a head that was not only black as midnight but oozed with thick viscous liquid. It was only above and below the eyes, a postbox slot of skin not covered by the niqab, that was normal. A pale dryness upon slimy ebony.

'Don't like what you see?' Afeza chortled in a deep voice, so different from her girlish one. Her hair was straight and long, falling down to her knees. 'My oily skin not to your liking?'

Then using her black thumb and forefinger, she ripped off that patch of normal-looking, human skin around her eyes to reveal the same greasy blackness. She dangled the limp mask before his eyes.

'Latex,' she said. 'Just to make us look human behind the niqab.'

On either side of him, two similar oily heads, Maffy and Naleen, loomed. Grinning, they ripped off their latex masks with their black fingers and threw them on the coffee table, on top of the mini-eclairs and biscuits. Then they pushed their heads close to his.

Fidrus screamed.

Both older women were bald with only a few strands of hair protruding from their oily scalps.

Maffy lurched at him and rained kisses on his forearm and when she withdrew, Fidrus saw it plastered with oily patches.

'Please, noooooo . . .'

The room spun. He felt like fainting.

You shouldn't be the only one naked,' Afeza giggled.

The three women pulled off their dark gowns to reveal skin blacker than black. Their midnight shoulders, breasts, stomach, hips, thighs, knees leaked with oil. It was the same familiar smell in the lift but it hit him hard. Now he understood. These loathsome black creatures wore perfume to hide their greasy petroleum stink.

'We're hungry,' Maffy grunted. 'Starving!'

Her grinning mouth opened wide to reveal sharp, glinting pearl-white teeth.

Naleen licked her lips. Her tongue was bright red like a flame against her sable leering, leaking face.

'Yes,' Afeza snarled, mouth open wide, her long straight hair swishing against her bare knees. 'Hungry for you, my darling.'

The sharp, sharp teeth of the three oily creatures fell upon Fidrus even as screamed. But Fidrus couldn't quite scream because Afeza's mouth was upon his, biting out his mouth and tongue.

The creatures tore at his body.

The neck. The genitals. The stomach.

All ripped red. Blood mixed with oil.

A feast upon his pale, pale, young flesh.

* * *

Fidrus's father glanced at the rearview mirror, eyes fixed on the receding image for slightly longer than necessary. He needed to see something.

Anything.

But there was nothing to see. No sign, no hint.

No hope.

Perhaps he had expected to see a hazy image of his son standing under a tree? Or waving at him beside a monsoon drain?

He grimaced, drove past the traffic lights and turned the car towards the condo.

'We've been invited to dinner on Friday,' his wife said. She sat beside him, wearing a green-patterned *tudung*, holding her phone close to her bosom. 'Do you want to go?'

'I don't feel like it.'

He couldn't be bothered asking whose invitation it was. Maybe it was her sister, a cousin or a friend. He didn't want to see anybody.

The condo's twin tower blocks loomed against a grey, hazy sky. How could they still be standing there with their son gone? This was now week three.

Can he be dead?

He didn't dare think it.

His wife turned towards him and touched his shoulder.

'It'll be good for us to see other people.'

He swallowed.

'I don't want to.'

'Aunty Nita asked us over. We should go. She's asked a few times now.'

'No . . .'

'Please think about it.'

He grunted.

She glanced at her phone. 'Oh, we need someone to look at the washing machine. It's making that funny noise again.'

'Yes, I heard it yesterday. I think there's a sticker with a service number on the side.'

'I'll have a look . . .'

The couple rarely spoke of their son nowadays. Neither wanted the other to grieve.

They had called everyone they knew and had visited the police station so often that the staff and officers there knew them by name.

Their private investigator, an ex-police detective, had come up empty handed too. He could produce nothing but a big invoice.

Their only lead were the messages Fidrus had sent his friend the day he vanished. Something about going on a date with a girl in a nikab. The police wanted to interview everyone who wore the face-covering in the condo but the religious authorities stepped in. They said it was wrong to target good Muslims and anyway religious people didn't commit crimes.

But, after handing the manager a wad of cash, he got their apartment numbers. But it was fruitless quest. All of them said, behind their veiled mouths, that they had never seen his son.

His disappearance was a big mystery.

Where has our boy gone?

He wanted to groan. Even scream out.

But he held the words coiled inside as he tightly clutched the steering wheel. Tried to keep life going as before.

But how can it ever be the same without him?

Their handsome, kind obliging boy. The light of their lives.

And now he was gone. He had no hope left. It was Allah's will, their friends said. But why would the Compassionate, the Merciful want to take their son away? He couldn't understand it. Didn't want to understand anything.

The hollowness in his stomach was now unbearable.

'Will we ever see him again?' he whispered.

He didn't dare look at his wife.

She stayed silent but he could hear her soft breathing. That same familiar sound when she lay in bed pretending to sleep and he beside her, right on the edge of the mattress, not daring to take her hand for what could he offer her other than his sorrow?

Still she said nothing.

He turned into the condo driveway whose porch pillars were greying and mouldy.

Three women in niqabs came out of the entrance, pushing past the glass doors. One of them, the slim one, wore an orange backpack. They trotted down the steps, moving like a single black cloud or perhaps a storm of bees towards a waiting black Toyota Alphard. The vehicle reminded him of an oversized hearse.

The women, its deadly mourners.

He recognised the short, dumpy one. He had spoken to her at the front door of her condo just last week. She was wearing dark glasses then as she was wearing them now.

So very sorry, she had muttered through her veil. *We haven't seen your boy. We hope you find him soon. Insha-Allah.*

She asked him to wait and brought out a pamphlet. It looked like a religious one.

It will help you, she said in a conspiring tone.

He declined the gift.

He had seen the slimmer one too. She was inside the condo sitting on the floor beside a coffee table flipping through a magazine. He guessed that she was in her early 20s.

Now as he drove past, her backpack glinting bright in the sunlight, she turned towards him and their eyes met. Behind her mascara and eyeshadow, her eyes were so cold that a chill went through him. The hairs on his arms rose.

Clutching the steering wheel tightly, he drove down the ramp leading to the carpark, wondering what made ordinary people so extraordinarily religious. And what would they do if he ripped off their face coverings?

'I . . . I don't know where he is,' his wife said. Her voice was quaking. 'Our boy. Our darling boy.'

He struggled to find something to say. There would be nothing in the rearview mirror. No hope. Just memories. There was nothing ahead either.

Just sorrow.

He made a left at the bottom of the ramp. He struggled to keep tears away.

His wife unwrapped her headscarf, yanked it off and, with a sigh, flung it against the windshield.

'I don't want this damn *tudung* anymore. Don't want to wear *tudungs* again. Those three women . . .'

'What . . . what about them?'

'They make me feel ill. Sick in the stomach. Don't know why.'

He parked the car at their allocated spot beside the lift lobby. With the engine still running, he turned to his wife, her hair curling free down to her shoulders, her face pale and quivering.

For awhile they said nothing but just stared at each other.

Finally, he took her hands, brought them to his lips and tears, like midnight rain, fell from their eyes.

COPYRIGHT
ACKNOWLEDGEMENTS

"The Rape of Martha Teoh" and "Biggest Baddest Bomoh" were first published in The Rape of Martha Teoh and Other Chilling Stories (Pelanduk, 1997)

"Emil and the Lurking Shadow", "Ladiah" and "Mr Petronas" were first published in BloodHaze: 15 Chilling Tales (Pelanduk, 1999)

"Malay Magick" was first published in The Woman Who Grew Horns and Other Works (Pelanduk, 2001)

"44 Cemetery Road" was first published in 44 Cemetery Road: The Best of Tunku Halim (MPH Group Publishing, 2007)

"Black Death" and "Gravedigger's Kiss" were first published in Gravedigger's Kiss: More of Tunku Halim (MPH Group Publishing, 2007)

"Kyoto Kitchen", "Shrine", "In the Village of Setang" and "The App" were first published in 7 Days to Midnight (MPH Group Publishing, 2013)

"Man on the 22nd Floor" was first published in Little Basket 2016 (Buku Fixi, 2016)

"Black Honda Jazz", "Mr Skull" , "No Kiss Goodbye" and "Midnight Rain" were first published in The Rape of Nancy Ng: 13 Nightmares (Buku Fixi, 2018)

"The Black Bridge" was first published in Best Asian Speculative Fiction (Kitaab, 2018)